I0682598

Mauveine

A Contemporary Ghost Story
By Roy Baldwin

Creative Gateway

Acknowledgement

The genesis of this book arose after I was encouraged to enter the 2013 NaNoWriMo writing competition for the first time. NaNoWriMo is a fantastic opportunity for all writers, new or experienced, to create a 50,000 word novel within the disciplined timeframe of the thirty days of November, supported and encouraged online by a vast community of other local and international writers. In its fifteenth year, NaNoWriMo anticipates a record half a million people to join the largest writing event in the world, from across seven continents including Antarctica. Through its Young Writers Programme, NaNoWriMo also provides free resources and curriculum globally to over 80,000 students and educators in 2,000 classrooms. In addition a host of volunteers provide write-ins and events in 500 regions. NaNoWriMo is an awesome writer movement which I am proud to support.

I decided to use my personal NaNoWriMo time as a kick-start to attempt something new and different, so Mauveine, a contemporary ghost story, was conceived the last week of October and a plotline and description formulated in time for writing commencement on November 1st onwards. All I can say is working to that discipline is amazingly cathartic and highly energising. Fortunately, the words flew, the keyboard smoked and unexpected characters emerged, ferociously taking over the entire plot and writing process. For thirty days I lived in another fantasy world for the whole time, enabling me to research on the go, write, polish, edit, format, create the cover and finally publish, by November 30th. So the novel you are about to read is, like an original painting, a summative totality of all my creative effort. Mauveine, I'm afraid, defies simple categorisation and is a cross-genre mashup of horror, fantasy, history, science, art, romance and adventure. Mauveine does however closely follow the complex and challenging emotional journey of two female protagonists trying to find their true destinies. Unfortunately a third joins them on the trail but not quite of this time ...

However this novel was not done alone, benefiting hugely from the inspiration and support of others who I would like to take the opportunity to thank profusely, especially:

§: My family for putting up with a grumpy, reclusive and uncommunicative hermit for a month.

§: My friends and international writer network for the fantastic encouragement and for forgiveness that I neither read nor replied to their emails, tweets or blogs for a month.

§: And lastly Rowena Beighton-Dykes for her superb heritage knowledge of dyes, textiles and paints to point me the right way, and Aliyah Marr who never fails, through her own uniquely talented art and design ability, to be a continuous source and inspiration for the necessary creativity and drive to get the work done.

Thank you NaNoWriMo and dear reader, enjoy the journey ...

Roy Baldwin 2013

About the Author

Roy Baldwin was born in South Lancashire and has lived and worked around the UK in various mathematical and scientific guises as an educationalist, civil servant, musician, house conservator and management consultant. Mauveine was conceived, written, edited and published in thirty days during the NaNoWriMo 2013 competition and is his fourth book. In between full time writing and book design, he also tries to enjoy and be inspired by the fabulous beauty of the Norfolk countryside and seashore where he now lives.

Other published novels (2016) include Prism of Purpurine, Morag, Rhapsody of Restraint, Rhapsody of Power, Rhapsody of Fate, Rhapsody of Succession and Rhapsody of Moon.

Further information can be obtained from the author's site: http://www.creativepubtalk.com

Author twitter: http://twitter.com/creativepubtalk

Author linkedin: https://www.linkedin.com/in/creativepubtalk

Chapter One

1990 on a canal in West Lancashire:

Working her way back home along the towpath from her friend Annie's house, Victoria McKenzie reflected long and hard. The gloom of dusk was descending and she vainly attempted to dodge the holes and ruts in the scrappy gravel surface, full of water from the earlier storm deluge. Why, Victoria concluded, doesn't anybody care about what she thinks, what she wears and how she spends her time? It was like living in another bygone era in that God-awful cottage. She and Annie had thoroughly enjoyed their music session earlier, paying a fevered homage alongside a few cans of lager to their favourite Black Sabbath and Frank Zappa weekly indulgence, especially since Annie's father had managed to track down an original 'Paranoid' album in that musty old record shop in Paradise Street where he worked.

She liked Annie's parents, Zeb and Katrina. They had met in an old shoe shop in 1965 on London's Carnaby Street, when it was all the vogue pretending to be hippies. Katrina was from posh Finchley but he hailed from the dark, scruffy end of Liverpool, an unlikely coupling if ever there was, but they were the days of wild abandonment when the fashions had become awesome and daring, with Mary Quant, miniskirts and the pill. Zeb and Katrina had made her laugh all evening, parading around in purple flares, thick-soled brown clumpy boots and her white miniskirt. Katrina still had amazing legs and a figure to die for. Everything was so normal at Annie's unlike with her own horrendous parents who continued to live in a yesteryear she neither understood nor empathised with. It wasn't her fault they were so old. Shit … Jack, her father, was already drawing his pension when she was born, and her mother was forty-three. They were still constantly going on about the thirties and the fucking war years, especially her, and how bad it all was and how they never had any proper food, and their damned religious obsession of going to church more noon and night, but never together, always separate. In fact she hoped, when her father sneaked out on a Friday night, ostensibly to pray, that he was really having some wild affair with the greengrocer who forever spoke warmly about him like they were all still living the good life of 1948. Not much hope of that though. He never spoke about his past, or his thoughts for her, or his ambitions, or his politics, or indeed anything please God, only the occasional mumbling about his weird obsession with arachnids, in various states of pinned, dissected and hanging formats on boards, next to the four cages of live tarantulas and black widows down that fucking dark cellar. Considering he had been a science teacher all his life in a hallowed private girls' school three miles away, she could never understand his constant closed inner world and perpetual silences. He was obviously bright, an outstanding biology scholar and had even been to Cambridge taking natural sciences, but took zero interest in her own progress at school. They never went to parents evenings. He just sloped off every Friday, on his own without a word said. Christ, she thought, something in his past must have really messed up his brain.

Her mother, Beatrice, regularly taunted him. Real men fought in the war overseas in trenches, parrying fire and bullets to each other whilst he avoided conscription unfairly, as a teacher, chalking rubbish on a blackboard to kids whose well-to-do parents had more money than conscience. Whenever that regular barrage started, he would slope off down to his spiders and not be seen for days.

In the meantime, Beatrice would rail off on her instead, with a daily berating for just about everything she did, wore, listened to or said and of course being the biggest disappointment in her life imaginable. Fuck. The Berlin Wall had just come down, soon the whole of Europe and Great Britain would unite, communism was dead and the world outside was getting interesting, but you wouldn't know it in Cinderblack Lane. So why on earth would her mother be interested in that long past period of doom, gloom and make do and mend, day in and day out? What was especially incomprehensible was that her mother had once been a fashionable and sought after model up to her mid twenties and had been brought up in another culture. She was American, the ultimate paradox, and so incredibly overbearing it was unreal. The only homage to some sense of past normality was the occasional break from her forties dance band obsession, and listening to early Elvis Presley records. Once she even caught her mother almost animated, rocking to Chuck Berry, but that was hastily turned off when Victoria walked into the room …

As Victoria continued walking, she realised she should have left Annie's much earlier. Darkness was approaching very quickly and she still had at least a mile to walk before reaching the edge of the town. It was quiet, chilly and eerie, only the gentle lap-lapping of the dark, murky water at the side of the canal breaking the silence around her. She stared over the fields between a break in the bushes, where the land was quite flat and observed the large old mansion in the black of the distance, the setting sun casting an eerie yellowy glow behind it, emphasising the stark bareness of the many chimneys and high rooftops. Someone was still living there. One room could be seen dimly lit through the misty haze over the marshy terrain in between. As a child she was told never ever to go over there, as the place was near derelict and dangerous and bad people lived inside. At one stage the forbidden house fascinated her as a little girl. She and Edwin, her older cousin, used to regularly play and cycle on the towpath; then when she was eight, they discovered a dirt track behind the bushes and long grass, snaking through the marsh towards the mystery building. She had no idea who lived there. Nobody knew or talked about it, except wild rumours from her friends of some old woman, who her mother would describe as a witch and who would boil up children alive if she caught them around the house, so Victoria never had to go there. She remembered that one day when, after a heated discussion of should they or shouldn't they, she persuaded Edwin to push his bicycle through the hedgerow, with a worked out plan to sneak up and peer surreptitiously through the windows. But they only got ten yards, when her mother sprang out from nowhere, just behind the trees. How or why her mother was there Victoria had no idea, but her face was immediately slapped hard and Edwin was told to go home, and that she would tell his mother and for him to expect a spanking that evening. He ran off terrified whilst she just cried and cried, being dragged mercilessly all the way back home, her face badly swollen with the blow. Her mother had never hit her before, and never did again, but that fear at such a tender age, had instilled such an innate horror of the place that she put it fully out of her mind from that time onwards.

She continued plodding along steadily, pondering again. She really shouldn't be down there at this time of night on her own. Finally the canal bent around the rolling lay of the land

and she crossed over the rickety wooden bridge which at one stage, using a rope, could be swung completely across on some sort of swivel to let the barges through; but there were no barges now and the choking weeds in the canal and general neglect and decay was badly evident. The bridge had eventually been repaired, raised up and bolted onto fixed concrete pillars, and extended either end, so any intrepid boaters, and there were one or two, could pass underneath, just, with the owners lying flat on their decks.

There were once even plans for a swish metal framed replacement, but the dithering Council, in the end, couldn't be bothered and claimed they had other priorities to spend scarce money on. So it continued to be repaired and renovated, looking distinctly ramshackle and worn out. As she continued onto the other side, the reeds on the side of the bank had grown noticeably larger. She made her way carefully onwards, feeling very wary of falling in, as the darkness had now descended firmly and only the faint light of the near full moon was to be her guiding salvation from accidental drowning.

It was there that she saw it, vaguely through the reeds in the water. Victoria stopped, and looked again, peering into the murky gloom and blackness. Something was sat in the water, covered in some weird type of purple sheeting, like a shroud. The wind suddenly began to get up and her heart pounded fiercely. Oh God, it was a body, a corpse floating in the water. She could see a head and long brown hair all bloated and oozing horrible coloured fluids, and the whole thing started rising up out of the water. A hand, at least it looked like a hand, emerged from the sheeting and was pointing in the direction she had just come. She screamed and screamed, totally unable to move, paralysed, her feet stuck to the ground like massive lead weights she couldn't shift and run whilst the purple shroud bobbed and blobbed about, like a jelly inside a piece of polythene, flubbing in the water. All she could do was continue to scream, and then she finally found herself able to move, turning violently and running blindly back, anywhere, away from this dreadful nightmare when she was caught, trapped inside the outstretched arms of someone huge, wearing a black cape, in front of her.

She looked up into the eyes of the monster …

"Hey, c'mon what on earth is going on 'ere young lady? You're fine now, c'mon calm down. There's nothing 'ere to be frightened of."

Will Hargreaves, the local police sergeant from the Burscough police station, was holding her firmly as she shook and shivered violently. He was a tall, well-built man, probably close to retirement, and was indeed wearing a long black overcoat but the relief, seeing his friendly face, was so palpable that she cried with emotion and gratitude.

"Mr Hargreaves, thank God it's you, but can't you see it, that thing, the dead body, floating in the water, the hand, pointing at us?" she screamed out.

He let her go and she pointed back towards the reeds and the gloom of the Leeds and Liverpool canal, turning into the bend ahead. There was something there floating, near the edge, just visible in the moonlight, not in the middle of the water and white and rounded, but there was no sign of any hand and the wind had vanished; everywhere was calm, exactly as it had been when she set off.

"Good heavens, Victoria, what on earth is going on in your head. It's only from that damned old tannery at Ranbolding, another dead pig, stripped of hide, that some idiot has thrown in the cut rather than disposing it via the proper waste facilities. There used to be a lot of this years ago, haven't seen it for a long time. Mind you it's floated some miles on to get this far. I shall report it to the Council in the morning, no doubt the health inspectors will be over there again. It really is time that place was closed down for good, but at least they've now fenced off the lime pit properly. If you fell in there you would know about it."

"But honestly, Mr Hargreaves, I'm sure I saw …"

"Listen, I have to ask you, but as it's you and I know Beatrice and Jack well, it will be informal. Have you been drinking or drugs? Tell me now."

"No absolutely not, Mr Hargreaves. Annie and I aren't into that; I'm just sure that …"

"Ah Annie Warburton, I assume. A nice family. Is she your best friend?"

"Yes, we spent the evening listening to records and talking, I'm just on my way back home. I must admit I was miles away when I thought I saw … obviously something else."

"Yes, sometimes our imaginations can do funny things in the dark. You really shouldn't be walking down the towpath this time of night on your own, I know we don't get much crime around here but you never know. There are some funny buggers around. I'm sure your parents wouldn't be happy either."

Victoria shrugged. "I do it a lot, I like the walk usually, but I think after tonight I'll get the bus back, despite the cost. Actually I'm starting a part time job next week, at weekends in the supermarket, so I can afford to be sensible."

Sergeant Hargreaves laughed his usual deep belly laugh. "I think that is a much better idea Victoria."

She looked at him gratefully, a comforting relic from the past really, and probably the last of his generation; the rural copper that everyone knows and respects. He was a welcome presence. Perhaps, she thought, some aspects of her parent's past were not all bad because the next generation of police will sadly have lost that local engagement and commitment to the community and knowing everyone like Sergeant Hargreaves, for whom policing had run in the family for half a century or more.

He continued. "Tell you what; my patrol car is just by the bridge. I shall take you home young lady; we don't want any more creating down the canal this evening."

"Thanks Mr Hargreaves, gratefully accepted. Please don't tell my mother will you, it would just be easier if ..."

"Don't worry, I understand. Sometimes we oldies don't comprehend your generation as well as we should. But hey, hasn't it always been like that? My parents never understood me one iota at all!"

She smiled and they walked back over the old bridge, and she got into his warm Landrover. She looked into the back and his Alsatian dog, Maxwell, was lying peacefully on the back seat, raising a mild eyebrow as Victoria stepped in, before nodding back into a peaceful slumber again.

As they drove off he carried on the conversation. "Actually I haven't seen Jack, your father for ages. Is he keeping well? He taught my daughter, Joanna, over at Cradwell. He was a teacher there a long time wasn't he. She got a scholarship, could never have afforded it otherwise on a copper's wages." He laughed again. "She loved his classes, eventually did medicine at uni and is a GP in London now, doing well and all down to your father."

Victoria felt quite startled at that revelation. She couldn't for the life of her imagine what her father could have been like in a classroom, let alone vaguely interesting, especially in a girls' school. "Really, that's ... mmm ... well actually he never talks about his past pupils. Yes he was at Cradwell all his life, straight after university, never taught anywhere else. Retired fully now, keeps himself to himself and doesn't go out much, which is probably why you haven't seen him."

"Give him my regards Victoria; I'll buy him a pint at the George when he's in next. I knew your mother when she was still modelling, she was a real cracker in those days," he joked.

Victoria smiled and thought; little did he know how she is now around the house, slovenly, dirty and lazy. A real trollope. It wasn't surprising her father was always down the cellar. She still dolled up with heavy makeup when she went out to the local shops, so nobody would even guess, and they never got visitors, well who would want to go there. In fact the main reason she took the cookery option at school was so she could make some decent meals once in a while. And she was doing really well academically at school, not that either of them gave a toss. She remembered telling her father she came top in each of the three separate science subjects, physics, chemistry and biology, but all he could say was what was wrong with mathematics, because she came second, and then went off to feed Edna the tarantula, who got fifty times more attention.

Most of her friends except Emmy, whose mum had always been single, all seemed to have cool fathers except her, and she was getting fed up with the bitching and sniggering when parents were mentioned by some of the silly cows in the class below, who would have liked to bully her, but when she walloped the ringleader behind the bicycle sheds in the face, they backed off for good. Fuck all of those losers. She was going to do well and get to university, out of this hellhole for good. Mind you, she sniggered to herself, after punching Amy Dickenson later in the mouth, it won her some tasty male admiration from a few interesting sixth formers, especially

Brian. At least she went on the pill straightaway, heaven knows what her mother would say if she knew, but she wouldn't even guess, living in that weird netherworld of hers. Okay, Brian was eighteen and definitely heading for Oxford next year to do engineering, but they had a cool time together for now, and Annie was going out with his younger brother too which was fun. But no way could they all go drinking in the George anymore after some bastard told her mother in the newsagents. She denied it of course but the vituperative slanging and nagging went on for days and days. How she was fucked off with living in that dreary cottage with that pair of idiots. Something was going to have to give, she didn't know if she could stand it much longer. Maybe Zeb and Katrina could adopt her …

They drove slowly down Cinderblack Lane to the small semi detached cottage at the end, and her thoughts jolted back to reality. She gazed up at the building in the haze of the streetlamp in front. It must have been at least one hundred and fifty years old, and as draughty and cold inside as it probably was then, although at least they probably stayed warm with roaring coal fires rather than a dodgy oil heating system which smelled at night. The thatching needed stripping off and replacing and her bedroom was always full of insects in the summer. She noticed a big crack in the grey rendering near the end chimney breast; a general air of decrepitude and lack of maintenance was evident. She caught Will Hargreaves perusing too with a look suggesting joint agreement.

"I'll just drop you off here Victoria, I won't bother to call in. Now take this." He handed her a large peppermint from a bag on the dashboard. "Suck hard and lay off the lager a bit next time. I can smell your breath, okay?"

She smiled; Sergeant Hargreaves was a nice bloke.

She sauntered towards the front door, thinking that actually those cans of lager were a bit strong and giggled. In fact probably mixing them with cider wasn't such a good idea. All Brian's fault, talking about snakebites the other night when they had gone in his car to the disco at the Kings Arms in Chorley, away from prying eyes and twitching village curtains. That explains seeing the purple pig. Gosh, that really scared the bejeebers out of her ... at least that must be the explanation mustn't it ...

As she pulled out her front door key, she peered in through the uncurtained window, lights blazing and her mother sat there, staring into space with a distinctly angry look on her face. Her father was nowhere to be seen and the cellar window was dark. But of course it was Friday night, when he was probably out shagging Nelly the potato woman, or something equally gross. She was going to get it in the neck that was for sure, but perhaps if she was quick enough she could get to her bedroom before her mother struggled up from the chair, especially if the whisky bottle had been full enough earlier.

Racing up the stairs, out of her mother's way, her mind focussed on one thing. How long could she keep this ludicrous and demeaning situation up for, time was running out, she was fifteen and no longer the child to be bossed around ...

Late spring had arrived, and Victoria was walking calmly from her final GCSE examination, which happened to be in her favourite subject, chemistry. She had torn into the paper and finished half an hour before everyone else and was confident of an A star, as she was with the other sciences and mathematics. Only English Literature might let her down with a B because she hated reading fiction and was happiest with her head in a book of practical experiments or reading about the history of science, which she had used for her project on women in chemistry in the 19th century. Since the peculiar episode on the canal, she had kept well away from the towpath, ditched Brian because he was becoming far too clingy, and she just wanted to get on with her own life, and work extremely hard at her studies. Whatever her father was up to she never knew, nor cared; he now slept permanently in the attic guest room. The only sign of life he was still alive was the drifting smell of cigarettes in the bathroom after he had been in the morning and the sight of the back of his black raincoat in the distance as he sloped off to the potato woman on Friday evenings.

Her slovenly mother was becoming even more of a pain in the neck, hardly doing any housework, which Victoria began to do every morning before school, and the cooking later because she couldn't stand the internal chaos and needed a sense of order around her to effectively study. At least her mother could still gather enough wits to head out to the supermarket occasionally, in the old battered green Volvo she had hung onto for years. Anyway, she needed to get there to keep stocked up with Bells, which was disappearing down her gullet at an ever increasing rate.

Victoria had entered for four extra examinations on top of the eight academic ones, including art, computing and music, which she enjoyed hugely and even had to pay for them out of her own pocket as they didn't want to know.

Her mother was getting balmier; perhaps it was the drink or she was always that way. Years ago they would have locked her mother up in the Burscough lunatic asylum. Victoria cared little except for one thing. The constant visions and the feelings. Her mother kept babbling on about a bad presence, and evil vibrations in the cottage, and was forever pouring over a large old bible. She had always gone on about being psychic when Victoria was a little girl and half scared the life out of her then, although sometimes, Victoria had to freely admit that there were times when she felt uncomfortable in the place and didn't know why, especially after that upsetting night on the canal.

It was her chemistry teacher, Dr Eva Pfennig who had triggered the most insane idea, but it gripped her mercilessly. Today was the day of action. She would do it, without any further hesitation. Eva was in her mid twenties and single, and they had gotten on together so well, and she even offered extra chemistry tutorials after school, a great help with practical work. The idiot slags at the bottom of the class, who liked to mess about all day rather than learn anything useful for their futures, used to call her Everest because she was so tall, but Victoria made sure they got a kicking when no one was looking. Nobody bullied her anymore. Eva was German, her mother had fled to England after being released from Auschwitz and Eva had studied science at Leiden University in Holland, a place of real academic learning, like the Dutch equivalent of Cambridge. She was going to do the same, she was inspired. It was time to run, her patience had finished, she was sixteen and the weekend job had been good. She had saved over a thousand pounds, all locked up and hidden away in her moneybox.

She hadn't packed much, just enough to all go in her rucksack. She had kept up the regular record sessions with Annie and had also developed an odd urge to wear a lot of purple, which she now loved as a fashion shade, both of them dolling up for the Kings Arms on Saturday nights, in a sort of matching gothic rock style. That was one thing she was going to miss, but Annie was not as academic and had decided to do beauty therapy at the local further education college in Ormskirk, so they would likely go their own ways in due course anyway, but she would remain her best friend forever.

Most importantly, Annie's parents were stars. They understood everything. Zeb, amazingly, had given her an address of a place at somewhere called the Pinsengracht, in Amsterdam, and the names of Beth and Andromeda. They were old friends of his and had bought one of the big old merchant houses along there and set up some sort of hippy academic commune of environmentalists. Zeb just said turn up and mention his name, and she would be good to go with a roof over her head. Zeb had joked that she would feel totally at home being alongside a canal and anyway, there were lots more canals in Amsterdam to explore. She had bought her map, got her passport and exchanged a hundred pounds of her money into Dutch guilders and was feeling very excited, her stomach dancing about with the anticipation.

Following a lengthy and tearful set of goodbyes, good luck and hugs from Annie and her parents, she jumped into the waiting taxi and set off towards Ormskirk station and the ferries. Once in Calais she would hitch to Holland. But on the way, she was perusing her map realising that the Andromeda household was near Ann Frank's House, an interesting place she looked forward to visiting, which made her think immediately of someone also very special. Almost causing the taxi to swerve, she asked immediately for a detour to Eva's, who lived about a mile from Burscough station so she would get the train from there instead.

She knocked nervously at the door; she knew the address but had never been there. Eva slowly opened it and looked wide-eyed at Victoria, her long hair in a ponytail, all kitted out with hiking boots, heavy rucksack and wax jacket.

"Hi Eva, I just wanted to see you before I go and thank you for all you did to help me, the chemistry exam was a cinch today."

Eva looked up and down the road carefully then waved Victoria in. She stepped straight into the living room of a small two-up and two-down Edwardian town house. The room was beautifully furnished with antique furniture, and a lovely old re-covered red couch and matching armchairs. An old stereo system, with a mixture of tapes, records and CDs stacked in a glass cupboard sat in one corner. The heavy velvet curtains were drawn tightly and the room dimly lit by a couple of wall lights, the walls nicely decorated with prints of female scientists. The dour unsmiling Marie Curie took pride of place over the fireplace. She could hear a television on slightly in the dining room next door. Having physically grown a lot in her previous school year, Victoria was almost as tall now as Eva, both a commanding presence and probably the only useful thing she took from her mother.

Eva, lifting off the heavy rucksack onto the floor, beckoned her to the couch and sat next to her, taken aback and intrigued, expecting Victoria, next term, to join the sixth form.

Victoria began to explain and felt her heart pound as a small tear rolled down Eva's left cheek. Blimey ... she certainly hadn't wanted to upset the best teacher she ever had by miles. But Eva finally smiled and said she was humbled to have inspired Victoria to do something so exciting, and how wonderful it would be at Leiden University, but that she would have to learn Dutch, despite half the courses being run in English. Some more advanced study first before being admitted was also emphasised and being vital. And Eva would happily write her a glowing reference if required.

Victoria was over the moon, and forgetting for a moment that Eva was her teacher not Annie, went to kiss her on the cheek to thank her … but suddenly found their lips meeting passionately for a good five minutes instead. It made her heart thump wildly, she had never realised before, having a set of blinkers on, and now realised why Eva was so upset. Everything suddenly made sense. Eventually Eva drew away, flushed and embarrassed.

Victoria stood up calmly and confidently. "Don't worry Dr Pfennig. I'm sorry I must go; I can't afford to miss that last ferry tonight. Tell you what; perhaps I should call you Eva from now on, if that's OK? And hey, promise me you will come and visit in Amsterdam some time and I will write regularly. Anyway I'll probably need some help soon with organic chemistry!"

Eva smiled. "Maybe I'll just do that Victoria. Keep in touch. Good luck."

Victoria was quickly out of the door, and with a final wave sauntered happily down the road toward the train station. She would just make it to London and then onwards to Dover and freedom. Skipping along she hummed to herself quietly, "Gosh, *I've kissed a girl*, so the hippies in Amsterdam won't know what will hit them. Bring it all on!" She mused mischievously that kissing a girl was likely much better than kissing a ghost, which she would have had to do if she'd stayed in Cinderblack Lane a day longer. Hopefully, the terse note left behind telling them not to bother looking for her, as she won't be coming back, would keep any further demons from following on behind …

Chapter Two

1866 at a coal tar distilling plant near Burscough:

Slumbering quietly in his large sitting room, James McKenzie could feel his eyes closing and the collection of heavy papers slipping slowly out of his grasp. He was so exhausted from the day's activity at his factory opposite, and they finally slipped from his fingers onto the floor with a hefty rustle. The gas light flame was beginning to flicker smokily again. At least, he pondered, they were so much better than the old oil lamps and the awful kerosene they used, but he began to think hard about what could improve the light even more. They needed something that the flame heated up and which would then glow very brightly ... that would do the trick.

As a successful amateur scientist and business entrepreneur it shouldn't be beyond his wit to invent something. Anyway, he was luckier than most in the nearby villages who couldn't afford gas even if they piped it into the houses. At least the streets were better lit, and crime at night had definitely gone down. Hargreaves, the local bobby, was less frantic than he used to be, he thought, laughing at the recent sight of his overweight friend running down the street with his truncheon waving, trying to catch some petty pickpockets. It was definitely serendipity that after bumping into Lord Ottersburn in the George they all agreed to jointly fund the setting up of a small gasworks in the town. In fact being so near the canal was ideal as the boat people could deliver endless cargoes of coal to keep the furnace fuelled up constantly. That had given him the idea to convert those redundant cowsheds and stables at the other end of the yard into a coal tar manufacturing plant, as it was relatively easy for him to add orders in alongside the gasworks requirements, and with the canal running at the back of the estate, Jake Gibbons and his men could keep the yard well stacked up. One excellent by-product of his entrepreneurial spirit was he could light all his own house up with gas lights for free, as well as pipe additional gas into the town network for the benefit of the community, although that pumping station needed some improving.

But those boat people could be a pain in the proverbial neck. At least, he mused, the Edwards family were mostly reliable and Jim Edwards, head boatman of his prolific clan, could be depended upon to ensure reasonably regular loads, even though he forever complained of the cost of horse feeds and his low wages, until it was suggested maybe he had fewer children, at which point he retorted, in jest. 'What else is there to do at night stuck in a boat in Wigan? I could play the fiddle, get drunk or fuck the wife.' Well one had to agree, after hearing the fiddle playing and then looking at his delectably buxom and red-haired young wife.

James McKenzie was enjoying his reminiscences and reveries, with a small Scotch by his side and the coal fire burning as hot as Hades in the room. He really had to get Lucy to moderate her size of shovels. Suddenly there was an almighty racket outside as the factory siren began whistling like the devil and a heavy clumping of feet and shouting could be heard running up the hallway, with Lucy screaming for them to get their boots off. The heavy oak door burst open and Jake rushed in, followed by his deputy and a couple of workmen holding shovels, their faces and clothes all covered in soot and filthy wet grime.

"Sir, sincere apologies for disturbing you, please, you've got to come quickly, there's been a calamity in the plant. The new cylinder for producing nitrobenzol has blown sky high. Joe Gregson got covered in acid and ran screaming out the back and dived into the canal. We fished him out with a large boathook but he's looking bad sir, I don't think he's going to make it. Albert has shot off on one of the horses into town to get Dr Gill, but Gregson looks terrible, burnt to hell."

James McKenzie shot up from his chair, grabbing his coat off the table. "Jesus Christ, Jake," he shouted out in a rage. "Some stupid fool has probably tipped in the nitrate of sodium far too quickly, which has reacted with the sulphuric acid to form nitrous fumes and nitric acid. I told you that reaction really generates some heat and you have to go easy. Fuck it all, the whole reason for setting up that cylinder was to get us to produce our own nitrobenzol rather than buying it in to get the aniline. Goddam it that will set us back."

"I'm sorry sir, I take full responsibility; I was out having a smoke and the apprentice turned the screw handle the wrong way, I don't know how many times I told the thick idiot. We've got to have better training sir; I can't do it and look after all the plant as well."

"Don't worry Jake, we'll have to sort it. Damnation, let's get over and see how Joe is …"

They were interrupted as Albert rushed in. He doffed his cap to James McKenzie then turned to Jake. "Doctor's 'ere, Jake. Ah've taken him yonder t' shed, he needs bandages and stuff."

"Okay, thanks …" James replied. "Lucy," he shouted as his housekeeper ran in petrified at the mess everywhere. "Take a couple of these men to the basement and get that trunk with all

19

that stuff I brought back from the Crimea. It's full of bandages and medicines. Let's go Jake and see what Gill can do. Does Gregson have a family?"

"Yes sir, eight children all under ten, one lad thirteen and his wife with pleurisy."

"Hells bells, c'mon."

Slowly they carried Gregson, bandaged up like a mummy and groaning in pain, to the horse and trap to get him quickly to the local hospital. James handed some pound notes to Jake to ensure medical expenses were paid for presently. They had poured whisky down his throat to deaden his senses but even if he recovered, which was highly debatable, he would not work for a long time if ever. James McKenzie had already begun contemplating some sort of basic worker compensation scheme to at least make sure families were fed if these things happened. They were working with highly dangerous processes and this was the second serious accident in a month, although the last one, when one of the stokers tripped and fell into the coke bed was his own fault for being too lazy or more likely too drunk after three hours in the George, to put the guarding up.

James McKenzie had always felt a social responsibility towards the local town and community and definitely leaned politically towards Disraeli and the Conservatives, presently in power and he had contributed to Lord Ottersburn's committee to help draft up the next Reform Act to give more rural working people the vote. He had no time for those mealy mouthed spouting Liberals under Gladstone who worked against the sound principles of conservatism, especially as business and industry now could be clearly seen to be changing the whole landscape of society and wealth distribution. He accepted he was privileged although the McKenzies had earned their wealth through science and engineering applications since the mid 1600s, the aptitude, amazingly passing on from generation to generation. His grandfather and father had been active developing steam engine manufacturing, and doing their bit towards the growing industrialisation that had shot ahead since the 1830s, especially with the canal being extended, and the coal traffic moving from Yorkshire down to Liverpool, a port buzzing with new activity and wealth creation.

But, unlike his father and grandfather he was a scientist, a chemist indeed, down to his boots and was committed to making his own family mark with a new industrial application in the plant. The accidental discovery of the first artificial dye made from coal tar by Perkins ten years back was an astoundingly important development for textiles. Whilst much progress had been made on the chemistry of the processes which he had been studying assiduously since, and producing the violet dye and indigo from aniline, there was still much to do to effect decent commercialisation, and what a huge market would lay ahead for those at the forefront. This dye work was as big as the first steam engine or the spinning jenny. James McKenzie was determined to be at that forefront, and get seriously rich from the pickings. The accident was a definite setback. If only he could engineer some better processes ...

Word was returning from the hospital, as Lucy rushed in to tell the news. Gregson was burned over seventy percent of his body with sulphuric acid and unlikely to live until daylight. His family were distraught. McKenzie went down the yard to talk to Jake who was gathered with other workers inside the plant mess area.

"Sir, I'm afraid it isn't looking good ..."

21

"Yes, I know. Jake. What were we paying Joe Gregson? I have decided to set up a compensation scheme which will come from investing some of our profits into a sort of new pension arrangement. My accountant is inside; he will be drawing it up."

"But Mr McKenzie," Robert Thompson, the head stoker interjected. "Them down road in spinning factory, they get nowt if someone's injured. We know risks. That's what we working men do, it goes with the job. You don't need to ..."

James McKenzie raised his arm and stopped the discussion. "That idiot Turner over in the textiles factory isn't using his brains. The better protected and supported worker conditions become, then the more productive the output and more profits and wages for everyone. I really believe that principle and we must, from today, institute a better training system. Safety and safe processes will become our guiding mission; I don't want corners cut which endanger lives any more. Thompson, I want you to head that up with your experience. Jake, the answer to my question please."

Jake shuffled on his stool, individual wages were not high and Gregson had been unskilled labour. "I paid him three shillings and ninepence weekly sir that was a full six days and ten hours a day. Those of us skilled we're paid more."

"Okay. From tomorrow then, assuming Gregson doesn't make it, his widow and family will continue to be paid half wages, reviewed in a year, so at least with that and the extra from poor allowance in the parish, those children will be kept fed and a roof over their heads."

The men looked stunned at the generosity but all felt a huge wave of gratitude to the boss. McKenzie was different and Jake thought, if he gets the vote next year from the Government then he will vote for Mr McKenzie to lead the Town Council.

"Thank you Mr McKenzie, I will see to it that injury pay is sorted first thing tomorrow. Gregson's oldest lad will be on the boats next year, the family have been canal people for generations, so money will start to come back in as well, but in the meantime, your scheme will be a great help for all of us if anything happens again, God willing it won't." Jake turned to his deputy. "What are we all hanging about for? We have a full night's stoking to do, let's get to it."

James McKenzie went back to the house. It had been a very long day but a momentous one in so many ways. Fatigue drew him to bed as he heard Lucy putting a hot water bottle under the covers. It was a cold night and hopefully she will have lit a fire in there too. He was looking forward to the research work he had planned in his new basement laboratory in eight hours time. Who else could dream about coal tar dye colours? Except probably his beautiful laboratory assistant.

McKenzie was up even earlier than usual, his brain blowing steam like a leaky governor, on a plethora of ideas to develop the business further. He'd had a strange dream, and was inside a crowded railway carriage travelling across Europe to Vienna, his mind always saturated with music and he loved the Waltz. He was in his pyjamas, embarrassed as everyone around was dressed in fine clothes. A beautiful blonde Russian woman with bright blue eyes, and her hair in a tight bun, sidled up and sat alongside him staring non-stop into his eyes. She wore the most beautiful, multicoloured silk gown, all greens, oranges and yellows in intricate patterns. She began a conversation. Her name was Natalya and she needed desperately to converse with someone about opera and dresses. She looked deeply into his eyes and sang an aria gently, the most beautiful voice he had ever heard and it aroused him in all kinds of ways. Finally, under his dressing gown, she moved her hand and held his erection tightly. He was both petrified and mesmerised by her beauty and sensuality. He tells her she must follow her passion, seek her destiny and become a singer, and she smiles back saying she would never leave him again. Then in the seat opposite three children sat down and smiled at them, accompanied by a good looking young man with dark brown hair and a large beard. The children were a spitting likeness of her, three girls under the age of puberty, with the same piercing eyes and stare, and they were dressed identically in beautiful bright red long dresses and shiny, expensive black boots. The man is staring at the children and then blankly out of the window, then at her, then blankly again out of the window, his eyes transfixed into the distance, as the train slowly rattles along. He is trapped, unable to move between the beautiful woman and other people, crowded on all sides. The children all continue to stare back at him and smile and she moves her hand, under his dressing gown between his thighs, whilst the man continues to stare blankly, non-plussed, obviously the father and her husband and what is he to do ...?

He had woken up in a sweat, bedding in disarray, but immediately felt inspired. His mind had unlocked on where to go next with his dyeing experiments in the laboratory. He was frustrated with only finding ever more variants of that perfidious mauve colour; light violets, dark violets, green violets even golden violets. He had indeed made much sound progress and written up four papers to present to the Manchester Chemical Society, and his correspondence with the chemist Hoffman, a strange man but they got on well, who he had met in London last year had proven apposite. Hoffman had hinted that, working on some new reactions with aniline and dichromate of potassium and then leaching with a photographic fix, he had fleetingly come across new colours, possible potential dyes, but had been struggling to replicate. That was the direction he and his laboratory assistant would need to go down; to create proper greens, yellows, and reds and orange with mordants which fix well and can be commercially developed in England. Those damn continentals, especially Germany, had been taking too much of a lead in dyes; England has and always will be the world leader in textiles.

Of course, the dream. Then it came to him. His recent meeting at that quaint London party of Lord Ottersburn. My God that man owned some impressive Georgian properties though. He was introduced to those two textiles people, William Morris and Thomas Wardle, who were collaborating on improving both dyeing techniques and print patterns, and had brought a small exhibition which everyone perused in the antechamber. Wardle was a silk dyer of some repute and a chemist too, but seemed to be obsessed with Indian silks and natural dyes.

He racked his brain and his thoughts continued to assemble with a contented smile ...

When he had mentioned the researching of coal tar processes, not only for dyes but other industrial uses, they became very interested and he had politely accepted an invitation in the New Year to one of their sessions in Leek of all places, where Wardle had a dye works. A godforsaken part of the country to travel around at that time of year, he had put it out of his mind, especially with the pressure at home to get that damned cast iron retort made for distilling aniline. The other gentleman, Morris, was an interesting character, a real creative jack of all trades; not just a textile designer but had written and published poetry, painted, wrote fiction and even translated mediaeval texts. Morris was a charismatic dilettante, a huge intellectual, full of amazing ideas. James McKenzie felt a potential bond could develop with Morris, as their breadth of artistic interests mutually matched. However, he believed Wardle displayed some hints of professional jealousy and concerns of plagiarism, always far from his mind, but Wardle was gruff and forcefully obsessive about silk and India, neither of which was uppermost in his priorities. Nevertheless, he could clearly see that their collaboration had much potential to encourage innovation and growth in the textiles and dyes sector.

But of course, then he finally realised ... his dream. The woman must have been lurking at the back of his inner mind. Morris had been accompanied by his wife, a striking beauty, refined and astoundingly knowledgeable about Pre-Raphaelite painting. She was hugely flirtatious and desirable, apparently a model as well, but somehow, although on the surface Jane and her husband appeared in love and devoted, there also seemed to be a cold distance between them, obvious by her need to talk constantly about the arts, deliberately unconnected with Morris' interests.

McKenzie pondered sadly for a moment and reflected on his status as a widower. Yes, he had all the luxury, goods and surroundings any man would wish for, but he was still lonely. His scientific work absorbed him that was true, but it had been five years since Susanna had died from the pox, that stupid but admirable insistence to care for the dying in the Burscough sanatorium after that virulent outbreak in '61. Perhaps it was time to think again about ... mmm... in fact maybe he will travel to Leek after all, and he could take his beautiful and talented assistant with him as well. She would undoubtedly impress Wardle with her knowledge of dyeing processes. It was a shame that the rights of women, and women's scientific

26

education were so stunted in the country, such a huge waste of talent and potential. He had also been taken with the brief conversation on that very issue that he had shared with Morris who obviously had strong leanings to social equality and community well being, akin to his own. Ottersburn was recommending him for a knighthood next year so perhaps he could make it a double celebration with Morris in Leek, and see again the intriguing and mesmerising Jane.

He remembered the very violent argument he had last meeting with those ridiculously prejudiced, and so called senior scientists and elder statesmen at the Royal Society Lecture, when some idiot was castigating women for debasing the natural tendencies of men in science by working in laboratories and how they must be expelled immediately from such inane and seditious thoughts and actions, because there was only one acceptable ambition for women and that was marriage, the home and children.

What utter nonsense, but without doubt if he had not personally schooled his female laboratory assistant from a young age in chemistry and mathematics and taken care of her education and well being, she would well have ended up illiterate, with seven children and wasting her life away in one of those damned barges on the canal. She had showed talent and ability from an early age, from the moment in fact she was brought to the house having been found, by his boatman, abandoned on the canal edge near Ormskirk. Susanna was insistent that we should bring her up without hesitation. When Susanna died she had been formally adopted immediately, and the legalities could never be challenged again. Now she was almost seventeen, beautiful and totally absorbed intellectually and practically in the dyeing research and laboratory science.

Indeed, he could not have continued his science work without her. But there was of course much more to it, and Jake must never ever know. Some secrets would have to be kept to the grave and beyond. He ruminated happily back to that moment when Harold, his head butler, brought her into the drawing room, all swaddled up in a purple coloured thin blanket and a matching purple woollen shawl around her head, obviously newborn; thank goodness it had been mid-summer and the weather sunny and warm. Susanna and Lucy took charge immediately with the bottle, and she grew strong and healthy quickly from that day and had remained so. Even now she enjoyed walking around with that shawl around her head, justifying the name he had chosen for her, on the spot. It seemed appropriate then, inspired even, and his cousins Madeleine and Eveline were also visiting, so the name even rhymed well. It was at that point of course that Mauveine emerged into the world and had since been remarkably living up to her name.

There was a loud knock on his bedroom door and Harold Rimmer, head butler, entered with a silver tray and bacon and eggs for breakfast.

"Rimmer, thank you. Can you find Jake, I'm sure he must be down in the plant. I need to have a meeting with him in an hour to go through the new design of a distilling retort which I have decided we will make to replace the old one wrecked in the disastrous accident yesterday."

"Of course sir, I will fetch him right away. In the drawing room?"

"Yes please and also Mauveine will likely be down in the laboratory already too. I know she is working on a new dyeing process and I want to supervise the initial experimentation, especially with that new glassware that had been made. I'm not

28

sure it is as leak proof as it should be. So I don't want her starting before I get down there, she can work on other things first."

"Yes sir, I believe that she is still sleeping actually, from what I heard Miss Lucy saying earlier, so shall we disturb her or let her sleep in today?"

"No problem. I think occasionally she should indulge in some beauty sleep and rest. She has been quite frenetic in the laboratory 'till all hours during the week, obviously with new ideas in her head, so it will be good for her."

"Of course sir."

However, not all in the McKenzie household was quite as straightforward as James had assumed. Having bunched up her blanket and sheets into a body-like shape to appear like she was still sleeping, as it was easy to fool Lucy, much of the time, Mauveine had sneaked out of the window onto the roof of the orangery, clambering to the back and out to the stables.

At such an early time nobody was around to catch sight of her purple shawl as she unbolted the door and sneaked in, picking up her long dress carefully from the mud in the entrance and gently patting Wilhelmina, her favourite white racing horse, chomping steadily on the great wedges of straw bales which had been thrown around her area.

The horse suddenly raised her head and whinnied softly. Someone was approaching, as she turned around and giggled loudly to see Isaac, creeping through the rear of the enclosure, skilfully dodging Ben, the black gelding, standing nearby. He walked towards her, furtively glancing through the window to make sure nobody was around then held Mauveine tightly in his arms.

"Isaac Fazackerley," she cried all laughing and giggly. "You have such a funny name and your breath is all steamy and warm as well."

"Your body feels warm under this dress too," he replied, laughing too as he moved his hands up and down her back and began to moan gently.

"Don't you think it's a bit early in the morning to be getting so passionate Isi?" she retorted, holding his slim waist and noting he had put on his best breeches and waistcoat just to see her, at the ungodly hour of six am, the sun having barely risen. But they had to choose their times and moments carefully. Undoubtedly James, which he had always insisted since a child, she called him, even though she knew she was his adopted daughter, would not approve, but there were times when a girl had to follow her heart and her heart was pounding whenever she saw Isi down in the gardens or working on the horses.

Isaac Fazackerley was a gardener for the McKenzie family and also was assigned to stable duty, as he had an almost mythical skill in being able to connect with horses by talking to them. He claimed it ran in his family and his grandfather had been equally blessed with the same gift, but the rest of his family, who had drawn barges up and down the Leeds and Liverpool canal for the last four generations, since the canal was first built and opened in 1773, did not approve of his move into the McKenzie estate to be a gardener rather than a boatman as expected. The jealousy and venom had become so bad his family had finally disowned him, apart from his younger brother, Nathanial, who he drank with occasionally in the Red Lion in Ormskirk. He had been so successful in bringing order and management to the stables, and cared so well for the horses, that James McKenzie had gifted him Ben the black gelding, which he rode around the district whenever he had any free time. That wasn't much outside of Sunday as he worked such long hours doing two jobs. But it kept him solvent and he now rented a nice town house, alone, in Burscough down Victoria Street, but kept away from his other family members who lived at the other end of the street.

Mauveine looked into Isi's deep set eyes. He was twenty five, tall, slightly bashful but with the most handsome face and body. Always he was chased by the local scrubbers in town and on the boats, but only had eyes for her. She adored his trendy new moustache and his flat brown cap, which, when he wore his best hunting jacket and coat, made him look so desirable she could eat him alive. And, they talked endlessly whenever they could about science, especially biology and plants that he was fascinated with, and she had over the last two years taught him to read and write well. She was seventeen in a week's time and old enough to do what she wanted. Many girls her own age, even some of her friends, were already engaged, or married and some had two or three children, She wanted to wait and study more with James and maybe get into a University, but that was so hard for a woman chemist. But she loved Isi deliriously and he adored her and she was confident, with her scientific knowledge of remedies that she could stave off being pregnant if she wanted to.

"We don't have too long Mauveine. It's my shift this morning to muck out the stables later and I have to attend to Wilhelmina's hooves and clean them out, as she has a slight fungal infection."

"I know just the cure for that, was reading up yesterday, Isi, so I'll make up a tincture later when I get into the laboratory. I'm so excited because I am sure that I've found a new chemical reaction to improve the colour range of the coal tar dyes James and I have been experimenting with. I have a flask sat in the corner, and he hasn't seen, of a red crimson-like dye, which I'm sure nobody has made yet. My calculations show it should be part of a family and could yield a range of other related colours of reds, gold, yellows. Isn't that exciting? And I've tried the reagent out on both silk and wool and it is holding fast. If the garments don't fade, and James and I can make the process commercial, it will make a lot of money for him and maybe for me too."

He held her closer and whispered gently in her ear. "And maybe Miss Mauveine, with the even funnier name than me, you would like to consider marrying me, so what do you say?"

"Are you actually asking me Isi Fazackerley? You have a very serious look on your face and why are you trembling then, afraid I'll say no? Of course I will," she shouted out giggling loudly and ecstatic at the thought of being the only Mauveine Fazackerley in the world.

"Shush," he whispered loudly, "Someone may hear us, keep your voice down. I love you too, Miss Dyehead and …"

But he never got any further words out as she pulled his head close to her hers, feeling his adorable tickly moustache against her lips and they began to kiss passionately. This was the moment she had been calculating on and, throwing his cap into the hay, she moved her hands down to the buckle on his breeches, rubbing her hand against his obvious erection.

"Now Isi, let's celebrate properly I want you so much and I can tell you want the same."

They began kissing passionately and he slowly unbuttoned the front of her dress. She was bare underneath as he clasped her small breasts and pushed his mouth around her large pink nipples. She soon had his shirt undone and in a flurry of groans and anticipation, they were soon totally unclothed, naked, together for the first time and began rolling over and over, laughing and joking, in the soft clean straw. Wilhelmina looked placidly on, with, Mauveine thought, a definite grin across her jaws. But, they had to be quick, there was not much time left and once he had pulled her naked bottom into position and pushed her gorgeous white thighs apart, she guided him deftly into her with a sharp intake of breath. It was her first time, but she had read some interesting old Chinese manuals secretly in James's library and worked out the most scientific way of arousing herself simultaneously. He came unsurprisingly quickly but she felt an immense wave of pleasure too. She knew he had been with other women before off the boats, but she didn't care about those slags because she loved him so much and he was now hers forever …

They lay together and held each other close, her arms wrapped around his warm sweaty body, with a horse blanket over them, in the warm afterglow of their now anointed engagement. She only had half an hour left and they chatted animatedly about all kinds of silly, harmless things that young couples do, looking forward to sharing his lovely town house which he had furnished with an amazing design eye, for a man. Their love had been secret and she had only one worry; how to break the news to James, although she had absolutely no intention of giving up her science and laboratory work.

However, what neither of them knew was that someone else was aware of their affair, someone who had silently crept out and followed her to the barn. He had been peering in, unseen, through a crack in the wooden wall, his trousers around his ankles, unable to contain himself at what he saw. But he was angry and bitter inside with a mind in turmoil, his long cherished dreams destroyed forever. Mauveine was never again going to be his … he would act, and quickly.

The commotion going on in the police house in Burscough was getting out of hand as PC George Hargreaves banged his truncheon down hard on the desk and shouted for order. There was no way he was going to have mayhem in his patch, but he could see from the look on Jake's face, standing quietly, white as a sheet, at the back of the crowd of workers from McKenzie's place that something serious had gone on.

The noise abated and PC Hargreaves asked Jake to come forward to the front and speak. Slowly and methodically he explained what he had found first thing that morning. Very quickly PC Hargreaves realised this incident was beyond his pay grade and expertise and quickly dialled for assistance on the telegraph to the County police headquarters. A reply came back swiftly from the Chief Constable that a senior detective was on his way and to gather as much of the facts and evidence as he could ...

The following morning PC Hargreaves, Jake and Inspector Thomas from Preston stood and watched in the stable as the male body was being cut down from the rafters.

"No human being could possibly have survived for long inside that vat of boiling dye, nobody," Jake whispered to the two bobbies. "Her body is beyond human recognition and gruesome to such a degree that no normal stomach will keep its contents down."

"What about her clothes?" The inspector queried. "Were any found? There may be some further evidence, but I'm not sure we need it now."

"We found them all neatly stacked up alongside the vat, all dyed mauve. They had been removed and dried off carefully in front of the oven. Her left hand had been hacked off first and placed on top."

"Good Lord above," the Inspector exclaimed, his expression pained and his face reddening. "Now I can see Hargreaves why you needed us immediately. But it looks like we may not need to delve any further. This man hanging? I understand he had been dallying about with the victim. What was his name again?"

"Isaac Fazackerley, Inspector," Hargreaves muttered slowly, now wishing he had done more work first as he could have got some credit for maybe solving it before HQ came into the case. "Head stable hand and gardener for James McKenzie the owner of the house, and legal guardian of the woman in question. Yes rumour has it that he had been sweet on her, and they were seen together a few times in the Red Lion, and riding the two horses which he looked after. However I have it also on good evidence that the woman in question was … well … how can I say it … somewhat fancy free with other lads in the town, especially the boatmen. And Inspector we also found her horse, with its throat cut, lying outside by the fence, and the other gelding, which belonged to Isaac Fazackerley, a gift from the master of the house, James McKenzie, has vanished, set free I wonder."

"And McKenzie, can we rule him out Constable?"

Jake then intervened. "I can confirm, Inspector, that Mr McKenzie could not possibly have anything to do with this gruesome murder. He loved his adopted daughter very much and in any case, he was with me and my men the whole time when it would have happened. We were in the plant for hours together setting up a new distilling cylinder. But I'm afraid Mr McKenzie is in no state to make any statement Inspector. We had to rush him to the hospital. On hearing the news he collapsed with some sort of heart attack or seizure and has gone mute. He is being looked after intensively over there."

"Distilling? Are you making liquor here man, do you have authorisation from the County?" the Inspector railed, as PC Hargreaves, standing behind, winked back at Jake.

"Err, no Inspector, we distil coal tar to make dyes. This is our business here and the victim was an important part of the work, a trainee chemist in the laboratory."

"So she knew the dangers of boiling vats. Couldn't have fallen in accidentally?"

"Hardly likely Inspector given the height of the sides, she would have had to have been hauled up on a pulley."

"And this man Fazackerley, is he one of those Fazackerley boat people? They have quite a reputation in this County, never up to any good. I have half a dozen locked up in the County jail in Preston."

"Yes Inspector, he was indeed," Hargreaves replied almost gleefully, which Jake, who liked Isaac very much was about to object to, but after a look from his deputy, bit his tongue.

Inspector Thomas became thoughtful for a few moments then began. "Well gentlemen, I think we have now solved this crime. It is very clear that Isaac Fazackerley, perhaps having learned of her misdeeds, got maniacally jealous and murdered her in a rage, a crime of passion, then suffered some sort of remorse and hanged himself immediately afterwards. All the evidence incontrovertibly stacks up. I am instructing, Constable Hargreaves, that this case be closed forthwith please. Odd name that woman had. Get the paperwork to my office by the end of next week and inform the Coroners Court. And can someone do something about those local press officials over the other side of the gate there? They can now have their story. Good day gentlemen."

Hargreaves smirked and led the Inspector off the premises. Jake just stood and shook his head as they bundled up the body of Isaac Fazackerley to be buried later ...

Chapter Three

2010 in the Erasmus Medical Centre, Rotterdam:

Lying in a hospital bed was not an experience that Victoria would have ever put high on her desirables priority list. It had been two days since she suddenly awoke, groggy and incoherent, from a week long coma. Even taking Eva to the local accident and emergency in Amsterdam, years back, when Eva fell over in the snow and sprained her ankle, filled her with dread. Perhaps it was that weird sort of hangover relationship from her childhood, when her mother used to constantly talk about the Ormskirk fever hospital and children screaming and dying from polio in the fifties all locked up in Dickensian old buildings with high windows with bars and extensive grounds with dogs patrolling. She knew, in her heart, hospitals were never really like that and her mother's imagination was going through another paranoid turn, but the subconscious stuck. But as she looked around, that old childhood obsession began to dissipate fast. She was in bed in a private room, all light and airy, with lots of comforting equipment around her. As a scientist that gave her a lift of confidence, perusing the tubes and medications lying on the table. Obviously some of that gear had been plugged into her before she woke up, fluids, sensors, alarms rigged, but the equipment was now discretely pushed away. Thank God she had forged back into life under her own steam by some miracle guardian angel watching over. What an odd thing to think, she mused, being an ardent atheist and humanist. No such thing as that guardian angel nonsense, eyeing the gorgeous long mauve velvet curtains hanging conspicuously in front of her. This was an expensive set up. Her employer must be being uncharacteristically generous as she could certainly never have afforded it. Those curtains were the first thing she saw, when she first came round, only they weren't curtains, just a blur of purple light, all kinds of shades and hues of violet, some green, some golden and some … mmm … crimson, shimmering and shading from one to another in a warm and welcoming blur of intricate patterns. If it wasn't for Abby and her obsession with colour schemes, she would never have known so many shades of violet existed … strange … it was like one of those dreams where you're flying at a hundred miles an hour, soaring into the sky and never wanting to leave … and then she woke up to a sea of smiling faces in white coats. And she was alive again.

Only now could she begin to think properly, although what got her there in the first place was still hazy. She remembered the sirens wailing mournfully, louder and louder, then a huge flash and that was that. She would have to work on exercising her brain, and began recreating a mental portfolio of her life since coming to Holland …

Suddenly the door opened with a knock and two nurses, one carrying a tray of porridge and berries with some toast and a glass of hot tea, entered. They smiled and began to speak to her in English. She sat up and they plumped her pillows and fluffed her sheets then wheeled over a large bed trolley to put the food onto.

"Ms McKenzie, we are so glad to see you awake. It's time to eat some proper food now. Are you feeling peckish? I am Annemieke and my colleague is Wilhelmina."

Victoria stared at their badges and smiled. She was certainly feeling hungry … gosh, this was the first real meal she had seen; yesterday had only been chicken soup. Wilhelmina? What a lovely name. She had never heard that before.

"Actually it's Miss, not Ms McKenzie I'm not quite that liberated, but hey just call me Vikki, no need for the formality. And thank you so much for the care, the food and … well keeping me alive."

They laughed. "All part of the service Vikki, but hopefully you won't do it again!" Wilhelmina replied with a broad grin and a mouth full of big white teeth, a bit like a horse but somehow very attractive. Victoria was quite amused, they were so Dutch, and not just the blonde hair in small pigtails and the sharp blue eyes but the way they spoke English, that trademark, stilted accent and precise wording that few Dutch seem to lose.

Annemieke took her temperature and blood pressure, and finally a quick heart scan with weird electrode sensors placed on her body as they lifted her white nightgown up, realising she had a pair of matching knickers on underneath but nothing else. She tucked into the steaming porridge and fruit with relish, real food at last, whilst the two nurses quietly wrote up her notes for the delicious looking Dr Ahmed, who would be visiting again later morning to check on her progress. She felt relieved when they began wheeling out the contraption with lights, bottles, fluids and tubes all over it, like a monster electronic octopus.

Annemieke came back over. "We'll leave you to your breakfast, I am so glad you have your appetite returned well. It is quite possible, I think, that only one more day you may be here? We will see what Dr Ahmed says later."

As they walked towards the door, Wilhelmina made some remarks in Dutch to Annemieke, both of them grinning.

Victoria raised her hand and also grinned. "Hey both of you, I speak fluent Dutch. Thanks for the vote of confidence."

Wilhelmina turned and smiled back, her eyes flashing. "Yes, Vikki, I know," she grinned and they closed the door, chattering away down the corridor outside.

Victoria started to butter the toast with marmalade, the tea was nice but she still hated that awful Dutch habit of serving tea in a glass, she would never get used to that ever. It really bucked her up to hear Wilhelmina say how attractive she was and that her progress from coming out of the coma was nothing short of miraculous. That was just what a girl wants to hear stuck in hospital.

She decided to work her brain further before Dr Ahmed arrived, and convince herself all was well. She began running through as many organic chemical structures and formulae as she could, saying out the compound loud and repeating the formulation, although why her head was suddenly focussed on coal tar derivatives she had no idea, not having studied those since she left Leiden University, but aniline she immediately rattled off $C_{27}H_{24}N_4$ … or was it actually that complex a molecule?

As she was happily working through an array of organic compound formulae, and pleased with how much recall she could muster, a second knock sounded and the door swept open. A tall, unaccompanied elderly Asian man walked briskly up to the bed, closing the door behind him. She peered through her glasses, as he held out his hand.

"Ah, Dr McKenzie, I am Mr Ahmed, Principal Consultant in this establishment for trauma injuries. I think now we should decide what to do next, do you agree?"

She looked up confused. "I'm sorry, I did see a Dr Ahmed but unless my brain is playing tricks he was …"

"Yes, I agree, much younger, definitely more handsome and dashing, but not quite as wise … yet …"

She had no idea who this character was or what he was talking about, but at least he got her title correct for the first time. She had worked long and hard for that PhD, so he wasn't totally bonkers, feeling for the intruder panic button just in case.

The consultant laughed. "Dr Ahmed is my son, registrar in Accident and Emergency, but in fact whilst you were sleeping peacefully over the last seven days, you were transferred then into my care. And, I must say, I am astounded by your rate of recovery, considering how you were when you came in. We have had nobody like you before Dr McKenzie so I can only put it down to strong Scottish genes." He grinned. "The good news, having reviewed your notes and spoken to all of my team of specialists, is we fully concur that tomorrow you can be on your way home at lunchtime. I'd just like a final twenty four hours to be sure. Can someone pick you up?"

She grinned wildly, in fact quite inanely really, it was so unexpected. She had anticipated being in for weeks and weeks. "That's amazing, Mr Ahmed, thank you so much for what you have done, whatever was in those bottles of fluids worked some magic. I'll call my flatmate Abby shortly, she'll pick me up."

"All down to you this time. Tell me what did you do your doctorate in?"

"Polymer chemistry, at Leiden."

"An interesting choice and excellent university. Me too, but then I retrained as a doctor instead. In Pakistan, my country, there were more opportunities for work, but, as a young man many years back, I enjoyed chemistry as an intellectual challenge much more. Does your friend Abby have short spiky pink hair, tattoos over her arms and dresses all in black?"

Victoria laughed, feeling immediately hugely elated and warm all over. "That is definitely Abby, not many around this sort of hospital with that description, Mr Ahmed."

"No, quite," he replied, shaking her hand. "She's outside waiting in the nurse's station, keeping them amused by the sound of it, so no need to phone. Otherwise, goodbye Dr McKenzie, get up later and walk around for a while, don't over exert yourself until you feel your energy back. I might consider a job, if I were you, in a nice quiet research laboratory rather than that awful refinery. There have been rumours for a while of serious problems down there."

She grimaced for a moment. He was probably right. Anyway first things first and she just wanted to see Abby.

As he walked out through the door, a whirlwind of excited pink haired babble roared in and plonked itself down by the side of Victoria's bed before jumping up and giving her a warm and gentle hug. "Wow chuck, you look totally fabulous considering what has been happening. Have I been worried about you? But they wouldn't tell me sod all over the phone, as I wasn't a relative, even though I tried to tell them you had no relatives and I was your next of kin. Tomorrow we'll have you out of here and as my next web design commission meeting isn't until next week, yours truly can pamper you like wicked. How does that sound? And you'll never guess, that guy in the flat opposite has been …"

Victoria, pleased as punch, put a gentle finger over Abby's lips. "Steady on Ms Tornado, let me ring for some tea, then you can start again, only slowly, and I want you to bring my skinny black jeans in tomorrow as this liquid diet over the last week has definitely improved my dress size."

They giggled and began a non-stop catch-up, definitely likely to last until at least lunchtime …

43

During the afternoon, once Abby had gone to see a client, Victoria made the effort to get up for the first time, wrap a dressing gown around herself and walk slowly but steadily to the lovely garden outside. It was a warm and sunny late summer day, a little noisy from the traffic, but the roses were all out in bloom along with loads of chrysanthemums and flowering shrubs as she plonked herself on a bench. Other patients in varying degrees of recovery, on crutches and in wheelchairs, were doing the same all watched over discretely by a couple of nurses near the door. She still couldn't understand why she felt so well, just a little tired, but she had felt like that much of the time in her stressful job anyway and wasn't complaining.

Living with her best friend Abby for the last three years in their compact two bedroomed apartment had been a bit of an experience. She still missed Eva occasionally, but that was a long time ago now. Eva was so amazing, coming over nearly every weekend, helping her to settle into the Dutch college system and environment but more than anything teaching her how … well… about life, normal things, relating with people for the first time; Eva had so many great friends in Amsterdam. She had seriously calmed down, began to appreciate there was more to music than Motorhead and Led Zeppelin, and developed a shared adoration of opera and jazz. She finally grew up, and she learned for the first time how to truly love another human being and do and be all the normal things she should have learned from her mother and father; Eva had provided the caring surrogate, but in a compressed timeframe. Their relationship became intense, wonderful and accepted, and Eva made sure she got into Leiden University, where she continued to study hard and she got her top degree in chemistry a year earlier than normal. Of course after a year she outgrew the commune in Amsterdam, and with Eva's help, she got a small bedsit in Leiden which they both furnished and decorated. And the weekend job which Eva found for her, testing in the laboratories of a bread factory in Delft, paid well, so she had become a truly independent scientist at last. That was the best period of her life, a constant balancing act requiring lots of determination, trust and organisation, but she loved it and found she really did have an aptitude to be normal. She laughed thinking about the moment when a large can of paint tipped off the ladder over Eva's head; fortunately it was water-based, although the bath never looked quite the same again...

But like all good things they always have to come to an end, perhaps when you didn't expect it, alongside the inevitable trouble coming in threes. She was in the last year of her PhD. She noticed Eva a little edgy and distant, then it all came out. Eva had been promoted to Head of Science in a girls' private school near Wigan, but it seemed that the less than subtle and determined wiles and subterfuge of her Head of English colleague had been too much to resist. They had been having a torrid affair for the previous two years and finally were living together; Jasmine, or whatever stupid name it was, had now become a full time writer of literary short stories or some crap or other. Victoria had never heard again from her mother and father, but then that same week as Eva broke the news that it was best not to come over to Holland again, she received an email letter from Annie, now working in a beauty salon and living with Eric, Brian's old friend, in Liverpool, who had been trying for years to track her down and finally managed through social media, via the new Facebook page Eva had forced her to put up.

Her father, it appeared, had died two years before and her mother had sold the cottage in Cinderblack Lane and vanished back to America! A cold and clammy sensation swept across her, just for a moment and she remembered in a flash, as you do in moments like that, a couple of happy periods in her childhood. And she cried for hours, not particularly for her father and certainly not for her mother, but for the great gaping hole of uncertainty and unreality for so long in her life that only now had been filled. That was until Eva provided the *'it's all over'* bombshell, and then the third thing; her landlord threatened her with eviction because he wanted the flat for his sister.

Obviously the runes had been truly shaken, her life had to restart a new phase, and that was when, on the hoof, she moved to Rotterdam, got a job in the testing laboratory in the Ahrendolie refinery and rediscovered men, sex and eventually Abby, a crazy ex-fashion designer from Manchester, who worked in the Turkish kebab shop, and still did, in between her precarious design freelancing … but now she could see best friend Abby walking up the path to reception with a large bag of clothes … great … it was time to depart.

Pouring out a tea, sat in a cafe alongside the harbour in Rotterdam, Abby grabbed the last teacake and stared quizzically at Victoria. "So, are you going to tell me what happened in there? You've kept very silent. I still don't know how you can work in that awful place, the stench that comes out constantly."

Victoria looked thoughtful. Abby had a fair point, but in fact quite possibly events could take a life of their own, as she would find out the following day. She had been signed off by her doctor to return to work but the refinery had asked her to meet with both the Chief Executive and her boss, the Operations Director first thing. "I may not have a job actually Abby. Things got sort of complicated?"

"What you mean finding yourself blown out of a building, the only one alive, with a massive explosion. It sounds like serious negligence to me and a big compensation payout."

"I don't know. Tell you what. If you go and get some lagers, then I'll tell you, because I need to try and make sense ..."

Abby could see that Victoria was looking tense and strained.

"No problem, in fact as it's coming up to lunch time I shall treat you to your favourite ham and cheese omelette with a big salad too."

Victoria smiled back and nodded.

"Good, that's more like it, exactly what best friends are for," Abby replied and sidled off to the crowded bar area to order the food.

Victoria began to reflect carefully. After ten years in the laboratory and some useful promotions, management had put her on a fast track leadership programme and she now headed and directed a small team of analysts who undertook constant sampling analysis of products for both safety and purity. She enjoyed her job and was well paid, enabling her to now afford a big mortgage on her luxury apartment, which whilst compact, was beautifully set up and furnished with an impressive modern kitchen and appliances. Then of course when, one night, she was picking up some kebabs at Ali's around the corner, and when Abby had discretely asked if she knew of any lodgings, it seemed a sensible move to let the other bedroom. They got on well from the beginning. Abby had quickly become like Annie, a soul mate friend and they shared the same love of eating out, rock music, clubbing, clothes and men. Now both in their mid thirties, neither wanted any permanent relationships, which always only lasted a couple of months, then they each moved on to the next conquests. Abby was a highly qualified fashion and textiles designer with her own small label, but had suffered a bad business deal five years before and was made bankrupt, surviving on Ali's continuing largesse to employ her three days a week and the occasional design work, mainly on websites as she was a whizz with computers.

Abby plonked the lager glasses down on the table. "You know Vikki, it's a desert out there with any decent guys our own age. Do you think it's because we're getting old, crotchety spinsters or something? I'm getting a bit sick of toyboys to be honest, especially that dick Adrian I've been seeing lately, because actually they all seem to fuck the same way and have nothing decent to say."

Victoria sighed. "You may be right, I'm giving it a miss for a while. I fancy a bit of a celibate spell and get my head together."

"I reckon it's time you went out with an older man, what's the oldest bloke you've been out with?"

"Twenty-nine."

"What?" Abby roared laughing as everyone looked around, her pink spiky hair dominating the colour scene of the drab cafe area. "And you're thirty five, Jesus. At least I've dated some forty year olds, big paunches and not so big …"

Victoria interrupted smiling. She loved Abby's never getting serious moments. But she had to get serious. "I think I get the picture, okay you want to hear? Then drink up and the food's coming. Here goes. My team had been given a rather tricky job, there was suspected corrosion in the distillation tower which produces heavy naphtha and I was asked to organise some analytical work on the pipes."

"Naphtha?"

"Yes, a smelly and very volatile liquid, a normal by-product of the usual distillation process of crude oil, used for a lot of solvents and in the bitumen business for roads, you know, that sort of thing. It also used to be produced from coal tar years ago when gas was made from heated coal. Not something you want to breathe so we wear protective suits, masks that sort of thing and rely on effective ventilation pumping to keep levels low when you work in there. But this job wasn't routine. The refinery is quite small by modern standards and these days, unless they are huge concerns like in India and Russia, many refineries are struggling. Costs and staffing have been cut back in our plant and sometimes maintenance has been slacker. But you never heard me say that did you Abby."

Abby gazed wide eyed at her friend who was sounding much more officious and formal than she had heard before, and Victoria's hands were shaking. "No of course not. Hey carry on, I'm all ears and this big mouth is firmly zipped shut, like so," drawing her finger across.

Victoria laughed again. "Okay, are you ever not crazy? Anyway when we were inside, after about half an hour, we had a number of pipes undone and were taking samples. I heard my deputy shouting into the intercom to get the fucking pumps sorted quickly, as apparently the main pump to the tower, keeping us protected, had seized up and the technicians were running around outside to find someone who knew how to start up the backup as the normal guys were all on nightshift. It was chaos apparently out there and then we all heard a hissing sound as vapour started escaping from a crack in the venting further along the shaft. My deputy looked at me and I immediately gave the instruction to exit immediately, but once we got to the main doors, they had self locked, God only knows why. Imagine it. You have nine people crowded together in a narrow shaft, nowhere to go and a brown vapour seeping through various holes in the wall. Some panicked and literally started screaming and banging like crazy on the side and the doors but we couldn't hear a thing and our arm buzzers began sounding, detecting that levels of gaseous toxins were reaching a danger point beyond the capabilities of our gas masks."

"Jesus Christ, Vikki, the place sounds like a death trap before you even went in there."

"But that's the point Abby, that's why nothing makes sense. Because when we first went in everything inside was shiny, clean and modern but suddenly all the lighting had dimmed like we were in candlelight, the walls looked like they were covered in great swathes of brown sticky slime, there was soot everywhere, and there is nothing in the processing that produces soot like that. And then in the background a thud thudding sound and hissing like a reciprocating hammer hitting a piece of metal and getting louder and louder to the point it hurt your ears. It was total bedlam and the guys were going balmy, I've never seen such fear on people's faces, yet I somehow seemed to manage to stay calm and shouted instructions to stay near the entrance, help was coming, but nobody was listening, they were terrified and then I saw and smelled it ..."

Abby leaned forward, her face terse, unable to comprehend then suddenly she began feeling strange ... oh God no ... because she hadn't felt those things for ages and it had suddenly come back ...

"Abby, your face has gone white. I'm sorry, fuck I didn't mean to frighten you what's the matter?"

Abby began taking deep breaths; she leant back then put her head between her knees for half a minute before coming back up, sweat pouring from her face. "I've had one of my ... errmm

… one of my turns, but you have to finish this now. What did you see? You must tell me."

Victoria held her arm as Abby's breathing slowly went back to normal and then she wiped Abby's brow with her serviette.

"Sorry," Abby replied. "I think the stuffy heat in here got to me for a minute and I've had too much lager again, ha-ha! Carry on please Dr Polymer."

"It was the smoky vapour. It had turned from brown to a bright purple colour, and was seeping like crazy out of the end pipe near me alongside a dripping clear mauve liquid. None of that made any sense whatsoever. I know my organic chemistry very well; Eva and Leiden University have taught me everything. That vapour wasn't naphtha but from the smell some sort of benzene compound, but nothing can possibly produce a purple gas."

"What about the liquid?"

"It looked like a dye and yes there are dyes produced that colour from aniline, which is a related compound, but any vapour is colourless. I remember staring at this great swathe of purple gas and then there was a huge flash of light and that's all I remember. Next thing I recall is waking up in that hospital bed, of all things, looking at purple curtains in the room!"

"Nothing was reported like that Vikki. The press just said there was an explosion, eight people died and one survived but they declined to release names or any detail as an investigation by the refinery is ongoing."

"The side of the distillation tower blew out, something ignited. The other eight of my team were found outside, all so horribly burnt and disfigured they couldn't have been formally identified except by DNA. But they found me alongside, unconscious, assumed head injuries and of course it took me a week to wake up, but I looked completely normal, not even my suit was ripped. The investigators when they interviewed me at the hospital all believed that I had got out through the door, well ahead of everyone and slammed it shut accidentally but it wasn't like that. I was at the very back, right inside. I could see that saying otherwise wasn't going to help my cause, especially when I said I had seen purple vapour and brown slimy walls like tar and they had to test immediately for samples of what it was. They just laughed and wrote down severe shock and after effects. As far as the plant is concerned it all points to the naphtha having ignited and a series of avoidable mishaps which will have to be explained to the national Dutch Health and Safety Executive, probably resulting in a big fine and making the plant even less viable. I can sense it Abby, I'm going to be set up as the cause of the accident somehow and be the scapegoat to save the backsides of the Executive. But I still don't understand what went on in there, it was really weird. Everyone, and I'm sure you too now, obviously thinks I'm blast bonkers."

Abby went quiet and thoughtful for a few seconds. "Actually I do believe you, because I sensed it not only when it happened but also a minute ago."

"Heh?" Victoria retorted, swigging down the last of her lager, having consumed half of Abby's omelette as well as her own. "Bloody hell, Abby, you're not starting again on that psychic crap are you, you sound just like my mother did. I'm sorry but there is a rational scientific explanation somewhere and I won't rest until I find out."

"It's not silly Vikki, seriously, I've always had a strong sixth sense of ... well things which couldn't be explained and as a child I used to sometimes see things?"

"What sort of things, did they have clanking chains and moan a lot?"

"Don't mock, there are things and energies around us which can't always be explained. As a scientist I thought you would have a more open mind. My mother was the same and her mother before her, and so was my brother, but not my father — these things do run in families. In fact I'm surprised, if your mother claimed to be psychic, that you haven't … well … sometime had feelings too."

"My mother only saw one kind of spirit, a brown liquid with a large bell on the side of the bottle. Anyway I was no different from any other kid, all children see things! It's their over excited, prepubescent imaginations, sort of goes with the turf, until they get their kicks later from sex!"

Abby laughed. "Okay, let's leave this to another time. We should get back, it looks like a thunderstorm is on its way and you need to sort out your best clobber if you're seeing the big chief tomorrow."

As they walked back and Victoria began telling her the story about the Ahmeds at the hospital and how deliciously fanciable both younger and older Ahmeds were, Abby decided not to mention any more. But in the evening, the moment she felt and knew something serious had happened to Victoria, before it all came on the television, she had dealt herself from her favourite pack of tarot cards. She had done three cards, five cards and even a Celtic cross spread, but each time there was always one discernible similarity. The card of lovers and the card of hangman appearing together on every deal, with either wands or swords. Heaven knows what that might be, but it made her uneasy …

Victoria began looking at the impressive array of Van Gogh prints on the wall. She always loved sunflowers; they were about the only thing that grew every year in their tiny back

53

garden in Cinderblack Lane. It was quiet except for the mild clack-clacking of computer keyboards, as a batch of secretaries were attacking a big pile of reports.

"Victoria, how great to see you so quickly and looking so well," a voice boomed out. "Please come into my office."

She turned and a very tall thin man held out his hand, the reclusive CEO, Joss van der Dyke. She had only seen him on TV; he was never at the plant but always gadding around the world in search of whatever he did. She felt some trepidation. This didn't feel like it was going to be exactly pleasant, as he opened the door for her.

"I'm glad you like the prints, we did have some originals once but I'm afraid they were sold off to pay a tax bill years ago, long before my time," he laughed.

"Hello Roland," she muttered looking at her boss standing by the window, a severe expression across his face. He raised a smile when she walked over, and kissed her cheeks three times in Dutch fashion.

"Victoria, you look amazingly well considering what we found out there. You reacted very fast to get out before the blast; damned door locks jammed then of course ..."

"Actually Roland, it wasn't like ..." then she stopped. What was the point? She could sense they had made up their minds and fire her anyway.

"Please take a seat Victoria," van der Dyke requested, in a calm but measured tone. "Now, I won't beat about the bush, we've assessed the initial reports from the health and safety team and also your ... err ... comments and recommendations from the hospital. There is a lot of stuff still to be done, sieving through the remains, analysis and then a rebuild, you know the sort of thing. Roland and I are concerned that you are able to take the time to make a full recovery, both physically and of course from the trauma. So we would like you to take leave of six months, effective immediately, on full pay of course, and with your bonus all tax free. On condition … err… part of the arrangement too is we have booked some sessions, all paid for, at the Delta Hospital with a Doctor Mieke Bennink, which we would like you to attend."

She looked at her boss. "Roland, that place is a mental asylum isn't it?"

He looked at the floor then stared back into her eyes forcing a smile. "Actually a very highly respected psychological clinic who provide top-notch trauma counselling; we know you must have had quite a shock inside the distillation tower. Then you can come back and hit the ground running."

Van der Dyke interrupted. "What Roland means Victoria is that we will review the situation in six months and jointly agree the best way forward in your job."

She knew instinctively what that meant. He had a reputation as ruthless to the core, so any requested deviation from what was on offer or asking for additional compensation, would likely be tied up already with a huge load of hassle and aggro and she really couldn't be bothered. She needed a holiday anyway, and hadn't taken this year's allocation yet, so another month would be added on. Technically at least she would be employed still, better to move on from. Fuck van der Dyke and Roland too, that squirming bastard; the break would give her some breathing space.

He continued. "Is that acceptable to you Victoria?"

She nodded. "Thank you, it's good to be working for a company that looks after its employees so well."

Roland looked away out of the window; he sensed her tone but van der Dyke simply waved to his secretary.

"Excellent. In that case, Lana will see you out, and we'll see you in six months time, have a pleasant break."

She was out of his office and out of the building in an instant. She got into her pickup truck and was quickly through the security gate, and just like Cinderblack Lane, she didn't look back and never would again.

The early morning sun drove a hazy beam of light through her half closed blinds. Victoria pulled off her duvet and headed down the stairs to her newly renovated kitchen. Abby was late coming in. She stumbled over a pair of wrangler jeans on the first two steps, noting the logical mathematical sequencing of a trail of clothes resembling knickers, a top, boxer shorts, shirt and finally a bra entwined around the banister knob. Abby's door was closed but a distinctive sound of snoring could be heard which was definitely at a tonal Abby frequency she was familiar with. Victoria sighed and smiled. One more notch on the bedpost, shit, there wasn't room for any more notches.

She switched on the coffee pot and started to make a brew. She had all the time in the world for a change and it felt good, like a big stone off her back. Two rather pale faces with towels wrapped around the rest and looking distinctly worse for wear popped their heads around the door.

"Hey you guys, I've made enough coffee for three, want some?"

There was a groan or was it a grunt of vague approval as Abby shuffled in. "Snakebites again. Victoria, this is Vittorio, I think I got that the right way round."

The olive skinned male, with dark hair and ever so trimmed designer stubble, was actually rather delectable under that worn out gaze; Abby could be a real taskmistress. He smiled. "Hi

Victorina, I am ah from … ah … Rome and … ah … I will be leaving in a boat … umm … very shortly."

"Well that's cool Victor, because my friend Abby and I will be going on a long vacation ourselves this afternoon, so I'll say ciao, ci vediamo, in advance, as I'm now going for a morning constitutional stroll around the harbour. Porridge either of you?" looking behind at a grinning Abby mouthing *are we*?

When she returned an hour later, having bumped into Sandy and Christa, former colleagues, for a good gossip, and wolfed through a large plate of bacon, eggs, beans, a fried egg and three rounds of toast down at Ali's, who kept perpetually asking where his lovely Abby had got to, and that was just her portion, she realised that the brief Italian invasion was over. Abby, now showered, perfumed and dressed in her skinny Zara jeans and pink floral jacquard crop top, had both tidied up and vacuumed, and not a boxer short could be seen and she was quietly even polishing the dining table.

"Vikki, I know that was a bit fleeting, even for me … so what's this about a long holiday? What happened then with the big boss, I assume they fired you?"

"Not quite, but I have the next six months fancy free, on full pay so I thought we might take a week in the sun … gosh I have a big hankering for Ibiza, really hit the clubs?"

"Mmm … that sounds right good, chuck, but what about Ali, the love of my life?"

"He thinks you've done a bunk anyway so he won't miss you for another week and holiday is on me, a celebration and big thank you for being the best and most entertaining friend ever."

"You mean even better than the astounding and incredible Eva?"

Victoria grimaced; she knew Abby's humour of old. "Maybe but Eva touched those parts others have failed to reach …?"

Abby roared laughing. "I don't think we'll go into that, not this time of day, and I am definitely not doing any lezzy threesomes."

"Hey neither am I ever again, but it was … umm … good while it lasted. So I shall get onto the laptop and book us the raunchiest week I can find …?"

"Cool and there's the postman too so get to it. I'll just get the letters."

Victoria was well into scouring the worst and noisiest Ibiza hotels she could dredge onto the screen. Abby sauntered back with two teas and a handful of brown envelopes, all bills. As they slurped their drinks, Abby suddenly got up and ran back out to the hallway.

"I forgot, there was one for you as well, from the UK actually, in fact Liverpool on the stamp … well … go on open it."

Victoria glanced at the envelope and immediately noticed the fine paper; this wasn't another missive from Annie who had got bored on Facebook and started writing letters for goodness sake. She opened it carefully, took out the letter and began to read it. But Abby felt an immediate pang of concern seeing Victoria's expression change from licentious nonchalance to a very serious and hard frowning at the contents.

"Blimey, get it over with, what sort of bad news is it?"

Victoria was silent for a minute staring into space, obviously in deep thought.

"Well?"

"Actually it isn't bad news, sort of the opposite and quite amazing, but I don't understand at all. You're not going to believe this, but it looks like I've inherited a property in England."

"My goodness, that's serendipity. Whose property? I thought all your family were dead?"

"So did I, and it's not just any old property but a mansion, and a sum of money. Jesus Christ Abby, the house is Orsbrick Hall."

"Pardon?"

"That big old house I talked about. The one that always scared the life out of me as a child and I was never allowed to visit."

"You mean in Lancashire, where you lived?"

"Yes. This letter is from a solicitor, Green and Burgess in Liverpool. It says there are conditions and I must visit the office immediately in person and only see Lynton Grey, Principal Partner. I'm going to have to go to Liverpool, damn, I hate the place."

Abby looked hard, smiled and patted her arm. "Close that laptop, forget Ibiza. I'll come with you, always fancied a magical mystery tour back to Liverpool. You forget, I did my undergraduate fine art degree there, it was my MA I did in fashion design in London. Wonder if the Cavern is still there?"

Victoria grinned and mused. Well, why not? And she could always surprise Annie too, although with four kids and living in a council house in Speke, maybe she would give that a miss.

"Okay Ms Psycho, bloody hell that was Freudian, I mean Ms Psychic, you're on! In fact I think there are flights from Rotterdam to John Lennon Airport, on me."

Abby had the laptop open again. "On to it, tomorrow morning at seven o clock sharp, booking, booking, booked. Thank goodness Vittorio has gone!"

They shrieked with laughter and began frantically looking for their rucksacks.

Chapter Four

Catching her heel in a bumpy pavement on Dale Street, Victoria almost ended her five-day holiday in the first half an hour, but was saved from disaster by the quick reactions of Abby, who grabbed her arm and hauled her away from the approaching shop window in an instant.

"Hey, the last thing we want is you back in the hospital again. If you want to practise head butting, can you save it for your boss when you see him next rather than launching yourself at HMV's shiny frontage?"

"Thanks," Victoria whispered, seeing other shoppers staring. "That was close. These damned five inch heels; I knew I should have worn sensible shoes."

"Just take your time girl, there's no big hurry. You can sue Liverpool Council another time. Anyway, I'm dying for a coffee. What about the Costa over there? … Gosh this area is all environmentally restored. I do like the way they've renovated the beautiful historic buildings here; you know once it was full of sailors and wayward women."

"Yes, and you're back again now!" Victoria responded with a grin. "Forget coffee, look over there, I can see Process Street, this solicitor office, Green and Burgess, is up there somewhere."

"I wonder if we can find Hitler's restaurant."

"Pardon?"

"Actually it was his half brother Alois who ran it on Dale Street with his wife in the early part of the last century and who maintained Hitler stayed with them there for some time, draft dodging from the First World War. Mmm, that street ... looks more like a back-alley that you find dingy nightclubs down."

"You continue to be an amazing mine of historic facts, I thought you were supposed to be a textile designer?"

"I'm a woman of many talents. At least those heels give you a statuesque imposing look, good for getting your own way with Green's Burgess, especially with the deep crimson coat. What made you choose that colour, although it suits you actually?"

"I don't know, just woke up yesterday and fancied it badly."

They crossed the road and turned into the side street, noticing a small cobbled alleyway about twenty yards up. Here was a distinct feeling of a return to yesteryear, seeing the gold sign of Green and Burgess, barely legible, hanging from black chains in front of a dirty old Victorian four storey building, which somehow had missed the clean-up scheme everywhere else.

"You first," Abby whispered at the front door. "Looks a bit creepy, up there ... press that bell."

A young female voice answered wrapped in a thick Liverpool accent. "Err ... can I 'elp, like?"

They looked at each other, mildly surprised, as Victoria drew back and in her poshest voice, acquired since Eva had meticulously taught her to speak in BBC Radio Four English tone like her, rather than Victoria's former broad Lancashire, replied confidently. "It's Dr Victoria McKenzie, with my colleague Dr Abigail Warren. I have an appointment with a Mr Lynton Grey at ten thirty?"

"Err, just 'ang on whilst I check. Yeh, no problem, just push the door when the buzzer goes like, know what I mean?"

Abby stifled a laugh as Victoria nudged her, and they entered a quite dimly lit small reception area, most of which was taken up with a large mahogany desk. Staring first at the conspicuously odd silver plate with Sally - Receptionist in bold print, stamped on the front, they then looked up, and the grinning Sally, in a black micro skirt, matching tights and white tee-shirt walked through, shook hands and pointed to the narrow, rickety old stairs in the corner.

"Err, it's the boss himself, up there right to the fifth floor, I'm afraid the lift's sort of knackered today, is that okay?"

"Oh, no problem, thank you Sally, we can walk up," Victoria proffered, seeing Abby wince. They set off up the creaking wooden stairs which went round and round, like in a castle.

"Business isn't exactly booming in here is it?" Victoria whispered back to Abby behind, already puffing and panting and they were only at the third floor. "I reckon you eat too many of those kebabs you cook, time to get to the gym with me I think."

"Ha-ha, but I agree. I always thought solicitors were those guys, like bankers, who have Lamborghinis and give a girl a good time."

"Not Mr Grey, I would concur. Anyway, there's the door, it looks like the only room on this corridor."

"That's because we're in the attic."

Suddenly the door at the far end creaked opened and a tall, well built man, mid thirties, with a trimmed beard and a very expensive looking blue suit walked out to greet them.

"Ah, Dr McKenzie and your colleague my name is Grey, Lynton Grey, owner of this practice."

Victoria ignored Abby who immediately whispered. "Shaken not stirred. Gosh he is a dream boat, would you credit it?"

Victoria readily admitted that the expected character from a murky Dickens novel looked more like he had just stepped out from a Vogue modelling shoot. They shook hands and were directed inside towards the seating around the teak coffee table with elephant carved legs. Victoria saw Abby's face drop as they both scanned the gorgeous antique Georgian furniture and his huge desk, the rich warm, velvety draped armchairs and thick rug carpeting. Abby immediately began to peer closely over the array of paintings on the wall, realising that that the middle two were original, but reframed obscure Rossetti Pre-Raphaelites, probably around 1870, and looking at the female face, when the painter was favouring a move of muses from Fanny Cornforth to his favourite sitter, Alexa Wilding. At the end was an excellent print of the famous Lady Lilith, making Abby immediately decide she would grow her hair long, frizzy and orange rather than short, spiky and pink. Mr Grey had disappeared into the adjacent kitchen and was brewing coffee and returned with three Japanese printed mugs, black coffee, milk and sugar on a bakelite tray.

Victoria sat down, primly and quietly, rustling in her bag for a notepad, and watching with amazement as he sidled over, gaze transfixed on the brazen Dr Warren.

"Ah ... err ... Abigail isn't it. Do you like art?"

"My first degree was fine art, and my postgraduate was in textiles design, but yes, what wonderful paintings," as she continued to gaze avidly, not noticing how intensely, solicitor Grey was eyeing her up and down.

He smiled, as she looked back. "I'm afraid I couldn't afford the original Lady Lilith but this was done by a student at the

Liverpool College of Art and it was so good I bought it immediately. Collecting Victorian work is a passion of mine, I have a private gallery in Southport, perhaps you might like to see some more, if you get any time?"

"Do you have etchings too?"

Victoria stifled a cough as her coffee went down the wrong way, amazed at the never before seen doe-eyed look in Abby's eyes, whilst he was obviously equally transfixed.

He grinned, the irony obviously not lost. "Of course, in fact I recently acquired a couple of etchings and engravings by David Law, but from my father, who retired last year. This was his business which I have bought out, the original Green and Burgess having passed on many years back. I'm in the middle of … a serious updating and upgrade of the practice …"

"Really? A founder member of the Royal Society of Painter Etchers? He was also an excellent map-maker for many years."

"You are very knowledgeable Abigail … err … Ms …?"

"Warren, Dr Abby Warren."

Victoria looked from one to the other, barely able to contain herself, now totally frozen out with the rapturous Grey-Warren show unfolding before her gaze. She coughed politely, a gentle reminder that this was supposed to be her formal meeting … and she had an inheritance to nail down … like.

"I'm so sorry Victoria," he said softly, walking to his desk. "Now if you would both like to enjoy the coffee for a moment, whilst I collect the files. I think the critical one has been left in my safe across the corridor. I'll just be a moment. Oh and I'm sorry I have some bad news for you Abby?"

They both looked up, mystified, as he shot out through the door.

"Bloody hell, that didn't last long, Vikki," Abby murmured, slurping down her hot drink. "He was growing on me sort of big time. Very nice coffee though."

"Yes, I can see that. Hey this is my meeting today, I have work to do; not getting you laid," Victoria replied, mildly irritated.

"I'm sorry chuck but ..." Abby didn't have time to finish the sentence as Lynton Grey returned.

"Now, the terms of this disposal are rather complex and unusual and must be discussed in private. I'm afraid, Abby, I will have to continue with Victoria on her own. Will you be able to find something to do in town? We'll be about an hour. Actually the College of Art isn't far and they have an exhibition on presently. I'm a governor."

Victoria smirked as Abby's face dropped, but then lit up again when he handed her his card with the mobile number ringed, in case, he said, you also need the services of a reliable solicitor in the future.

"That's a shame Abby," Victoria quipped, "But when Mr Grey and I have finished, I'll give you a ring on the mobile and meet you at the College of Art. We can probably have lunch there; it sounds like you would enjoy the exhibition."

Abby gave her a fleeting glance of a knowing glare and then smiled at both. "Exhibition it is. Well goodbye Mr Grey, it was a pleasure meeting you."

"Me too," he replied shaking Abby's hand and eyeing her over again. "Don't forget, if you are ever at a loose end in Southport, you will be very welcome at my gallery."

"I won't. See you later." She tripped out of the door and clattered down the stairs with a new found energy. Victoria breathed a quiet sigh of relief. Now she could get on with getting to the bottom of this increasingly unfathomable intrigue.

After more coffee toppings up, Lynton Gray proceeded to explain the detail, guiding Victoria through various contracts and strange legal wordings, which she was quite happy leaving to him, as to whether to sign the bits of paper or not. What she really wanted to know was how she had inherited the place, seeing as all the known family were dead, although obviously now that had not been the case. But Orsbrick Hall? How could she possibly be the owner of that awful place which she was never allowed to visit, and smarting in her head again from the memory of the vicious swipe over the cheeks she got from her mother the day she was caught on her bicycle when about to head up there?

After half an hour of contorted legal discussions about the contents of the will, Victoria realised that she still hadn't been told any more about who owned it, only that he had gone through all the complexities and property background with a fine tooth comb and could see no legal reason for her not to sign it, except for a couple of quite specific requirements.

"I have been particularly requested *not* to tell you who owns this property, Dr McKenzie," he uttered, suddenly getting formal. "All I can provide you with is the address of the person, through whom I am acting and that you are asked to go and visit before making up your mind whether to sign up to the legacy or not. Her name is Eveline West, and she was in fact the original beneficiary of Orsbrick Hall but has specifically relinquished all rights to you, if you comply with all the conditions."

"Which are?"

"That you visit her very soon, live in the property for at least twelve months and at that point you will be the recipient of a trust fund which has been set aside. The money is residing in a London bank under our control here, until that eligibility is fulfilled."

"How much is the trust fund?"

"I'm not allowed to say either, but I can certainly confirm that it is all accumulated McKenzie wealth passed on through many generations in your family, Victoria."

Victoria was completely amazed, transfixed on such a remarkable turn of events. But why on earth was there all this mystery? And, being a rational scientist used to debating the fineries of decision making, with clear experimental evidence in front of her from which she can make logical conclusions, she was uneasy with the weird obfuscation.

She stopped gazing at the papers and turned to him directly. "None of this Mr Grey …"

"Please, I think you can call me Lynton now …"

She noticed he blushed which amused her. "Well Lynton, it doesn't make sense because all of my family are dead. My father certainly never mentioned any family wealth, he was a science teacher in a minor public school for all his life, we lived quite frugally in a small cottage, and if there had been any money my mother would certainly have gotten her hands on it."

"Your mother? Is she still alive?"

"To be honest I don't know. Once I left home almost twenty years ago, I never heard from her again and she sold our cottage and disappeared back to America, and I only picked that up and my father's death accidentally two years after it all happened. So could she then be a benef …"

He interrupted her promptly. "No, she is not and cannot."

"But why?"

"I'm not permitted to say."

"And Orsbrick Hall, I remember always seeing it at a distance as a child; we were never allowed to go near it. So I assume a relative of mine was living there. That is so peculiar, and who is Eveline West?"

"I'm sorry Victoria," handing her an envelope, "but I can't tell you that either, in fact I don't really know her background. Here is a card with her address."

She opened the small brown envelope carefully and gazed at the flowery and ornate card. Miss Eveline West, Textile Artist, Appleby Lodge, Parbold.

"A textile artist?"

"I'm sure she will tell you. But I should advise, Appleby Lodge is a private care home and Miss West is in her nineties and rather frail, so I wouldn't leave it long."

"No, I won't," she replied calmly, thinking that she would hire a car pronto. "Thank you for all your work Lynton, it is much appreciated. Now I can see you're very busy with that mountain of paperwork on your desk, so I'll see myself out and no doubt we will be in touch one way or the other."

"A pleasure Victoria. Oh, can you tell your friend, Abby, err Dr Warren ... that I have quite an interesting collection of Victorian etchings I am sure she would enjoy perusing. I actually live near Southport."

"I'm sure she would, I won't forget," Victoria replied with a grin. "Is your wife an art collector too?"

"No, I'm not married ... a widower actually," he mumbled, again blushing slightly.

"I'm so sorry Lynton, it must be ... well ... sort of difficult readjusting."

"It was some time back, and my work keeps me very busy. Good day then Dr McKenzie," he replied, polite but determined, obviously, she thought, cutting off any further discussion of that topic, still patently painful.

She sauntered slowly down the stairs, her brain whirring madly with all kinds of data assembly and synthesis of what she had learned so far, when she suddenly became aware of a strange pungent smell. Stopping on the third floor, she looked around. Total silence, There didn't seem to be anyone else in the building but that smell was strong, like some sort of coal tar, benzene or aniline again. Her mind immediately flew backwards to the refinery, the same smell when she was in the distillation tower, just before ... she felt frightened and began to clatter down the stairs, throwing the final door open to reception to be greeted by a smiling Sally once again.

"Everything go like, okay with the boss then Dr McKenzie?"

"Fine thank you Sally, what is that awful smell on the stairs?"

"I'm sorry?"

Victoria looked into Sally's face, totally blank and uncomprehending. She breathed in again ... and couldn't smell a thing, only a vague sense of a recent furniture polish on the shiny desk.

"It was probably the door open to the toilet on the second floor, we did have some trouble with the drains in there, but I thought they'd like been fixed, I'd better ..."

But Victoria wasn't listening because her attention had been drawn outside through the window. A woman, certainly young but hard to tell her age, and very pretty, was standing at the window staring at her, with a long and very wistful gaze, like they knew each other. She couldn't tell the age because the woman was wearing a very striking mauve shawl around her head and a long black coat. Perhaps, actually, it was Sally's attention the woman was trying to catch.

She turned to Sally. "Do you know who that woman is outside looking through the window with the shawl …?"

They both turned around and not a sign of anyone. Sally looked at her rather bemused as Victoria felt her cheeks reddening with embarrassment. What on earth was the matter with her?

"I'm sorry Sally, I was sure there was a woman standing there, trying to catch attention from in here … I know I've only come from Holland, but maybe I've got a touch of jet lag or something."

Sally smiled. "Eh, don't worry yerself. I know just the thing like to cure that feeling, a few vodkas and tonics do wonders for me, know what I mean?"

Victoria laughed and headed to the door. "I'll be in touch, bye."

"See yeh, Dr McKenzie."

She got into the tiny street and looked around, intending to head back to Dale Street and then phone Abby. Turning to the left she started to wander down the street, but after a few further turnoffs, she realised she had gone totally the wrong way. Everywhere around was quite deserted, the street had got narrower and the buildings either side were tall and bleak, either warehouses or, as she noticed from the sign, converted night clubs, probably heaving and lively at night but completely dead in the day.

She became aware of footsteps following her and began to feel panicky, hastening her step as the footsteps got louder. Suddenly two hands were around her waist pulling at her from behind and a second guy, Chinese, in a hoodie confronted her, pulling at her handbag. "Giss your bag and your phone you fucking bitch, that's all we want, or we'll split your face open."

Bloody hell, she thought frantically, she was being mugged in broad daylight. She couldn't scream as the one behind had a big gloved hand across her mouth and eyes, but she struggled like mad. Despite her recent ordeal she was gym fit and strong, and was determined to hang on to her bag come hell or high water. They all struggled in a blur for another five or ten seconds, as she managed to bang the person at the back against a wall and he released his grip on her head, when suddenly a large hand shot out of the blackness of a doorway at a fast velocity and connected directly with the face of the Chinese mugger, sending him sprawling, over and over the pavement, blood pouring from his nose all splattered open. The person holding her released his grip and she dived to one side, staring now at her other attacker. He was black Asian and quite burly but equally taken by surprise at seeing his friend prostrate on the ground.

A very tall man in a long brown coat, collar up hiding much of his face emerged from the shadows. But it was enough for Victoria to see he was probably in his late forties or early fifties, slim, a thick head of curly grey hair, a silk scarf across his neck and piercing blue eyes, which settled unerringly on the Asian guy through gold rimmed spectacles. The Asian was looking like he would square up, as Victoria watched the pair of them, but whoever this man was, his gaze must have penetrated right to the core of that guy, because he simply stood, rooted to the spot, and shivered. The grey-haired man, without averting his gaze on the assailant, or even blinking, pushed his hand inside his coat and withdrew a short machete.

"More of the same, young man?" he said in a deep and quite cultured voice, with a hint of an accent, but not really Liverpool or Lancashire, more like a sort of odd hybrid including Cockney London.

The Asian turned, and looked at his friend. "Fuck you. C'mon Chin, let's leave these shitheads to it." He ran off, pulling his friend still groaning and bleeding badly up off the floor and the pair stumbled away down the alley, disappearing into a side street …

Victoria, essentially unhurt, and her bag undamaged, was just shaken, but something similar had happened to her once before in Amsterdam, so it somehow felt less bad a second time. She turned to her mystery grey-haired knight in brown shining armour, who had returned the machete into his coat, and held out her hand. "Thank you so much. That was pretty amazing. God knows what they might have done if you hadn't been there? I'm Victoria," wondering actually why he was there because there was absolutely nothing down that street to attract anyone except scallywags and muggers.

He held out his hand and shook her warmly. "Hi I'm Julian. I was just taking a short cut to be honest and bought that butcher's knife for boning meat from a specialist ironmonger further down that way. Cooking is a sort of a hobby. The cleaver came in handy, although many years back, when I was younger, I did some stints with the Territorial Army and learned a few tricks for taking care of oneself."

She laughed. He and it both came in handy, noting the mischievous twinkle in his serious gaze behind those academic looking spectacles; what with wire frames?

"Just as well. Are you by any chance heading towards Dale Street? I think I got a little lost, I'm visiting Liverpool on business, don't know my way around, silly really," she muttered coyly, although why, she didn't know. Doing shy, especially with men, wasn't normally one of her core attributes.

"Yes, as it happens I am, but I must advise, you're going in the exact opposite direction. Tell you what, you look like you

73

could do with a drink and not far from here, in Dale Street, there's an excellent pub, the Ship and Mitre. It's an old traditional place with real ales and a long history, one of my favourites in Liverpool."

"That sounds like a good idea, okay then. Do you have time Julian?"

"Yes, all the time in the world. I'm a writer, so I don't have a real job or a boss to answer to."

She laughed, neither did she anymore. They began to walk together back up the street, when she could feel herself feeling a little unsteady, perhaps a bit of aftershock or something else, she thought.

He noticed immediately and gazed down at her five inch heels. "Listen, just put your arm through mine and hold tight, you'll be fine, I won't let you fall. Not far to go."

They set off, her arm firmly linked into his. She looked up at him and smiled. She was well over six foot in those heels, but he was at least a couple of inches taller and she felt instantly comfortable, cosy and warm, especially as there had been a distinct and unseasonal approaching autumn chill, all the time they had been in Liverpool. She suddenly thought of Abby, talking about wanton women and sailors. What on earth would Abby think now? But she decided, knowing well how self contained and time unaware Abby always was, especially in an art exhibition, to ring her a little later. This was proving to be an unexpected but delectable distraction with Julian the writer whoever he was. And she realised she was quite intrigued to know more about her mystery saviour.

Along the way he described in meticulous detail the historic background of the streets they walked through, of seafaring, skullduggery and merchants and a generally hard life for many and rich pickings for a few, especially during the 19th century.

She listened, fascinated by his deep local heritage knowledge, saying nothing about her own background, but knowing that the terminus of the Leeds and Liverpool canal, which had sustained many forbears of her friends and childhood acquaintances, was not far away. They arrived quickly at the front of the pub and she immediately looked up and pulled out her iPhone to take a picture. You couldn't miss the place, standing out uniquely from the other buildings, with its stark white block stone frontage and unusual placement of very tall slatted windows. He took her inside and they headed for a quieter area of a large bar. She was impressed by the design where everywhere was decked out like the inside of a ship, taking the name of the pub to its true meaning. Julian was certainly correct about the range of unusual beers, many from tiny breweries around the UK. He ordered both of them a three-cheese quiche and generous helping of salad, she was feeling decidedly peckish again, along with a large bottle of Belgian beer. The shakes she had earlier had vanished.

She quickly learned that Julian Endersby-Finnis had done a degree in English Literature at Oxford and been a journalist for a long time with a national newspaper and covered some conflict zones, including the Iraq war in Kuwait. But having made sufficient money he decided, some years back, to do what he always wanted to do at university and become a writer and was on his fourth published novel and that year, for the first time, was earning more money than he had spent. She gazed at him, unable to get a word in edgeways, the epitome of a dreamy academic, as he rambled on, oblivious to his surroundings and obviously totally enmeshed inside a world of strange characters, weird plots and unlikely happenings of another era totally. She realised as she counted the appearing wrinkles on his forehead and lines around his eyes, that despite his good head of grey hair he was probably in his early fifties, but in his tight fitting jeans, smart checked shirt and trendy jacket, he looked very cool.

Eventually she decided to cut in as they were halfway through the delicious salad. "So, tell me what exactly is steampunk, Julian? All I know is it involves the Victorian period and science which interests me. I'm not really a lover of genre fiction." He missed the cue, so she would return to science shortly.

He looked vaguely horrified at the thought of steampunk being classed as a simplistic base genre like chicklit and went into a diatribe of an alternative history of Victorian England, steam powered machinery and post-apocalyptic futures of fantasy worlds powered by steam. He was obviously, she thought, a marvellous storyteller as she continued quite entranced, gulping down her beer and now tucking into a large oozing profiterole. She felt he was drawing her into his world, that he sketched and moulded every day with words, visions and deeds, which she had no idea could be so imaginative. He concluded by saying that steampunk was a hybrid specialised category of literary fiction drawing on science fiction and that it was really a culture, now influencing fashion as well as philosophy. Despite his obvious leanings to the hyperbole, she was impressed with his enthusiasm and commitment to his writing and especially his wonderful imagination and communication. Perhaps being cooped up with technicians year after year had dulled her own artistic creativity too much. She loved science but somehow he gave her a different perspective which she had never felt before and she wanted to give him a hug for making her feel so good after that terrible ordeal nearly two weeks ago, that could have destroyed her entirely.

"Would you like another beer Victoria, I hope it wasn't too strong? I guessed it would suit your taste, and of course you are named directly from that era too."

"Mmm … true I suppose. Yes please, anyway Julian, how come you guessed I would like Belgian beer?"

He smiled, went quiet for the first time and looked directly into her eyes with that beguiling twinkle. "A very faint hint of a Dutch accent, which I have pinpointed to likely Rotterdam. Am I correct?"

"Yes, I've lived and worked there for many years, but you're the first person to ever notice. I am very English with the accent to prove it, okay actually from Burscough originally. Now do you want to know what I do?"

He grinned and moved closer, as she felt herself take a mild gulp. What was the matter with her insides, she needed really to call Abby … well … soon …

"Of course," he replied slowly. "I'll just get the beers first. Okay, confession. I lived in Rotterdam for three years, taught liberal arts and sciences at Erasmus University and researched my first book there. So what's it like being a boat person?"

"Really? What a coincidence. I'm a scientist, with a doctorate in polymer chemistry, have worked for a long time in the refining sector, but I'm not a boat person, although many of my former school friends were. You seem to have a much greater affinity for life on the water?"

He looked straight through her. "Probably. A scientist, now that is quite fascinating, so what are you doing here?"

She decided this was not the moment to talk about being in between jobs, inheritances or any of the other weird things going on in her life right then. "Oh, you know, just having a bit of a break, seeing some family and school friends and visiting, haven't been back for years."

He continued looking at her, but made no comment. She could tell by a twitch of his mouth and a very slight change of focus of attention that he didn't believe her. She had almost finished her second bottle and was feeling decidedly ... no, not drunk, just ... remarkably relaxed. "Oh," she continued, realising that she almost slurred. "I'm here with my friend Abby, who has just gone to look at the art exhibition at the College. She did her degree there. Actually I must phone her and tell her I'm here."

"Of course. Anyway, I must go, have to meet a colleague in Aigburth, possible short journalism assignment. This has been a marvellous lunch Victoria."

She looked and blinked. She really didn't want him to leave although if she was truthful to herself she didn't know what she wanted, and she was slightly pissed anyway and didn't do the swapping mobile numbers, she was too old for that. "I agree, and thank you so much for saving me."

He grinned, the laugh lines around his fifty-three year old eyes, moving about sensuously. She knew he was fifty-three because he had left his wallet on the table when he went to the toilet and she had peeked inside quickly and seen his driving licence. He looked good for his age but then she didn't know what that really meant as she had no proper benchmarks, not even knowing her own father in his mid fifties. She had certainly never dated or slept with any fifty-three year olds ... and wondered ... gosh ... that beer was strong.

He bent down and kissed her cheek, his clean shaven face smelling of some expensive aftershave. "Oh, before I forget, please take my card, in case you need any future advice on steampunk, although I'm also pretty good at house repairs too. I own a large former sea merchant's house in Toxteth, live in one apartment and let out the rest. Do-it-yourself keeps me exercised in between sitting in front of my laptop." He ringed the mobile number and passed it to her and her stomach jumped a little again.

Touché Dr Warren, she thought. Then, why she said it she couldn't fathom but blurted out, "And Mrs Julian, does she help with the do-it-yourself too?"

He roared with laughter. She suddenly felt hugely embarrassed, her cheeks burning wildly. What on earth had got into her?

"No, Victoria, I never got around to marrying any past conquests, no Mrs Julian in fact no Mrs Anyone right now, far too busy on this new book," he joked, his eyes flashing again. He waved on his way out. "Bye."

"Bye…" she whispered back, feeling stupidly forlorn and then thought about Abby and felt a distinct perking up again, plus she was or could be the owner of a big house soon. She stared back down the busy galley bar and he had gone already. Then, someone near the window caught her attention. It was her again, that woman, still with the bright mauve shawl wrapped around her head, standing near a table and staring vacantly through the window outside. Victoria immediately surmised the woman had followed her into the pub, and decided to confront her once and for all and find out why she was following her. She got up, determined to march over and demand an explanation.

But, as Victoria got up out of her seat, the woman slowly turned around and stared. She was very beautiful, possibly early twenties or so, and Victoria could see under the shawl, she had long mousy hair, but the woman's expression seemed pained and troubled, like she had some terrible problem she wanted to unburden. Victoria began to look down for her handbag, which had fallen onto the floor off the back of the seat, threw it over her shoulder and began a sprint to the window ... and couldn't believe her eyes ... no sign of her anywhere. Bloody hell she was quick to move. She dashed over to the table where two couples were sat talking and canoodling. The shaven headed guy nearest to the window, looked up, obviously irritated that his kissing and fondling of a black-haired companion with her skimpy skirt up to her matching underwear had been rudely interrupted.

"Can I help you or what," he uttered with a deep growl and heavy accent, pulling up his shirt sleeves to reveal a great muscled mass of purple and red tattoos of tall ships with sails and rigging.

Victoria felt distinctly uncomfortable. "I'm sorry, may I ask you? That woman who was standing next to your table a minute ago, with the purple shawl, did you see which way she went?"

"Sorry love, there was no woman at all standing here ..." he replied curtly, looking distinctly unpleasant.

Now she realised too, his accent was really awful West Lancashire, like she used to hear as a child on the barges, especially the scruffy ones. "But you must have seen her; she was right next to ..."

He got up out of his seat. "Listen, how many times do I have to say it, there was no fucker here. You been on the ale or what you soft bitch."

The other three friends all laughed gratuitously, their mouths slathery, staring at her like she was some demented moron.

She backed away. "I'm sorry, you're probably right, not used to the beer in here," forcing a laugh and then departed sharply back to her seat, quite ruffled and irritated. She got out her mobile and earphone mike.

Abby answered immediately. "Where on earth have you got to? I've been worried sick for the last hour, your phone was on permanent voicemail and I left three messages. Are you alright, not fallen down a hole or something?"

"Sorry. I'm in the Ship and Mitre."

"At the top of Dale Street? What are you doing there? It's a great pub mind, used to be a 1930s art deco place, a very in scene."

"Yes, I know." She was slurring a little. "I haven't been on my own," looking then into her phone.

"Oh, I see, Mr Grey quickly shifting allegiances already then? Bugger, he's a nifty worker alright and you sound pissed. Knickers intact?"

"Abby sometimes you get a bit over the top," she replied sharply. "No, not the 'I only have eyes for Abigail please see my etchings' Mr Grey but someone else I met in the street called Julian, a steampunk writer and he took me for lunch."

"Good Lord, I only leave you alone for five minutes and you're off cavorting with strangers. The sea air in Liverpool isn't good for you, brings out that hidden wanton woman. I'll be there in five minutes and where is this Julian guy now?"

"He's vanished into the mists of time …"

"Bloody hell Vikki, I'll be there pronto. You sound a bit edgy actually, are you sure you're alright?"

"Thanks, I'll be waiting outside."

She buttoned up her coat and hurried to the exit, seeing those inebriated idiots out of the corner of her eye on that window table, pointing and laughing at her again.

Some shopping at Zara in the afternoon and a search for the former Cavern club, now car-parked over, soon consoled her earlier confused state of mind. And it was a pleasant relief to be back in the Adelphi Hotel, put her feet up in the lounge and peruse the evening meal menu for a reservation for the two of them she had made during afternoon tea. Abby was relaxing in the swimming pool, both of them worn out and having already decided they needed a holiday to get over the holiday, and this was only day one. She smiled at Abby's mesmerised expression when she described the mugging and then the delectable Julian saving her from a fate worse than a night out with her former boss, but she wanted some time on her own to reflect on the day's events.

She had happily ventured all the gossip on lunch with Julian and after copious giggling in Costa, causing even their staff to glare, they agreed that the combination of arty Lynton and bookish Julian, might be worth cultivating further if they get bored, although the likelihood was looking pretty slim. Once Abby heard excitedly about the required discussion with the enigmatic Eveline West, especially the fact she was a textile artist, she had insisted that sooner rather than later meant first thing in the morning.

Victoria had asked reception to book her a hire car for after breakfast. She was now determined to set off on the trail to Parbold and find the elderly lady, and actually having Abby with her would be really useful. They had no maps of course, but reception would get them a car with a built-in satnav so logistics problem scientifically solved, especially as she realised, it had been so long since she was last in Liverpool, that everywhere seemed like an alien city, the surroundings had changed so much. She could easily have been in Moscow for all the recognition it was making on her senses, and undoubtedly the same would be said for her former childhood haunts in West Lancashire, once they got there.

But she decided not to mention anything about the weird woman in the purple shawl. Whoever it was must have recognised her from school or something, probably a young sister of one of her old friends, although why the woman hadn't said anything she couldn't fathom. She had to admit, when she got a better look in the pub, the woman's long dark dress was fashionable but actually quite unusual, it looked like linen, and not a style she had seen in the places she normally shopped, but certainly wouldn't have looked out of place in Laura Ashley or maybe a museum, like the woman was making some sort of retro statement. It was perplexing, and undoubtedly the woman had something bothering her, but once she and Abby left the city centre that would be it and the incident quickly forgotten. Pity Julian hadn't been with her when she turned up, he may have had something to say about the dress style.

Abby came bounding in, her hair all wet, wearing a track suit top and bottoms. "I'll just get a quick shower first, and then I'll be down. Tell you what, I really like this hotel now, but has it changed! From its former grand old days in the past when only the gentry or those with serious money could afford to stay here, the place is now quite urban chic to appeal to the business hoi polloi."

"You mean like us?" Victoria replied with a wan look.

Abby glared back. "No, daft, we are the special ones."

"Well certainly with that wet pink hair you definitely are. Found your spaceship yet?"

"Ha-bloody-ha. But hey I'm enjoying this holiday so far, and thanks best friend for bringing me along for the treat!"

"Mmm ... you'd better be useful tomorrow on our magical mystery tour. It might make me freak revisiting those places, even before we get to Orsbrick Hall. You want to drive actually?"

"Yes please … must go, won't be a minute."

"I'll just find a seat over at the bar. Shall I get you a vodka and tonic too?"

"If that's how you mean to go on, go for it, then later we can slope off to the Blue Angel."

"What's that?"

"Used to be a nightclub near the Pier Head."

"Don't know about that, I need a clear head tomorrow."

"Gosh, not like you! Ah … joke! Actually you're right, we've had enough indulgence today with men and fantasies, and Downton Abbey is on the telly later."

Victoria sat at the bar munching some crisps with a double vodka and tonic, as Abby arrived in her trademark black miniskirt and crop top. "Your legs look quite tanned actually," she remarked. "What have you been up to?"

"The sun bed that Ali installed in one of his backrooms, especially for me, cos I said I liked his dark skin. I've beefed up the rest of me too, just as well in case Lynton calls. I'm sure Ali probably peeped through the cracks in the door when I was under, I miss him actually, and we do get on well. He even asked me to marry him once but he had been puffing on some hookah thing with his mates all night."

Victoria smiled. "I bet … wishful thinking. Anyway what are you going to order? I'm having the sea bass with potatoes and vegetables."

Abby looked over the menu, and her face lit up with a big grin. "Mmm … just the job not had that for years. Scouse, a plate of chips and pickled beetroot please."

"Pardon?"

Abby perused her friend quizzically. "I don't think you ever lived much when you were here as a child. Warming and nourishing on a chilly night, the seafaring and potato famine escapee Irish, of which there were many in Liverpool, brought scouse here generations ago and the food of the gods has sustained many a poor family."

"You mean scouse is a food, not slang for the Liverpool dialect?"

"Oh gosh Vikki. I don't suppose ... anyway ... talking about wanton women, do you know how much of a serious red light district this area by the station was in the old days? The hotel here has probably got all kinds of murky secrets lurking within the four walls of the old bedrooms."

"Really?"

"Obviously," Abby replied, dumbfounded with Victoria's ignorance. "You've never heard of Maggie Mae have you," and began to sing a variant of the old traditional Liverpool folk song in her quiet lilting voice.

Oh Maggie, Maggie Mae,
They have taken her away
And she'll never walk down Lime Street anymore
She robbed so many sailors
And captains of the whalers
That dirty robbing no good Maggie Mae

Victoria gaped, looking around at a myriad of male eyes focussed on the cute woman in the tiny black skirt and fishnet tights perched only just modestly on her bar stool. "Shush Abby," she whispered vehemently. "Everyone is staring!"

A chorus of clapping emerged from a group of businessmen further down, as Victoria went bright red and Abby stood up and took a bow. "Reckon we could be very well set up tonight, you can have the ugly one. Hey, cheer up, only kidding. And there goes our food over to that table," as she smiled at a waiter waving them over.

The rest of the evening, despite three more vodka and tonics, ended up quietly in their twin room and Downton Abbey. For Victoria at least, it was the perfect ending for the day.

Chapter Five

The wintry chill had finally abated. They emerged from the hotel doorway, the concierge chatting away as she led them to their hire car parked around the side of the building. The moment they turned the corner, Abby's face dropped looking at the large, gleaming black BMW X5 four by four SUV.

"Vikki?" she hissed. "What happened to the Ford Fiesta? I didn't expect to be driving this monster."

"A bit of a muddle with the booking because I wanted a satnav, anyway the hotel is taking responsibility and we are paying the price of your Ford Fiesta. Isn't that super?" Victoria beamed.

The concierge gave Abby, looking blank, the key. "Have a great day guys. Make sure you get to Southport, nice drive up there and great seafront," and left them to it.

Once they got the doors opened and jumped in, Abby began to smile again. "Mmm … I like the height of this beast, and the leather upholstery. This is yummy comfort for me. Oh shit Vikki, it's an automatic. I've never driven an auto before."

"Easy, put that stick into drive, foot down and away you go. Use your right foot for accelerator and brake as usual; left foot now is redundant, all cool. N is neutral for when you stop at lights and P is park when you stop for good. Switch on, so I can program the navigation screen. I've got the post code of the Appleby care home on this card."

They shot forward wheels spinning and Victoria whitening as Abby took a careful jerky cruise around the perimeter of the car park, stopping and starting a few times and getting the feel of the drive, then they shot out of the entrance, through the lights and into the busy city centre traffic.

"Wow, soon got this beast tamed. Thank goodness for the navigation screen because I don't recognise anywhere here. Blimey, the shops and the roads have changed like mega."

"I thought it was just me; anyway not far to go either, we should get there in three quarters of an hour. There's a new motorway here now so we'll follow that route, bypasses my old childhood haunts. We can backtrack later."

"You mean you want to see this Orsbrick Hall as well, today?"

"Depends on what Eveline has to say, but yes, why not. Get rid of some old demons at the same time. I'll tell you more later."

Despite the motorway distraction, Victoria was quite intrigued driving through places she hadn't seen for so long. Certainly there were changes; a lot more housing estates in what used to be quiet and isolated villages, new roads and business parks. But much of the unique rural nature of West Lancashire, once outside of the conurbation, came back to her instantly, thinking warmly of the evenings as a child when all she could hear were skylarks, singing and hovering over the canal and cornfields, and the lovely sunsets, perused out towards the flattened green landscape of Liverpool Bay.

"Parbold Hill," Victoria began before turning to Abby, concentrating on the winding road. "A sort of landmark, it even has a monument on top, and was always the first change of scenery from the flat green farmland. You then continue onwards towards the starkness of the dark Pennines and bleak moorland. The hill is only about a hundred metres high but you can see it for miles. The village nestles at the foot, and the Leeds and Liverpool canal winds through the outskirts."

"Sounds idyllic. You look relaxed and contented for the first time," Abby replied smiling. "Do you like it here again?"

Victoria couldn't quite understand why, but somehow she did feel very relaxed, despite all the desperate hurt, pain and turmoil of her childhood. The area still had an inviting charm, certainly far nicer than the noise and urban bustle around the refinery in Holland. Secretly, she had been feeling quite claustrophobic sometimes in Rotterdam, especially at the weekends sauntering around the shopping centre, when Abby wasn't dishing out kebabs; the amount of people around now in West Holland was becoming overwhelming.

"Did you say care home?"

"Yes, apparently Eveline is quite elderly and according to Lynton, rather frail, but he just refused to tell me any more, although I'm sure he knew plenty. Why are you smiling?"

"Oh, I forgot, I sort of got a text actually … from Lynton."

"Well? And how come he had your number?"

"I slipped him my card on the way out, whilst you were gazing at Lilith on the wall. Text just said Southport with a question mark."

Victoria laughed "Maybe we could ride the big beast out there."

"Which big beast?" Abby chimed in with a smirk.

They turned into another short cut lane and Victoria pulled down the visor to apply some red lipstick. Glancing into the mirror, she looked … then looked again … her heart nearly stopped dead.

They were not alone; they had a passenger in the rear. That woman was sitting there primly, purple shawl still wrapped around her head, same pained expression, staring hard at Victoria, except she raised her hand and pointed left.

"Oh fuck,"

"Jesus Christ, Vikki, what on earth is the matter with you?" Abby shouted. "You've gone as white as a sheet, I'm pulling in."

They stopped in a cutting between the hedgerows, everywhere quite deserted, just a small farmhouse, with a smoking chimney in the distance and some cows grazing in the adjacent field. Victoria was staring straight ahead and now shaking badly. "Just tell her to go Abby please, tell her to get out of this car and out of my life."

Abby stared at her. "Tell who to go? Okay, slowly please, what the fuck are you talking about?"

"That woman in the back with the purple shawl, please tell her to leave, I've had enough now."

Abby turned around and back again. "There's nothing there, look."

Victoria turned around, no sign of anything or anybody, but she smelt a faint whiff of something penetrating and unpleasant when she realised again, the same as in the solicitors; it was definitely aniline. She felt frightened once more.

"Actually," Abby said, suddenly opening her door, "I can smell something peculiar, like petrol gone off. Hope we haven't got a leak."

Victoria looked at her and her insides bounded back to normality; she wasn't going crazy, and threw her arms around the startled Abby, slobbering. "Oh Abby, thank goodness, it isn't just me, thank you Abby, thank you so much ..."

Abby gently lifted her arms off and looked sternly into Victoria's face. "Okay. I can sense you haven't told me

90

everything lately ... and maybe I haven't told you things either, so time for total honesty and a chat. There's a large garden centre according to this map not far from here, and we have a good hour yet ... probably with a tearoom. Deal?"

"Yes, deal. But that woman was vehemently pointing, pointing to the left. What's over there?"

Abby played with the satnav and altered the magnification to get a better view of the surroundings and moved her finger gently over the screen. "As the crow flies it leads directly to ... mmm ... the village of Orsbrick. Let's get to that cafe. Maybe having me with you is more than fortuitous."

"What do you mean? Has all this got something to do with Orsbrick Hall?"

"I suspect so and you must promise me something now Vikki. No more scientific rationality ranting and vitriolic scorn poured on things you don't understand or believe in. I want you now to have a very clear and open mind, just like you were doing a detailed and objective scientific investigation that you had no idea where it was going, understood? Do you promise?"

Victoria stared hard at Abby. It wasn't often she was serious and assertive but whatever was going on had touched Abby deeply as well. And she was so very, very grateful for her best friend being there, knowing that together they could muster and rustle together all kinds of skills and knowledge to get to the bottom of this weird stuff. Suddenly she felt an unexpected relief again, like nothing had happened, exactly the same as in the solicitor's office when she got outside.

"Tea and cakes on me, time to get fat both of us," she replied with a grin. "Well? Step on it, Lewis Hamilton."

Abby grinned back and they shot off towards the garden centre.

They were sat, pondering in front of a large red-spotted teapot and two giant slabs of lemon drizzle cake. Victoria now came clean and explained the odd sightings of the mysterious woman, both inside Green and Burgess and then at the Ship and Mitre. No longer, after the ghostly carjacking, could she put this out of her mind as some random non-event, as she was normally capable of scientifically doing. She stepped back from her thoughts and waited for Abby to respond.

"Whilst you were cavorting in the pub with the eccentric Julian, after the exhibition," Abby commenced, "I went up to the new Central Library and had a scour of information in the reading room."

"What sort of information? On what topic?"

"It was on a couple of things. Lately, I don't know why, I've been experiencing odd periods of serious inner unease and even had some recurring dreams of being in a laboratory, which as you well know is definitely not me. I distinctly remember wearing a white coat and holding flasks of coloured liquids; there were people around me, all men, I didn't recognise. Everywhere was hazy and smoky and smelled horrible and the equipment and the furniture were ancient, and there was someone at the end of the bench wearing a top hat and a long dark coat. I had the same dream three nights running, preceded each time by those bad feelings, like there was a presence but in my head. The last night was when you had your accident. And then there were the tarot cards, which I had dealt to myself.

"Tarot cards? You mean those crazy things that people believe in for predicting futures and ..."

"Vikki?"

"Sorry, I promise ... I am sticking with the deal, big zip on lips."

"Good. No matter how I dealt a selection, two cards kept coming up, each relatively harmless, not the death card, it doesn't matter now what they were, but I wanted to dig further into interpretations, my knowledge isn't that deep. I'm not really a practitioner."

"So what did you find? This is where I come in, analysis and synthesis of ideas in a logical and scientific thought process."

"Not everything follows that ideal dream ticket, I'm afraid. Anyway not as much as I wanted, because you rang and I had to get out of the reading room and find you. But, I did get time to look at some old papers and photographs. They were rare and under glass for protection and others had been microfiched, basically old sepias, between 1875 and 1890 done by a famous photographer in Liverpool. I'm now absolutely certain that the setting in my dreams wasn't as I first thought, some mental distortion of earlier school years in old chemistry labs, but a Victorian science laboratory, with lots of practical work going on. I've never seen or been in a Victorian laboratory Vikki."

"No neither have I. But how you describe it sounds plausible, thinking of the man in the top hat and coat too. But why didn't you tell me before?"

"Remember last time we tried to have a discussion about my so called psychic abilities and you went into one of your negative and endless debating rants that felt like I was being put on trial and convicted for fraud. I just didn't want to continue."

"Okay, after what has been happening to me over the last week or so, even I have to admit my über-scepticism has taken a serious knock, so a psychic rant-free zone has my full personal guarantee from now on. Victoria smiled and patted Abby's hand. "More cake?"

"Gosh no, I can only just fit into these jeans as it is," Abby replied laughing. "Anyway, I found something else. Curious about Orsbrick Hall, I had a search in some archives. Couldn't find anything, and then the archivist said any meaningful information would be held by the County Records Office in Preston or local parish records and possibly census data, much of it online. But she did have some old maps of the area, done in the early 1870s. What do you remember of Orsbrick Hall as a child, from a distance? I know you said you never went near the place, but you saw it presumably?"

"Yes, of course, from a distance. It was large, certainly old and looked dilapidated, a manor type house with obviously lots of rooms and big chimneys. All the gardens and land around it looked very neglected, but it's vague Abby. I was about eight at the time when I last remember and it was always misty and damp."

"And where did you see it from?"

"The canal of course, which ran in front of the house although I'm not sure now whether it was the front or the back, come to think of it. The perspective didn't click with my eight year old brain."

"It was the back. No other building then?"

"No, why?"

"Because the map shows what must have been a large factory, labelled of some sort in the grounds between the house and the canal, so whatever it was the canal probably supplied materials or was used to get goods to customers and probably both. The factory has been completely removed obviously or you wouldn't have been able to see the house. Unfortunately, no maps in between that period and now could be found."

"What are you trying to say?"

"Not sure yet but something seems to be being planted, reflecting circumstances, into our minds, but isn't making sense, at least not yet."

Victoria looked at her watch. "We'd better go and get to see what Eveline West has to say. She must hold the key to all of this. I'm glad we're going now and especially that you're coming with me too."

"Odd, isn't it?" Abby whispered. "Like I've been destined into the act too?"

"Mmm ... keys out, let's get a move on, I'll go and pay the bill ..."

Soon they were on the outskirts of Parbold having taken a quick detour up the hill so Abby could peruse and pat the monument.

"Good heavens Vikki, what an unusual design, the stone is carved out like a large bottle. What's the background do you know? Lovely view too."

"It's actually called the Parbold Bottle and made out of local grit stone. Apparently it was put up in 1832 to commemorate the Reform Act and give many more people a vote for the first time around the country," Victoria replied immediately, amazed with her own detailed recall of local history, which had been buried in her brain since school. "Although," she added, knowing Abby would be interested, "it was of course only males allowed to vote which was reinforced by the Bill wording and caused much resentment, from which the women's suffragette movement sprung up gradually."

Abby smiled. "See, you do have empathy with the locality really. Actually that Bill was also commemorated by the famous portrait painter George Hayter, now hanging in the National Gallery. What a great store of historical knowledge we two can muster up between us, I'm sure even Lynton and Julian would be impressed."

Vicky laughed loudly and they jumped back into the BMW and continued down. They soon took a left turn near the Leeds and Liverpool canal and drove slowly along a wide gravelled drive. The ornate iron gates ahead, with Appleby Lodge prominently displayed on a gold plate, swung open automatically and they parked with a gravelly crunch of tyres outside the main door. They appeared to be the only visitors there, although they could see a couple of old Landrovers at the side.

Abby stared across at the Lodge. "What a beautiful building, certainly Georgian by the windows and overall architecture, the brickwork is in amazingly good condition."

"I agree," Victoria replied softly. "The place is very well kept too, the gardens especially and the surroundings; look at those lovely oak trees and the flowers and roses out in the flower beds. This isn't your ordinary sort of care home, Abby. I am getting more intrigued by the minute."

They pushed the bell and the large red door opened. They were greeted by a smiling woman in her mid fifties wearing a smart blue suit and white blouse. A couple of other staff were hovering in the corridor, cleaning and taking trays out.

"Do come in, you must be Dr McKenzie to see Eveline. She's expecting you. My name is Betty Grable, no relation I'm afraid. I'm the warden of the Lodge. If you just wait over there, I'll see if Eveline is ready." She looked somewhat more sternly at Abby. "And you are?"

"Err ... Dr Abigail Warren, I'm Victoria's colleague."

"Ahh ... okay ... I'll mention it to Eveline first. She insisted we made some sandwiches, so I'll just get them topped up.

Before you head over there Dr McKenzie, I should just warn you."

Victoria felt some trepidation coming on, but Betty Grable sensed the anxiety and smiled. "Nothing serious don't worry, but Eveline is getting on and has a tendency to nod off unexpectedly when she's talking, it can be for just a minute or hours so be aware. Otherwise, for her age, she is in remarkable health and state of mind. I think her continued artistic work must be good for her."

"You mean she still does textile art work? Gosh," Abby interjected quietly, looking animated. "Sorry Mrs Grable, I'm also an artist, that's fabulous."

Betty Grable's demeanour suddenly changed and with a grin she replied. "I shall tell her that too …"

They waited for a few minutes, when Mrs Grable returned, with quick strides. "Eveline will be pleased to see both of you, I'll take you down."

"Actually Mrs Grable, may I use your facilities please?" Abby suddenly requested, looking uncomfortable. "I'm sorry Vikki."

"No problem, Dr Warren, down that corridor on the right. When you've finished I'll take you to Eveline's room separately."

Bette Grable and Victoria marched off through a large oak door and into the other corridor towards the back. The Lodge was quite spacious, spotlessly clean, but somehow retained a nineteenth century atmosphere, with the style of drapes and antique furniture everywhere. Passing one room, Victoria could hear the mellow tones of a cello being played, and what sounded like a choir somewhere in the distance. One of the residents suddenly came out of a room wearing a pair of goggles and overalls covered in paint and holding an easel. Victoria's eyes swivelled to watch him disappear happily into a large room.

"I can see Dr McKenzie that you don't know the background to Appleby Lodge. This is a special care home. All the residents in here are artists or musicians of various types; some continue active, others I'm afraid are beyond their former calling. We have fifteen residents who come from all around the country. Most are here only a few years, like in many homes, and we have a full range of facilities to accommodate physical needs and also dementia."

"It must be ... I'm sorry ... I don't want to appear rude as I don't know but, well, expensive?"

"All these things are relative aren't they, but yes the home would be out of the reach of your ordinary local resident. But it was set up with a trust for this purpose. Ahh ...we are here now. Eveline has one of the nicest suites in the Lodge with a lovely view from her windows."

She knocked on the pale green door and Victoria heard a firm but certainly elderly voice, in a very posh accent, reply. "Do please come in."

Mrs Grable held the door wide and Victoria walked into a large and very high ceilinged room, papered with a striped design she had never seen anywhere before and the walls finished off with a marbled Georgian coving. All around the walls were adorned with wonderful hanging pieces of fabrics, again like nothing she had seen, intricately designed and colourful, where she could make out themes of an outdoor nature, trees, water lilies, meadow flowers, orchids. She immediately thought of Abby, wondering why she was taking so long.

A high rear window, from floor to ceiling, which could be opened out, and letting in lots of daylight, especially noticeable with the sun shining in brightly, took her gaze. Standing in front, staring motionless at the view and holding onto two sticks stood a small elderly lady in a mauve cardigan and chocolate brown skirt, her hair white but thick. She turned around slowly, her soft complexion highlighted with a bright red lipstick and smiled. "Victoria, how wonderful to see you at last."

But Victoria, ready to move forward and kiss her cheek, stopped dead, frozen in her tracks as she looked into the beneficent face and her mouth dropped. The likeness was so uncanny, she couldn't believe it, it was like looking at herself in the mirror, admittedly a much older face, but Eveline had remarkably few lines, great skin and her thick white hair, cut in a fashionable bob, just a little shorter than her own blonde style. But the eyes and the intense look were identical.

Eveline looked quite amused and didn't seem in the least bit surprised. "Well, my dear, I must admit you have inherited the family likeness and are quite beautiful"

Victoria stared perplexed, who was this woman?

"I'm your aunt, Victoria, although obviously you would never have known, as I can see from your reaction. Just one of a number of things for you to learn today. Please, come and give your long lost aunt a big hug."

"Oh gosh," Victoria stuttered and rushed forward to hug Eveline and kiss each cheek, totally bowled over by this unexpected revelation.

Eveline took her hand with both of hers. Her grip was firm, but her pale skin was lined with lots of small brown spots. "Now take a seat, the armchair, by the coffee table. As you can see I've had some sandwiches made, cucumber and cheese, I hope they're acceptable, I'm a vegetarian I'm afraid. Tea? Earl Grey?"

"Lovely, thank you," Victoria replied as Eveline sat on the other armchair opposite and lifted the large pink teapot, and began slowly pouring out some tea into expensive Staffordshire china cups, sitting on delicate matching patterned saucers. Where on earth was Abby?

Suddenly the door knocked and opened and Abby came bounding in. "I'm so sorry, Mrs Grable insisted on showing me the most absolutely beautiful textile art objects in the conservatory," then looked first at Victoria and on to Eveline, both staring back at her. "Oh …"

"Abby, please meet Aunt Eveline," Victoria announced, with her best voice, in a formal kind of way, not her usual style.

Eveline, her eyes narrowed, was staring hard at Abby, with a concentrated frown across her brow, then she suddenly smiled and held out her hand as Abby moved forward to shake it.

"Abby, I'm so glad you're here, you're one of us aren't you."

"Yes …" Abby replied slowly. "I suppose I am."

Victoria, intrigued, looked from one to the other, not understanding what on earth her aunt was talking about, although obviously Abby certainly did, both their eyes still fixed firmly on the other, as Abby shook hands. Of course, Victoria muttered to herself. Artists; they are both artists.

"Excellent, now Abby my dear I assume you would like a cup as well. I hope you enjoyed the display in the conservatory, actually that is my latest nature collection, which I completed earlier this year. Lots of inspiration in the woods at the back. The residents love a bit of a show, especially Gerald."

"Gerald?" Victoria queried.

"My boyfriend. He still plays a beautiful cello but sadly, although ten years younger than me, he's gone a bit gaga.

Forgets everything the moment he goes out of the door, music is the last part of the mind to stay with dementia you know. But he's such a gentleman and it's like having a fresh date every night. I'm sure you know what I mean Abby, and do please call me Eveline, I hate Ms West. Pull up that rattan chair over there with the yellow cushion."

Victoria, once more dumbfounded, stared at Abby, who grinned and then blushed beetroot. "Of course. And your work is so wonderful Eveline," looking around the walls with huge admiration at the patchwork of colours and textures.

"Actually my dear I have a lot more on display, especially the fabrics I made as a young artist, around your age, in a gallery in Southport. It was then I developed and mastered my own technique. Everything is hand sewn, original and unique which I developed from my roots in painting. Each object evolves from an initial concept; I hand stitch each piece of fabric into place with layering, nets, shears, using scraps, wools and yarns, all that sort of thing and I dye materials as I desire them. Like you I was a visual artist. But that was a long time ago."

Abby grinned again and back at Victoria, both of them in their own ways realising that some things were making a little bit of sense.

"Now both of you, tuck into those sandwiches." She struggled up and quickly returned from a side room holding an ornate tray with three cut glass dishes containing jelly, fruit and a blob of fresh cream. "My studio is in there, I made this treat specially this morning. I have a small fridge where I keep the natural dyes I use to stop them going off."

Abby's eyes lit up as she delved into the large plate of sandwiches.

"Now Victoria," Eveline began, not brusque, but measured in a business-like tone. "The reason you are here. I want to tell you things about your family and the past which may surprise you, even shock you, but I understand you're a polymer scientist so you should have a strong stomach and what is done is done. Correct? Then, when I've finished you can decide, whether you want to accept ownership of Orsbrick Hall or not."

Victoria nodded, munching a cucumber sandwich slowly. But as Eveline began to slowly pursue her story, the revelations that emerged were so mind boggling as to almost be beyond belief, as she sat patiently, listening and trying hard to take it all in to her sharp memory. The questioning would come at the end. Abby simply listened, very interested, but unusually showing no emotion or reaction, almost as if all of these bombshells she knew all along, and that Eveline and her had been sharing intimacies for years. That observation, Victoria couldn't fathom at all, but was determined in her own mind, to do so as quickly as possible.

The first thing she learned was that her father, Jack, was even older than she thought, he had been born in 1907 and that Eveline was his younger sister. Amazingly, she was in her ninety eighth year. But even more astounding was the house, Orsbrick Hall, that she had never been allowed to go near as a child, belonged to her father's twin brother, William McKenzie. He was someone she had never known existed. Other relatives, mentioned vaguely once as a child, were all supposed to have been killed during the second world war during a bombing raid in Liverpool, obviously, she thought, a total lie. It appeared that her father and William had fallen out immediately after they graduated together at Cambridge, both in natural sciences with first class degrees.

"They were exceedingly clever, Victoria, my two brothers. William graduated top of his year at Cambridge, your father was sixth. That was when the resentment started. They fell out completely six months later over my best friend. She was an artist too, a muse and plenty of other things. She took them both for a ride, but they never spoke again. And your father never subsequently spoke to me."

But that was just the starter. Her mother was not her real mother, but her aunt and stepmother. Her natural mother had died of pancreatic cancer when Victoria was three weeks old and her father immediately married her mother's sister, one year older than her mother, who had been adopted as a baby. The family was just too big to feed, and she was brought up in America.

"But why all the secrecy Aunt Eveline? Why was all this kept from me? How did it all take place?"

It turned out that her real mother's family were hauliers of coal, up and down the Leeds and Liverpool canal and lived a nomadic life on gaily painted barges for generations. In other words they were boat people. Her mother's grandfather originally owned and lived in the cottage on Cinderblack Lane, but then in the depression life fell apart for the family and he went to work in Liverpool on the docks. He died in the war years but had rented the cottage to her father, who lived in it on his own as a bachelor teacher, exempt from war service as a reserved occupation. That was how he had met her real mother and they dated secretly for years. She used to clean the house and he became obsessive about privacy. When her grandfather died, she inherited the house, her father continued living there rent free, when one day after many years she got unexpectedly pregnant … with Victoria … and she was constantly ill with stomach pains but everyone assumed it was the pregnancy. She gave birth, died soon after and her sister, Beatrice, inherited the house, turned up penniless from America and she and her father got married. To the outside world Victoria was passed off as their baby, as they were both so reclusive at home, nobody guessed or cared.

Victoria sat back, staring into space, silent and contemplative, but taking in the logical sequencing of events, happenings and conversations and coming to the logical conclusion that much finally began to stack up and make sense. She wasn't especially bothered or even surprised about her so called 'mother', but despised her parents even more for the continual and forced deceit. She had obviously been close to finding out about Uncle William, when her mother caught her and hit her badly that day. If only she had known him. Gosh, he must have been at least 102 when he died, amazing. Of course her father was dead now too so what else could be said, except wherever Beatrice was now, she never wanted to see her again that was for sure. She idly picked up a dish of jelly and fruit and began to pick at the cream, watching Abby wolfing down hers. Eveline had gone quiet, having suddenly nodded off, her head slumped back in the armchair, snoring peacefully.

Abby turned to Victoria. "You certainly have an interesting family background, I'm sure Eveline was quite a raver in her day too."

"Yes, she obviously has just met a kindred spirit," Victoria replied, looking vacantly at Abby and still trying to take in the enormity of what Aunt Eveline had just said.

"Now, Victoria, the final piece of the jigsaw, Orsbrick Hall."

They both turned startled to see Eveline, perched on the edge of her chair awake and ready for more. The property went back a long way. It had been in the McKenzie family for generations, right from the mid seventeenth century, when an ancestor and friend of Isaac Newton had apparently built it. The family had not only been amateur dabblers and enthusiasts for science right the way through, but also acquired significant wealth during the first half of the nineteenth century, applying their science and engineering successfully to opportunities rapidly emerging with the industrial revolution. The male head of household in each generation always partook of a family ritual and went to Cambridge to study sciences or mathematics.

"Of course," Eveline added, "that opportunity wasn't open to women in the McKenzie family in those days. They had to stay at home, looking pretty and waiting only for marriage and children."

Victoria interjected. "I see how I've taken after the family and it is fantastic to learn all of that, but were there no women then interested in science or able to pursue it?"

"There was talk by my parents that there were some science women in the past, but they never would expand on it, to me or William or your father. To be honest, I simply was too young, a child, and not interested. My father, your grandfather, also a top Cambridge graduate, was a brilliant researcher into drugs and medicines as a young man and set up and ran a chemist's shop in Ormskirk with my mother. But they both died, within days of one another, in the flu epidemic of 1919, trying to treat people in the local sanatorium. I was of course living in Orsbrick Hall. I was seven and parcelled off, as was common then, to a cousin's house in Burscough and joined their household, a nuisance. There were no adults as such, both parents had been boat people and had just vanished, heaven knows where. My cousin Maud was nineteen, the eldest and head of the household. Ernest was seventeen and a boatman; he had missed the war because of his health and died when he was twenty from consumption. The other two girls, in their early teens were horrendous, seamstresses in the local textiles factory. I was like a fish out of water, artistic, clever, bored at school, bullied and ridiculed at home, and when I was fourteen ran away to Liverpool and became a model, and pretty quickly muse, to a famous society photographer."

Victoria sighed, feeling oodles of hidden guilt melting away. She had done the same thing as Aunt Eveline, well, apart from the muse part!

Eveline paused, as if ready to snooze again, but was simply reflecting, in a daze, her eyes glinting for minutes on what were obviously very happy memories. Abby smiled.

"Eventually I met and married a very handsome, rich and charismatic cotton merchant with a string of ships and warehouses. We had no children sadly and lived in a huge house near Sefton Park in Liverpool, where many seafarers and merchants lived then. He was a rogue and a serial philanderer, never at home for months on end. That was when I fully developed my textiles art, sold lots and made plenty of my own money, and lived at the heart of Liverpool's high society. Culture, jazz, dancing, everything. I made my own amusements of course when my husband was away. I had great parties, especially during the thirties." She winked at Abby, who blushed again. "One day my husband disappeared and never came back, presumed dead at sea, but I continued in the house … and only came here when it became too much for me."

"So do you remember Orsbrick Hall? What was it like? What happened after your parents died?" Victoria queried wide-eyed.

"Not a lot, although I was happy there as a young child, my parents were always laughing and joking. But there were parts of the house, locked and barred that I could never go to. They were very close, with a great sense of local community and purpose. It was tragic really; they were both only in their early forties. And you see William and Jack were at the Blue Coat private boarding school in Liverpool and stayed there. They never came back and went straight to Cambridge together. I don't know who managed the financial affairs, there must have been some legal executor. The other part I couldn't go to was in the factory outside, where my parents made drugs for their pharmacy and for sale. They distilled coal of course then for lots of things, including dyes, which is where I developed my interest in textiles. I learned my fine art at evening classes."

Abby spoke for the first time. "There was a factory in the grounds?"

"Of course Abby and had been there many years with various manifestations. I think it was built in the 1830s. But what you want to know is what happened to it don't you."

Victoria looked at both of them, like a private sub-conversation had been going on. She didn't understand, but no matter as this amazing outpouring of the past was blowing her mind so much she just wanted Eveline to carry on all day if she could, although her conversation was beginning to jump about, probably getting tired.

"Aunt Eveline, may I make us another nice cup of tea? Those sandwiches and the jelly were delicious."

Abby nodded with a grin.

"I'm so glad you both liked it. Use my studio, you'll find a sink and a Bunsen burner and kettle."

"Abby, can you help and bring the teapot please," Victoria said quietly with a mild stare, carrying the cups and saucers, as Eveline settled back for another snooze.

Once inside the studio, she quietly closed the door. "Okay, honesty and openness you said earlier. Now what is going on?

It's almost like you know this fantastical story already and have shared thoughts with Eveline before we got here?"

"Because I have."

Victoria looked at her friend, totally perplexed.

"Pardon?"

"Because Eveline is psychic Vikki, very psychic and she sensed me the moment I walked in the door as I did with her. No, we don't share thoughts in a language, like you and I speak, it's very hard to describe, a sort of language of feelings and intuition, anticipating ahead with triggers you can't explain. That was why she immediately said I was one of them."

"But I thought she meant being an artist."

"No, clever of her wasn't it. She wanted you to think that. I am just surprised you don't have the same sense. I think you do, but for some reason it's all locked in at the moment. Eveline will know we've been talking about this and she wants that to happen, because there are things that have gone on at Orsbrick Hall. I know now, and she can't tell you because her own psychic ability is acting as a shield to prevent her. Maybe because whatever it is was so awful. She is trying to use me to unlock the barrier and let you in to find out, because I'm sure, because of her age probably, I don't know just guessing, she is losing the will and capacity to find out herself. She's reached a delicate point in taking you this far. I know you're full of questions but my advice is this. Don't mention anything about women in purple shawls. She won't be able to tell you and in her mind it will create indescribable turmoil."

The Bunsen burner was slow but the kettle had just started whistling.

Victoria for the first time, not only bit her tongue but was grudgingly prepared to accept Abby's hypothesis, and because of her immediate growing attachment to her new aunt, was not willing at that moment to test it. Also, her own inner conclusion was she didn't have all the facts or evidence yet. It was as if a mantle of responsibility was being subtly passed on to the next and remaining member of the illustrious, scientific McKenzie family, her. Now she began to understand why Eveline wished to pass on the legacy of Orsbrick Hall to her, but she wanted to know more about her Uncle William. But she had also made up her mind on the other matter.

"Thanks Abby," she replied "You are quite amazing actually," catching the saucer quickly which had slipped from Abby's hand. "I believe you."

Abby grinned, stunned and quite incredulous that she was hearing that statement. "Gosh, that's a turn-up Vikki. I never expected to hear you say … well like … yes so easily."

"And," Victoria replied, "I've decided. I'm going to sign the contract and own the house. I feel a responsibility to continue such an amazing family legacy somehow, and try and solve whatever this mysterious bad deed is, but on one condition. Will you help me?"

"Try and keep me away, but you haven't heard all the other legal conditions of Lynton Grey yet?"

They walked in as Eveline was re-emerging from another quick snooze. "Ah, tea again. What a wonderful pair you are. Grab that biscuit tin Abby. I think, Victoria, we need to conclude shortly and you want to know some more about William and your father, don't you."

"Yes, I do. But can I ask? The solicitor said …"

"You mean Lynton? Such a sweet young man, he's been very kind and helpful."

"Yes, Mr Grey. He said there were conditions to fulfil if I accept the contract and take ownership of Orsbrick Hall?"

"Very simple my dear, you can sign the contract and take ownership anytime, as long as I approve. But if you want the financial legacy left as well, you will have to live in Orsbrick Hall for twelve months. At the end of that period the legacy will be released and the bank account unfrozen. You are then free to do what you like with the house and the money. So what do you think?"

"I've made up my mind Aunt Eveline. All the things you have told me today are so amazing and almost unbelievable and it will take a little while to sink in, but I'm so glad you have. I would never have believed there was such an historic and scientific legacy going back generations that I knew absolutely nothing about, and I feel both a responsibility and a huge inner drive to carry on that legacy in some way. So I want to sign up, find out more about the house and try and take the opportunity to ... do something positive somehow with the place ... I don't know fully yet, I have to go there and see. But I feel really enthusiastic."

"Good, my dear, because there is only you and me left now in the McKenzie family, and it would have to be down to you. I want to see my time out just doing more fabrics and painting, and of course having some fun with Gerald, whilst it lasts." Her eyes twinkled and a big grin broke out as Abby laughed loudly then stifled it quickly.

"As for living there," Victoria continued, slowly. "I do need to think about that. There is my work and life in Holland, lots of things to weigh up, and I need to see the place too. I'm not really bothered about the additional money, there is something more fundamental inside me wanting to own Orsbrick."

Victoria had already drawn the logical conclusion that any money remaining from all that wealth generation during the nineteenth century would be near worthless now with inflation,

110

demonstrated by the way the house, as she remembered it from a distance as a child, was so run down. Obviously Uncle William had little money himself.

"Well dear, that's excellent, I'm so pleased to hear it." She walked over to her sideboard and took out a small decorated silver metal box, with a beautiful patterned engraving etched onto the top. "Take this box Victoria. It's a cigarette case, which belonged to your great-great-grandfather. It was given to him, I believe, by the wife of someone called William Morris, another textile artist and I think a writer. Apparently he cherished it and carried it everywhere for the rest of his life. Inside is the key to Orsbrick Hall. The house is yours. Lynton Grey will sort out the boring legalities but there are no problems. I approve."

"Oh Aunt Eveline, thank you so much," Victoria cried out hugging her hard." I won't let the McKenzie family down."

"Enough of that Victoria," Eveline whispered hoarsely, catching her breath. "Now, let's take that tea before it gets cold."

"Congratulations Vikki. Ginger biscuit anyone?" Abby added warmly, holding the full tin out.

Eveline concluded the background to Jack, her father, and his twin brother William. "After I had been packed off to Burscough in 1919, Orsbrick Hall lay empty for the following seven years, until both William and Jack finished Cambridge, both quite young as they had gone up at age sixteen. William came back and reopened the house. In the intervening period the former housekeeper had kept an eye on the estate, ensuring the house didn't get too run down, although the grounds became completely overgrown and the factory had deteriorated badly. After the fallout between the two brothers, Jack went to

Africa for five years collecting and studying exotic insects on behalf of London Zoo."

Victoria had no idea. It was only when he came back again and moved into Cinderblack Lane that her father started teaching at the Cradwell private school for girls, where he stayed, reclusive for the rest of his life.

Eveline continued. "William was a totally different character to Jack, at least he was then, apparently full of life, a bon-viveur, and Orsbrick Hall became a social mecca in West Lancashire for high society rural jaunts, dancing, extravaganza and parties, as the roaring twenties continued. And William fell in love. She was a beautiful young red-haired debutante. Her name was Alicia, visiting the then Viscount Ottersburn. They began some sort of affair, it was 1928 and science was the last thing on his mind as he had access to his own independent means. He even had an MG Sports car, although where that ended up nobody knew. But something happened on the night of the 31st May. Only a servant saw it, they still had servants then and William had reappointed them back and even a butler. Alicia had got up in the middle of the night and gone downstairs for some water, not feeling well. Whatever she had seen that night turned her totally hysterical as she began screaming the place down and ran out into the gardens."

"But did Uncle William find her in the end?" Victoria asked not wishing to break the flow of the story but had to ask.

"Yes ..." Eveline responded softly but with some hesitation. "By then William was awake and with his servants began scouring the grounds without any luck. At daybreak they found her floating behind the reeds in the canal. She had jumped in and drowned herself. Nobody to this day knows why, but William changed overnight. He became depressed, reclusive, the parties stopped and nobody visited anymore. The following year he demolished the factory, razed it to the ground and of course eventually nature reclaimed the land back. He never went out again, the servants left or were sacked until all he was left with was the housekeeper and her daughter. The daughter eventually took over when her mother died and looked after him until the day he died."

Abby never moved; she was absorbing everything she could, conscious and subconscious. Something had begun formulating too in the back of Victoria's mind, but she put it to one side as she still had an important question.

"And you, Aunt Eveline? Were you not able to do something for Uncle William and what about my father when all this was happening?"

"Sadly dear, we had all become so estranged that nobody cared about the other, we each lived our own lives like the others never existed. That was often the way in those days. We simply shut each other out, mentally and physically. I never saw either your father or William again. I regret I didn't even go to Jack's funeral but I knew when he died. Well it wasn't quite so bad because when I moved here three years ago I decided to end this stupidity and go and see William, on his one hundredth birthday would you believe. It was quite an effort after all those years. That awful housekeeper was still there and he was not the man I remembered. He had become very frail and forgetful, but at various moments his mind returned as razor sharp as ever. He had reunited again quietly with science, rekindled his private interest in chemistry and had been dabbling with experiments somewhere in the place, but on what I haven't any idea. That is your domain my dear. Abby and I simply paint! But he knew you existed. How or why he wouldn't say, and he even knew you were a scientist living in Holland. But he insisted and I agreed that you be given the

McKenzie legacy and house to continue when he died. It was William who set the conditions. In his last year his mind finally went and I became the legal executor, but he died peacefully in his sleep. He is buried there."

"Buried?"

"Of course. Orsbrick Hall has its own private cemetery and small chapel at the rear. There are generations of McKenzie's buried there, although your father was, I believe, cremated."

Victoria's eyes widened and she glanced at Abby whose eyes still remained fixed and unmoving on Eveline.

"Well that's it I think for today. Victoria could you please tell Betty that we are finishing for the day, whilst I show Abby some more of these prints and paintings on the far wall."

"Certainly Aunt Eveline," Victoria replied, sensing now that after these massive but necessary revelations her aunt was looking decidedly weary. She headed to the door.

"Oh, before I forget," Eveline whispered loudly, her voice having become decidedly croaky. "You may, my dear, change your mind about the financial legacy when you know how much there is."

Victoria turned around. "How much is there?"

"Just over twenty five million pounds. You will never have to work again dear and will have enough to get the house back to normal. The house is still essentially very pretty but needs quite a lot of work doing on it. William let it run down dreadfully over all those years."

Victoria felt a disbelieving stunned sickness envelop her. That amount just couldn't be possible, surely? She smiled back weakly. "My goodness Aunt Eveline, yes ... certainly food for thought ... Oh gosh."

She went off in a daze down the corridor to look for Betty Grable, catching once again the melodic sound of Gerald's cello playing sweetly in the background.

Eveline grabbed hold of Abby's arm and led her into her bedroom where the walls were covered in paintings rather than fabrics. Abby gazed, open mouthed at the sheer sensuality, warm colours and bold brush strokes, vibrant summer scenes of fields and flowers but mixed with early Liverpool urban regeneration in the forties and fifties, where old and new buildings sat side by side in an uneasy alliance.

"The blitz destroyed some wonderful old buildings, Abby, in the war years. Liverpool got a pounding of course because of the docks, but the senseless destruction of heritage which never could be created again is still unforgiveable. Look what they put up in their place, like bad false teeth. I tried to capture the desolation I felt at the time through my painting. This was the period which slowly influenced my move to fabrics and sewing, I felt the brush was betraying me, do you understand my dear?"

"Absolutely Eveline ... But these are wonderful. I also felt the same, which took me into fashion design, but which hasn't been a big success unfortunately, I'm crap at business."

"Yes I know, I can sense it, I think you may want to return to your passion, fine art, one day."

"Hey, Eveline, maybe even textiles art ..."

"Maybe, Abby. But whilst Victoria is outside I want to tell you something else quickly. About her step-mother, that damned American, Beatrice. She came here three years ago and insisted I took her to Orsbrick Hall to see William. She was with some fat slimy looking Texan, younger than her, with the most awful accent and she looked a peculiar state, all tarted up like a Pier Head whore out of the 1940s. It made me feel quite queasy, especially when she began asserting that she had rights to inherit Orsbrick and would pursue a legal claim if she wasn't in the will as main benefactor. I insisted that her partner would not be appropriate to visit and he remained in the Adelphi Hotel in Liverpool. Next day we arrived near the entrance at Orsbrick in a taxi. She was in the rear and I was in the front, I loathe the back seats of cars. When … she suddenly started screaming hysterically and appeared to be wrestling with someone next to her, then she was gripped with some sort of seizure and fell over the seat. The taxi filled up with a strong smell too, like the kerosene we used to use to light oil lamps. The poor driver was hysterical. She never woke up and died two days later in the Royal Infirmary. The autopsy revealed she had actually died from the effects of acute alcoholic poisoning, her brain had gone to mush. That was obvious looking at her; she was an alcoholic, you could smell it. But the registrar at the Royal took me to one side and revealed that not only was her liver three times the normal size but it had gone a bright purple, same colour as the methylated spirits, mixed with whisky she had secretly been consuming. Nobody in the hospital had ever seen that before, so very odd. She was immediately cremated and the Texan disappeared back to America with an urn. So Victoria's mother, as she always sadly had only known, is quite dead my dear. I would like you to tell her at an appropriate time but I don't think it's wise right now. You know why I'm saying that my dear don't you. You must help her find herself."

Abby took a deep breath. Yes she certainly knew so much, and was as concerned as Victoria's Aunt Eveline. "Yes, I will, I promise."

"Excellent, now I'm surprised my little beauty at the end hasn't caught your eye yet."

Abby turned and looked to the far wall, near the large bay window, and her heart nearly jumped out of her mouth. "Oh my word, is that what I think it is?"

"Go and look my dear, and see for yourself."

Abby bounded to the window and peered at the framed painting of a young and stunning looking woman with thick, blonde hair adorned with water lilies and sitting in a billowing yellow crinoline dress, staring wantonly towards an open window. She squinted at the signature, now fading and shrieked with delight. "Gosh Eveline, it's a Rossetti, a genuine Rossetti … that is so awesome and amazing but who is the woman doing the sitting …?"

"Look carefully Abby. Who does she remind you of?"

Abby gazed hard, then it became so obvious, the eyes, the stare and the shape of the face, the likeness was so incredible. The painting was becoming a little faded, the face slightly distorted, not perhaps as well done as earlier works, probably she mused, towards the end of Dante Gabriel Rossetti's life when chloral and ill death dogged him badly.

"That was my grandmother Lydia, and Victoria's great-great aunt. She was nineteen at the time, a McKenzie, a young niece of Victoria's great-great grandfather, who owned the cigarette case. Rossetti had many muses in his time including Lydia. He loved women and especially painting them as you know of course."

"So Victoria's family, during that period, were not only scientists but also had close links with the arts?"

"Oh yes, they were very much part of the landed high society of the time, the arts and sciences were very intermixed, cultured men and some women, when they were allowed, were highly knowledgeable of both, it was a sort of rite of passage to demonstrate you had a top liberal education. Victoria's great-great- grandfather was probably at the pinnacle of that period."

"You mean he knew and mixed with Rossetti, Wardle, Morris and all those other people dabbling in arts and science and textiles?"

"Quite possibly my dear … I don't really know … ahh I can hear Victoria returning."

"Hello? Aunt Eveline, Abby, where are you?"

Abby and Eveline walked out of the bedroom to be greeted by Victoria, holding a large framed fabric piece alongside the smiling Bette Grable. "My fault, I apologise she was so long Eveline, but I had to show Dr McKenzie your little exhibition in the conservatory."

"And, Aunt Eveline, guess what, I've bought one, seeing as they had a price tag on them, ever the businesswoman aren't you?"

"I never miss a trick my dear, not even in here. Now what have you purchased? Ah, the water lilies, how nice, that has such happy memories when I did that."

"Really?"

"Yes, it was from a painting I made in the grounds of Orsbrick Hall," Eveline began, fidgeting with her sticks. "At the edge of the wooded area, there is a large and secluded natural pond, surrounded by reeds and tall grasses. That pond has a long history and was always an integral part of the family and growing up, because all the men of the McKenzie family loved to fish there, the children would have picnics and collect frogs and tadpoles and little sticklebacks in jam-jars." Her eyes danced mischievously. "And I'm sure on quiet sunny days it was a place where boyfriends and girlfriends would be taken for a bit of canoodling."

"You mean you painted all the water lilies in the pond, and then made this piece from it? But when was that?" Victoria quizzed, somehow not getting the timelines to make sense.

"It was only three years ago my dear and I wanted to do something meaningful to reconcile properly with William. You see for all those many years, deep down, I loved my elder brother. He was like me in his youth, mischievous and outgoing, a real extrovert, not I'm afraid like Jack, always the correct and studious type. They looked like twins but their personalities were so different. So for William's one hundredth birthday, I suggested taking him fishing at the pond, and he went with all his old gear and rods. It was a bit of a struggle, but we managed it and we even took a picnic and I painted. The housekeeper actually brought his old wind-up gramophone and we played old 78 records, they must still be there somewhere. William loved early jazz and dance bands. We had such a wonderful day and we talked and talked, his mind became so lucid again it was amazing, and we made up, after all those years. We never repeated it and he began to deteriorate quickly after that, but it was a day I shall never forget. Funny my dear how you picked that one isn't it. A lovely memento I'm sure."

"It's really fantastic, I feel so happy today," Victoria replied as Abby, standing behind Eveline, watched, pondered … and began to think even harder …

Chapter Six

Back in the garden centre and the weather was beginning to change, the wind whipping up sharply and darkening clouds were beginning to scud along the horizon. Victoria was quietly perusing the variegated white, yellow and purple water lilies for sale in the tub alongside a range of peculiarly shaped grey, shiny fibreglass pond moulds, and trying to imagine the former floating in the latter. She sauntered back to Abby who was finishing off the contents of a very large teapot, under the trellis canopy with sweet peas climbing up, of the outdoor cafe area.

"I've only just realised how much tea you can happily consume in a day," Victoria commented.

"I love tea," Abby replied slurping down the final dregs in her pink spotted green mug. "What is in that envelope you were handed on our way out?"

Victoria slowly fished inside the contents of her handbag, getting frustrated with finding everything else, as she started loading two phones, lipstick, packets of tissues, sweets, pens and her red leather purse onto the table. Abby watched, amused at the ever growing pile of stuff, when finally Victoria found it. Inside were a couple of faded sepia photographs ... of her pharmacy grandparents, taken, by the look of the dress, around the turn of the century when they had probably only just got married. In the first picture, her seated grandmother, wearing a pretty white blouse and dark skirt, had her dark hair pinned up.

They both looked stern but she was very attractive. Her grandfather, stylishly dressed in a dark tailored jacket, buttoned at the top, white high necked collared shirt and matching tie stood with one arm around her shoulder and his other arm posed behind his back like a wine waiter. They looked very up and coming, the epitome of educated professionals. Those strong McKenzie features with the sharp stare, oval face and prominent nose were very evident in his face, sporting a fashionable moustache uplifted at the ends and a thick head of dark, swept back hair. Oddly her father had quite weak features in comparison, although his eyes also had shown that same stare, which of course she, Victoria, along with Eveline, maintained.

"Gosh, your granddad was very fanciable in those days, I could quite have ..."

"Mmm, I'm sure, oh my goodness, just look at this other picture."

They both giggled at her grandmother, in a long dress down to her ankles and a Sunday bonnet, perched on the seat of a strange riding contraption and holding a pair of levers, her grandfather sitting behind. The photo was taken outside of Orsbrick Hall, the imposing frontage, rearing up behind them. A small wheel at the front and a slightly larger one at the back supported the frame with two large penny farthing type wheels on an axle either side of them, like some kind of original tandem cycle.

"Listen," Abby began. "I'm going to make a suggestion. You've had the most mind blowing revelations thrown at you today, and you look totally whacked out. How long do we have the beast, because I suggest you come back to see Orsbrick Hall, tomorrow or maybe the day after even. The house has been standing for over three hundred years, so another day or two isn't going to make much difference is it. You need to reflect properly and go in a fresh state of mind. What do you think?"

Victoria pondered, fingering the cigarette case in her hand lovingly. "I agree, you're right. I could do with a change of mind for a bit and let this lot sink in more. We have the beast for the whole week, remember it's really a Ford Fiesta."

"Super, because … for today's evening entertainment, I would like you to come and meet my younger brother Edward and his wacky girlfriend Eleanor. They've just bought a little semi on a new estate in Wigan and he's invited us to tea, knowing I was over from Holland. Not far, I'll drive and I don't want to drink for a change so you can have a celebratory sozzle and I'll get us back to Liverpool later, most of the journey is nice motorway."

Victoria laughed. "Okay, why not, let's head for Wigan Pier then or wherever," feeling as surreal as the book.

Within twenty minutes they were standing on the pavement outside of a brand new but box-like semi detached house at the edge of a small new housing estate, built in a space probably created from demolition looking at the other properties nearby. Abby immediately thought of Aunt Eveline and her description of forties period Liverpool and the post war reconstruction efforts.

Abby began to whisper. "Before I forget, they both work for the local Labour Party, did social services degrees, and Eleanor is a hardened Marxist. So whatever you do, don't get into politics, especially with your views on the shrunken state and business enterprise. They do have a two year old, so you can talk babies instead."

"I don't have a big repertoire on babies, what about science?"

"As long as you don't bring up how bad the NHS medical system is and that Holland is much better because we pay for it."

"How come you know all my favourite party lines?"

"This isn't a party; hey, stick to music. Both Edward and Eleanor are big rock fans, the heavier the better."

"Now you're talking Dr Weston, I can provide an uplifting analysis of Johnny Winter and the Chicago Blues movement …"

Whilst Abby did a flash tour, with her brother, of the house just about large enough to swing a cat in, Victoria listened with as much intense enthusiasm as she could muster, biting her lip, to Eleanor's diatribes about wanting to pump even more money into the welfare system as too many unemployed people were not having the quality of life that the state should support. But once Abby returned and they got into the commercial success and fantastic sound of Metallica, the atmosphere and conversation turned very convivial for Victoria, now holding centre stage, as they all supped wine and nibbled a plate of nuts. Although she was severely struggling with the vivid spectrum disconnect between Abby's bright pink, spiky, punk mop and the tightly trimmed orange curls of Eleanor, who spoke with an extremely tricky to understand thick Glaswegian accent.

"Jake is fast asleep now for the night, thank Christ, but we have a bit of a problem sis," Edward suddenly proffered in the middle of a track by track dissection of Cher's last album. "The oven's sort of packed in so the roast pork, and I know you love a big slab of meat, is still sat on the draining board."

Abby looked quite crestfallen.

"But," he continued. "The good news is there's a brilliant chippy round the corner that does real Pukka Pies ... and it's just opened."

Victoria interrupted. "Absolutely no problem. Abby and I will go and this is on me, I insist. Can I get another bottle of wine there too?"

"What, in a chippy?" Edward uttered, perplexed.

"What she means, thick head, is Joe the Wino's shop next door," Eleanor interjected, gripping the couch tightly. "Yes, let's get a couple of bottles. I'll come with you Vikki, these two look like they need to talk families, I'll just get my coat."

Grinning at Abby, Victoria made her way out with Eleanor, down the road, then across into an old, dingy Victorian terraced street. They walked past the front windows of long rows of two-up and two-down tiny abodes, which once must have housed the endlessly large families of cotton workers, crammed together in appalling conditions, probably all the kids sleeping top and tail. It was the same where she was brought up near Burscough, where lots of similar houses and tiny cottages were occupied by boat people. They could see the bright lights of a couple of shops further down.

It was crowded inside initially and getting dark as Victoria and Eleanor shuffled slowly up the queue, which began to thin out as they got to the front. Victoria began to peruse the menu, pondering and then started rummaging again in her handbag, this time for her purse which had disappeared into the depths of detritus. She could feel Eleanor's coat rustling against her leg.

"This damned bag Eleanor, I can never find what I want," she started to say, turning around casually. But immediately she stopped, and an icy deep cold flowed from the top of her head right down to the tips of her toes in a microsecond. It wasn't Eleanor's coat, flapping against her calf, but a dark brown, crinoline dress, all bunched out at the bottom. The woman was there, standing right next to her, wearing a matching coloured jacket but still with that bright purple shawl wrapped around her head. She smiled, a warm and genuine, even happy smile, quite unlike the pained and contorted expression before, her face now more visible behind that shawl. And those eyes and mouth and that look and the shape of her face, which Victoria could see clearly and unmistakably for the first time so close up. It was like looking at her sister, if she had one. Victoria was speechless, nobody around was batting an eyelid, as the woman grinned and pointed to the fish menu and the cod and then to the bread and butter. Victoria began to feel dizzy, the room was spinning oddly and everything was hazy, all she saw through a cloud and murky light on the board was the figure ninepence.

"Was it four pies and chips, love, you said?" the man behind the counter shouted over the clattering and din in the shop, "I didn't quite hear you." Her brain jolted and her vision suddenly sharpened back to life, as she turned to see Eleanor standing next to her, large as life.

"Sorry, Vikki, I just popped outside to get a frigging stone out of my shoe."

"What was it again love?" she heard again, his loud tone indicating the onset of irritability.

"I'm sorry. Err … can you make that three pies with chips and gravy and one cod instead with mushy peas and chips … oh, and I'll have the portion of bread and butter and a tea please?"

"No problem," he replied as his assistant began putting the hot food into bags.

"Vikki, why do you want a tea?"

"Oh ... err ... well, it's sort of all in isn't it. I'm so used to that in Rotterdam."

"Aye ... of course. Tell you what there's a funny paraffin smell in here isn't there. Hey Jimmy," Eleanor shouted over the counter to the fryer in the back. "Isn't it time you changed your fat, especially with these prices you charge?"

"You're a cheeky monkey aren't you," he shouted back, laughing, obviously used to Eleanor's Scottish humour. "Only the best sunflower oil in here, not like that old beef dripping lard they used to do the chips in a hundred years ago. Do you know you could buy the all-in-one meal your friend's ordered for just ninepence then?"

"Yeh and you've added a thousand percent inflation yearly on since then. No wonder you have that Merc outside and not a horse and cart!"

The shop roared laughing. Victoria just blinked, dumb, as Eleanor took the order bag and she handed over a twenty pound note.

"I'll just go quickly and grab two bottles of red from Joe's next door ..."

"You've been very quiet, so when did you meet with the ex-members of Cream then?" Edward slurred towards Victoria as they worked their way through the second bottle of fifteen percent Chilean red wine.

"Mmm ... what'd you say Edward? ... I can't really remember. You mean Gingery Eric?" Victoria slurred back, wishing the world would stay in a permanent haze of drunken light heartedness, because she always got wittier when she was pissed and bad memories were drowned out ...

"Actually Edward, I think Victoria and I should be heading back to Liverpool now," Abby suddenly chipped in, not having had a drop of alcohol, and feeling a definite big beast aversion to the notion, despite being a bad miscreant in the past. "She's very tired, we've had a long business day, haven't we Vikki … and she's not the only one."

They all turned to see Eleanor slumped, eyes closed on the couch and out for the count.

"It's been a great evening Edward, you stay there chuck, we can see ourselves out, I'll ring you soon, okay? Coming Vikki?"

"Guess so," she mumbled, as Abby ignominiously hauled her up from the comfortable armchair out of a distinctly slumped for the night position and they headed to the door, with a departing wave from her brother …

"Can we stop at the next service station please because I could really do with a pee," Victoria croaked, her voice oddly hoarse, as she swigged a bottle of welcome cold water down.

"Yes, in three miles, hope you can last, the beast won't like it if you unload over his posh leather seats. Tell me something. Why did you order fish, chips, peas, and that bread and butter and even a plastic tea? You missed out on a real Pukka Pie. That wasn't like you?"

"Because she told me to and it was absolutely delicious, just as she said, great value for ninepence."

Abby looked across and said nothing for a minute as they began to draw near to the service station entrance. She parked as near to the building as possible.

"It wasn't Eleanor who told you was it."

"No."

"You saw her again didn't you? What in the fish and chip shop? I don't believe it, out with it then I'll let you go."

"It wasn't quite like that. She didn't speak, just pointed at the menu and smiled, really grinned, like she was having fun." She relayed the rest of what she could remember and Eleanor's quips about the bad fat, making Abby roar with laughter.

"Honestly, I can just see the tabloid headline — I fed a ghost in a chippy — it can only happen to you! We have some serious work to do and I need to get back to the Central Library as well and follow up some things. I feel so much more ... what's the word ... empowered, no confident, since we met Eveline. A mountain of stuff to research there."

"A ghost? Do you really think that? I've never believed in ghosts, they make no scientific or logical sense to me in a rational universe."

"Are you so sure the universe is so rational? — open mind yes? Especially after your monster family learning session with Aunt Eveline."

"Yes, I promised and I'm going to stick to it but whatever, the woman looked somewhat happier than in the back of the beast. But what was so eerie, Abby, was the resemblance, like she was my kid sister or something."

Maybe she knows you're taking over Orsbrick Hall?"

"Good heavens, but I suppose ..."

Suddenly Victoria's mobile phone began ringing as she fumbled in her bag again, this accessory now top of her list for a definitive style change and soon. She peered down at the screen, not recognising the number and put it to her ear.

"Hello? Why Julian, how lovely for you to call. No. I'm not in Liverpool right now. What? Am I doing anything tomorrow? ..." excuse me Abby she mouthed, and opened the door diving out quickly towards the service station cafeteria, with a quick smirk at Abby gesticulating wildly for her to come back, so she could hear what was going on ...

She met Abby coming into the toilets as she was going out.

"Well?" Abby said, her arms folded.

"Err ... slight change of plan tomorrow, Julian has just come back from London and wondered if I was doing anything as he was taking a day off writing, having slogged his guts out doing some deep research into Sherlock Holmes and ..."

"I think I get the picture, Dr McKenzie," Abby sharply interrupted and then changed her sham annoyed look to a laugh. "Anticipating that your wanton woman hormones were firing up, the moment you said Julian, I decided to phone Lynton, who was having an evening at home."

"Perusing his etchings?"

"No, but he's actually bringing some into town tomorrow and asked me to lunch as he would value my opinion because he was meeting a very important client next week and would like ..."

"Okay Dr Weston, My turn for synthesising the wild data pouring forth from your trembling body, and also getting the picture. Mmm ... fun isn't it. Can't waste a good opportunity can we?"

They hugged and laughed. "No," Abby replied. "And I think it's good for you to do something different anyway, before we head to that new house of yours. I reckon it's a bit bigger than my brother's pad, don't you?"

As they walked back to the beast, Victoria became pensive, turning to Abby. "Actually, err ... Julian ... well he's a bit older than me."

Abby turned sharply, particularly inquisitive having being fed a continued diet of toyboy one night stands from her friend for the last fifteen months.

"How much older?"

"Err ... he's fifty-three, but he doesn't look it and he's fit for his age."

Abby frowned playfully. "Not an older man at long last Vikki? Really? So have you wondered what it will be like when …?"

"Don't you dare start on that track Dr Weston, as if … she immediately interrupted with a tell tale smirk. Maybe it does run in the family after all she thought to herself …

They jumped in and shot off into the night and back to the Adelphi, singing Maggie Mae …

Chapter Seven

"Yes madam, I can confirm, you have been put on the list of eligible drivers so you will have absolutely no problems. I'll print out a copy of the receipt. Here."

The hotel receptionist, on her own at a busy desk, appeared to be somewhat irritated by the three times repeated question, whilst Victoria was totally unaware of the large queue of business people building up behind her, in a hurry to check out and get on the road as business people do. But she was determined to be sure that her change of plan had no extraneous glitches, still smarting from being fined five hundred euros, sixth months before, whilst driving Abby's uninsured wreck of a Fiat Panda through Delft.

As she wandered towards the breakfast area, she spotted Abby coming in through the main door walking briskly towards her, wondering why her friend had disappeared into thin air when she awoke, obviously in a hurry for some reason.

"I thought you'd gone swimming. Had breakfast without me then?" she called out, hastily shoving car key of the beast into her jeans pocket.

"Sorry chuck, I've got to get on, I really want to do some work in the Central Library again before it gets busy and then, *as you know*," she continued in a dryly emphatic tone, "I'm having lunch with Lynton Grey. And before you start asking with that sharp brain, if he asks, I shall say that you have made progress with Eveline West and are weighing up the options, but we will of course be occupied professionally with his etchings that he wants a business valuation on."

"Yes ... purely business," Victoria replied grinning.

"So, are you joining us for lunch at the Ship and Mitre? Lynton has booked a table in the smart restaurant upstairs, he has an account of course. I'm sure you would be allowed to bring Julian."

"Err ... no ..." Victoria began, having to suddenly think on her feet because she had forgotten to ask Julian where they were meeting ... damn ... and she had other ideas and wanted the beast. "I'm heading for ... the Pier Head ..." she said confidently, the first thing that came into her head. "I shall meet Julian there, he's coming on the bus."

"The bus? Well, I suppose writers are always skint aren't they? Anyway I shall catch up with you later in the day, give you a ring."

"Look forward to it," Victoria replied, then gave Abby a big hug. "Have a great day, don't do anything ..."

"Yes, that you will probably be doing ... no I won't ... see you later, have fun breathing in the sea air, ferries are always romantic on first dates!" Abby shouted back jauntily, skittering out of the entrance in her respectably black fitted trouser suit, a sight rarely to be seen.

"It's not a date ..." Victoria tried to mouth back. She had other ideas, but she did have to admit she was quite looking forward to seeing Julian again. But it was his sharp research mind rather than his body that was the real focus of her plan. She had decided overnight to visit Orsbrick Hall after all. She simply had to go, especially after all that family enunciation yesterday and would drive the beast there herself. Having Julian with his deep knowledge of the nineteenth century would be a big bonus. She would simply ask him if he wanted to go for a ride out to the country, and then casually drop in that … she was becoming the owner of a big mansion and would he like to come with her and see it … She was aware that it might upset Abby not telling her, but … didn't want Abby discouraging her again. Ultimately she had to face down her family dilemmas and secrets herself, and was impatient to break the voodoo of never having crossed the threshold. Plus it was obvious Abby had the hots for Lynton Grey, and keeping him on board would also be beneficial. Okay, she perused, dishing out some fruit into a bowl and picking up a plate of scrambled egg on toast, it was risky but … she simply had to do it now not later. However there remained the problem of meeting Julian …

"Hi Julian," she said quietly into her phone earpiece, waving to the waiter for another Earl Grey tea.

"Ahh … Victoria," he answered immediately. "I'm glad you phoned because we never …"

"No," she interrupted impatiently. "That's why I called. Would you like to meet me at the Pier Head say in an hour?"

"Fine, always up for a little 'Ferry cross the Mersey' reminiscing. See you at the waterfront opposite the Liver Buildings. I'll get the bus."

Victoria laughed loudly down the phone.

"Sorry?"

"Nothing Julian … err … just thought of something amusing about the Searchers, look forward to seeing you then."

"Yeah, me too, bye."

"Yes! …" she uttered loudly as three businessmen glared across, whilst dousing her scrambled egg with salt and pepper.

Victoria certainly hadn't counted on the difficulty parking, or the volume of traffic down there, although she was confident in the BMW, having learned to drive in Andromeda's large old commune Landrover in Holland. Getting increasingly irritated going up and down Water Street five times in a continuous circle, she suddenly spotted a van leaving a parking meter and outmanoeuvred a Mini with a deft swing in; yes size does matter sometimes. Looking up at the clock on the tall and magnificent Georgian office building opposite, she realised she was going to be late and after retrieving a couple of hour's worth of meter change dashed down the road, finally grasping the railings and panting madly over the edge of the murky, fast running water. Where on earth was he?

She peered up at the clock on the top of the Liver Building behind; she was actually half an hour early. Breathing a sigh of relief, she reapplied some lipstick and contemplated what she was wearing. She would have liked to wear her new Kate Spade short red dress and leopard skin jacket that she had managed to stuff into the case, but decided to stick to her usual smart casual, best skinny jeans, ankle boots and black leather jacket, as she had no idea how decrepit and dirty it would be inside the house, grateful too that she had pulled on a thick jumper as it was decidedly breezy and chilly on the waterfront, but then, when she thought back, it always was. The surroundings were totally different from what she remembered as a child. Everywhere looked very touristy, but nice. Gazing up again at the eighteen foot metal cormorant and famous historical symbol of Liverpool city, perched on each tower of the equally famous and splendid Liver Building, her mind flashed back to the former 1970s TV series the Liver Birds, depicting the daily mishaps of scatty female flat mates, like her and Abby, which her mother was constantly watching repeats of as a child ... and even then she always had a whisky by the side of her ...

"It was originally supposed to be an eagle you know, in King John's time ..." a deep voice sounded out, making her jump. "Hey, don't fall in, I wouldn't really want to leap in there."

She turned to see a tall and smiling, grey-haired, Julian striding up briskly beside her, a giant scarf blowing about madly in the breeze. He had old fashioned brown brogues on, that fortunately matched her own smart casual look, albeit distinctive, with tight fitting, faded blue jeans and a barleycorn tweed jacket over a brown checked shirt, obviously he liked that style, or only owned the one. He was cleanly shaved, smelling of something expensively pleasant, as he bent down to kiss her once, twice and then three times on the cheek.

"Mmm ... Dutch style ... how nice Julian," she proffered jauntily, noting from his expression that he had caught a whiff of her favourite Jo Malone perfume. Good start ... but she needed to check his brain.

"Sorry Julian, you were saying about the Liver birds?" Which as hoped, he immediately provided her with an unwavering two minute diatribe of their histories, from the original King John Liverpool Charter in the thirteenth century to the present day. And she learned there were other Liver birds in the city too, a fact she didn't know at all. So historical brain seemed to be in focus ... excellent.

"Coffee?"

"Well ... actually, I wondered if you might like to go for a ride in the country, sort of accompany me on a little childhood reminiscing of West Lancashire."

"Haven't got my timetable with me, although I do know there are regular buses from somewhere around here out to Ormskirk."

"I'm driving no problem and I'll treat you to lunch. Car is just up the road, actually better hurry before the meter runs out."

"Excellent Victoria, why not, let's go."

They set off quickly towards Water Street, and she immediately hooked her arm into his like last time, a habit she decided, she definitely was fast warming to. She rather enjoyed being called Victoria for a change. The only other person who had always used her formal full name, apart from Aunt Eveline the day before, had been her father.

"I see you've got over the old shakes and jitters then?" he said and grinned across at her.

"Definitely," she retorted, as they began to gabble away at all kinds of nonsense, as he described his recent days researching into the Sherlock Holmes depths of London and 221B Baker Street and probing her for wider scientific insights to bring the two together into a new fictional variant.

Five minutes were left on the meter. "Over there," she pointed, as he began to head for the sporty Renault Clio, parked behind. "No, this one Julian," pressing the door unlock. She could read his expression beautifully.

"It was supposed to be a Ford Fiesta, but I ended up with the consolation prize after a booking muddle."

He roared laughing. She liked his laugh as his blue eyes definitely twinkled wickedly behind those thick lenses. They drove off, smoothly merging into the busy traffic, although she was glad she had pre-programmed Burscough into the navigation system, remembering where Orsbrick Hall was relative to the canal there.

"I really like driving the beast, the automatic is so responsive," she muttered happily over to him.

"The beast?"

She relayed about Abby liking to ride big beasts and that set him off again.

"So where is your friend today? I assume she found you at the Ship and Mitre?"

"Oh yes. Abby is very much into art and design and taken herself off to more galleries and museums and stuff, you know that sort of thing, but I get a little bored with it."

"Actually," he continued, "I like a lot of art, especially nineteenth century and do have a number of pre-Raphaelite prints, Rossetti, you know that sort of stuff. Couldn't afford the originals. I expect Abby is very knowledgeable about that period, isn't she?"

"Yes, I'm sure. Oh look, over to the left. Those huge warehouses along the docks, they used to store sugar and cotton and tobacco didn't they? But they've been renovated into what appears to be very upmarket flats," deciding that she needed to get his mind off Abby quick; good job she was off on a jaunt. He was peering into his iPhone as she pondered which girlfriend was probably texting him, when he immediately smirked.

"Yes, tell you about the dock history in a minute. Just found a great local history site on the net, about the boat people who lived on the canal, references to archives and parish records going back centuries. But you said in the pub that you weren't related to boat people were you."

Until she met Aunt Eveline she wasn't, but decided to skirt over that. "No, farming people who worked on the land, although there is probably some intermixed stray lineage that veered onto the canal at some stage."

"Yes, I'm sure. Lots of intermixing went on in the nineteenth century when the canal and the industrial revolution were in their heyday," he replied knowingly with a grin. "Some legitimate but a lot not so legitimate."

That made her think. Were all her forbears married legally? In fact she actually knew nothing of her own parent's marriage for that matter, it was never mentioned. She assumed the deed took place at the local parish church, but her stepmother was American, and where the hell she was now, she neither knew nor cared. But it made her realise, even after Aunt Eveline's remarkable unveiling of family facts, she still knew precious little else about her own background. She needed to find somewhere to stop and tell Julian where they were going, and indeed why. Well certainly not all of it but enough so he wasn't under the illusion they were off for a joyride around Ormskirk.

They continued further, along highways and through the conurbation she and Abby had driven into yesterday but no motorway this time. She would take the old road, more scenic, although again not unexpectedly there was a lot more build up of housing than when she last remembered, but eventually the urban commuter picture cleared and the familiar flatter green plains, farmland and rural idyll she remembered as a child reappeared.

She felt her breathing increase, partly with anticipation that they were not far from Orsbrick Hall but also with an unexpected easing of tension again, same as the day before, near Appleby Lodge. An inner relaxation and comfort was enveloping her, like she had come home with a deep sense of belonging, which as a child she had never experienced, ever, until the day before. She suddenly glanced nervously through the rear mirror ... nothing, thank goodness, what would she do now with Julian there? She hadn't thought of that, how stupid ... then spotted a Little Chef cafe sign on the right and pulled into the parking lot with a deft swerve, jolting Julian from his iPhone perusing again.

"Coffee?"

"Mmm ... good idea, I'm getting thirsty."

"Actually Julian ... I want to tell where we are really going."

He looked at her quizzically. "Now I am intrigued. More mysteries? Great, after you Victoria."

Once inside and seated at an end quiet table, she ordered two large coffees and a lemon drizzle cake to share; it was too early for a whole one. Her mind had gone into its usual scientific synthesis mode again, weighing up the known data and juggling how to present the facts in the most economical, logical and clarifying way. But there were too many bits and pieces she didn't understand, nor could knit together into any sort of sensible or meaningful hypothesis. Talking of women in purple shawls, was definitely off the agenda, Julian would only think she was an escapee from a secure institution. So she had to focus on the key objective, the basics of Orsbrick Hall, minus inheritance money of course, and then allow the information to tickle his historical research fancy, and see if he pours forth as easily as his knowledge of nineteenth century Liverpool and London. The more she pondered the more of a silly long shot and fruitless escapade this would likely be. Oh well ... straight to the point.

He was silent, waiting for her to start, poking his fork into the cake.

"When I said earlier about my family working on the land, well that was only partly true."

"What does partly mean?" Julian replied, pulling off a large piece of cake, gently manoeuvring it to his mouth, before it fell off at the last post. And she giggled.

"Okay, it … well it means that they didn't just work on the land, they actually owned it, they were landowners."

"Like farmers?"

"No, more than that. The McKenzies were nineteenth century local landed gentry who had made money for generations back from exploiting the sciences and engineering of the time, the rural equivalent of the rich shipping merchants of Liverpool."

Now she really had caught his interest.

"You mean they were entrepreneurial industrial revolutionaries, original steampunks even?"

She laughed again, gazing intently into his glasses, quietly, as the waitress came over and topped up their coffee. "Yes, what a beautifully quaint summary Mr Endersby-Finnis. Going by your name it sounds like you should be this side of the table saying this."

He smiled, not taking his eyes off her, and then supped his coffee gently. "No, I'm just a mongrel from all kinds of social detritus, not a squeak of a baronetcy anywhere near my forbears, I'm sure. Although I've been so busy researching everyone else in the 19th century, I never thought to ask before World War Two. Merely a case of a Miss Finnis being a stroppy independent lady and still is, marrying a Mr Endersby, who sadly passed on soon after but begetting me in between. Anyway, never mind me, so go on. It's like waiting for the next episode of Twenty-Four!"

"You don't have to now, I've got the full DVD collection," she replied softly, tapping his hand gently. "I only found out about my family yesterday. I've inherited the estate and that's where we are going … to see Orsbrick Hall for the first time."

He lowered his coffee, took off his glasses and rubbed them gently on the serviette. "Really?"

"Really."

"I don't know what to say, except … I don't know what to say. I think I should pay the bill and we go and find your piece of history. What sort of state is it in?"

She opened her bag, pulling out the cigarette case and opened it up, displaying the large brass key for the front door. "Not sure, but the impression I got from my Aunt Eveline, the only other remaining member of my family, is a bit run down. But I need your historic research mind to help me unravel some … well secrets, issues … tell you later … if that's alright. I think it was auspicious that we bumped into each other."

"Mmm … yes … know what you mean … I've been thinking about that since we met too. But apart from my brilliant mind you may need the old body a little too."

She looked, wide-eyed. Time to move on, he was getting personal at juggernaut speed. Maybe not so great an idea right then.

He caught the zeitgeist and laughed. "No, Victoria. I have another practical skill. Building restoration. Used to do voluntary work for the National Trust for relaxation, usually between girlfriends, and I have a maniacal compulsion for conservation, heritage and do-it-yourself. Comes in useful when you're a landlord of a listed building as well, the tenants would wreck my place, if let; so I practise pre-emptive strikes."

She smiled. "Two benefits now for the price of one, definitely fortuitous."

"We can't be far now to Burscough, just check my GPS map," peering again at his iPhone. "Bad addiction this, must cut it down. A couple of miles left. But where is Orsbrick Hall from there? I can't see anything on the map?" he replied looking puzzled.

"I'll know once we get there. Ready?"

She was beginning to feel hot and bothered as they walked slowly up and over the high iron girder bridge. The old rickety wooden bridge she remembered that once swung across to let the coal barges through had, as Sergeant Hargreaves predicted, been replaced by a modern architectural monstrosity, under which leisure canal boats busily sailed. She squinted in the bright sunlight as they stood on the tow path, looking up and down the once familiar terrain she used to play on as a child and walk along to Annie's. The environment was certainly a lot more pleasant, the canal looking like it had been dredged and widened in places, no old bicycles sticking out of the water, weeds and algae gone and definitely no dead pigs, the tannery having long been closed down and demolished. A flashback made her body shudder for a moment as she peered at the reeds, the same ones, she had once seen ... and been terrified at fifteen ... but nothing. Everywhere was tranquil and calm, brown billed ducks quacking as a male slowly swam in the clear water towards them expecting bread. She could even see a shoal of small fish nearby in the shallower edge.

The high hedgerows were thick, impenetrable and covered in ivy and berries as she tried to remember.

"I told you there was nothing on the map. I thought you said you knew where it was?" Julian ventured, cleaning his glasses on his scarf, flapping in the way to see the map properly.

"I did," she uttered impatiently. "Just need to think."

"Ooops, sorry, Victoria," he replied, struggling in the light breeze with putting the map flatter over a log. "Err ... my mistake I've been looking the wrong side of the canal, got my north and south mixed up, stupid orientation of the way it's printed. I can see an area now, with a building labelled Hall, some woods and outbuildings and ... mmm ... quite a large plot ... and ..."

"Here, give it to a scientist. Men!" she shouted laughing and snatching it from him. Immediately that confirmed her suspicion and her memory of eight years of age came flooding back. The rear of Orsbrick Hall was definitely behind those hedgerows.

"See Julian, there *is* a front entrance. I knew there was, and we even drove past, down that main road, but I didn't see a thing. That's why I got muddled up with myself."

"Possibly all overgrown by trees or boarded over or something. We can try later. Look, up the tow path, I can see a small gap in the hedgerow. He took her hand and they walked up about ten yards and he pulled back some old wooden fencing posts, gone rotten, and helped her through the brambly mess. His hand was warm and soft, she thought, not much calloused do-it-yourself in those mitts, but it felt nice ... gosh damn those prickles.

But it was worth the scratches. They both stopped and looked across the wet and marshy land. There, quite clear in the distance, the profile of Orsbrick Hall stood erect and proud in its own extensive grounds, the light yellowy-brown stone construction rearing majestically with the sun behind. Somehow it didn't compute with her memory of twenty seven years back, and it was much further back than she had realised so the detail wasn't clear. But definitely it was a huge house, and pleasingly symmetrical, three storeys with a large hip roof and rear gable in the middle and either side a smaller two storey extension. Abutting those were some kind of frame structures, possibly former conservatories but all the glass was missing or broken, as spiky reflections shone back. The main windows had been shuttered or boarded up for security. Orsbrick Hall looked both forlorn and imposing at the same time, certainly invoking an era of past splendour, but obviously now very neglected as were the grounds and gardens around it.

She couldn't speak trying to take it all in. One signature and it would be hers, but what on earth could she do with it?

"Gosh, Victoria," Julian croaked his voice crackly and emotive. "What a splendid looking place. It really is quite huge. I would estimate at a first glance from the number of windows facing us, there are at least fifteen bedrooms and six reception rooms. And I would say from the map boundaries there are at least six acres of land too, with woodland, there over to the right, and some also to the left; hard to tell here as the lay of the land is quite undulating and overgrown with an amazing flora."

"It's beautiful, come on, I want to get in ..." grabbing his hand, a habit she was acquiring to very readily.

But he stopped her immediately. "Hang on a second. Whilst there is some semblance of a path up there just look at where it's running through. The ground is very waterlogged, I can see a stream running slowly through those thick reeds or whatever they are, running in an oxbow, then veering away from the canal. This area has been terribly overgrown for many years, and whilst we're not dressed for clubbing, we're certainly not dressed for this terrain," looking at her smart Diesel boots.

She immediately turned to him and regretting it instantly said softly, "Would you like to go clubbing with me? I bet there was some dancing and partying here once upon a time?"

He laughed loudly, and took his glasses off again, rubbing his eyes. "Yes, that would be fun ... but shall we try the front door first?"

She had decided, moving forward ... she was going to kiss him there and then, she felt so excited ... but in an instant her nostrils filled up with that awful smell of bad kerosene. She looked around fearfully, her heart pounding but there was nothing.

"What's up? Something startle you?"

"Sorry Julian, it was a rustling, probably a rabbit or something. I agree, let's get back to the car and have another drive round the lane towards the front ... now we have scientifically identified the compass points!"

"Cheeky!"

He steadied her again through the hedge and they slowly walked back, with actual skylarks twittering in the background, hand in hand to the beast ... as she thought quietly, she really was going to have to tell Julian somehow about what she had been experiencing, but how would he react? Even the beast looked like he was fretting, waiting quietly at the canal edge.

Driving slowly down the main road from the tiny Orsbrick village itself, Julian craned his neck as she kept a sharp eye on the traffic. "There Victoria, over to the left, pull over, all hidden with twining ivy and those oak branches, I can just about see a set of large rusty gates in between some stone pillars."

She pulled in alongside the dropped kerbing. No wonder they missed it with all the overgrowth and leaves. The main gates hadn't been opened for some time, from the state of the large padlock and chain, but a small walk-in wooden gate, locked at the side and leading onto the gravel drive thick with moss and weeds, gave evidence of more recent comings and goings.

Julian fiddled with the padlock and chain, and finally dived into the beast's boot to find a small wheel lever, which with one sharp push pulled up the lock shackle. "I thought that might happen, rotted inside. This lock has been on here for at least twenty years looking at all the rust. Let's see if we can drive beastie inside"

Struggling together they unbolted the heavy gates, cleared the rubbish behind and with a few hard shoves pushed them back, creaking loudly on the old hinges. Heaven knows, she mused, when that was last done. Slowly driving over the moss-ridden gravel, they swept up what was once a magnificent tree-lined drive into a circular driving area and parked in front.

She jumped out and stood in front of a very large square stone porch entrance, a flat seating area with balustrades on the high top and fronted by a magnificent twelve foot archway, for which the space inside would have easily sheltered a former travelling coach and four horses. She felt overwhelmed and awestruck at the immensity of the place. Moss covered plywood boardings were screwed in over all the windows. She fumbled for her antique cigarette case and large brass key, noting the heavy looking big oak entrance doors.

"It's going to be dark inside Victoria, I noticed a halogen torch in the boot, I'll just go and get it," Julian shouted as she threw him the car keys.

Tentatively, she slid the door key, in turn, into each of the two separate mortise locks and turned both with remarkable ease and a comforting clunk. Turning the heavy round handle, the brass needing some polish, and one door opened smoothly, inside some kind of hallway. She was hit by an immediate overall damp, musty odour. As expected it was pitch black inside, the heavy curtains also having been drawn. Julian switched on the torch, swivelling it about as their senses were immediately hit by the sight of a magnificent sweeping marble staircase, where the hall corridor opened out, leading up each side from ground to first floor. They walked in slowly, staying close together, the torch shining a wide beam over the decorated walls and high ceilings, looking at least fifteen feet or more tall.

Everywhere appeared remarkably well kept, albeit dusty, the paintwork, a mixture of creams, light greens and white. They pushed open a high, double set of interior mahogany swinging wooden doors, the original stained glass still evident, and entered a massive square living room with sheeted over chairs and a sofa, and further rooms off it, the ceiling even higher, but sporting a beautifully latticed artex patterning and original Georgian coving. Decorative pillars set off the white and light olive green theme of the walls. Unusual wall lights adorned each side of the cast iron fireplace, still with half burned logs inside, and completed with an original tiled shiny brown patterned mantelpiece, which Julian insisted was late Victorian. Old heavy radiators lined the walls, piping through to adjacent rooms, so some kind of working heating system and a boiler were in evidence. There was a considerable amount of old but well polished furniture around including glass bookcases, filled with all kinds of ancient looking tomes, again only slightly dusty, indicating somebody had been coming in occasionally to keep some modicum of cleaning going, probably at least until the window boardings were put up.

They peered into a number of adjoining rooms to see a makeshift basic kitchen with an aga cooker, and cupboards and tops, sitting on a red quarry tiled floor. Finally they found a compact bedroom with a relatively modern ensuite bathroom constructed off it, plus a cosy study through a small door at the end, replete with antique desk, writing paper and the usual knickknacks including an odd cage hanging from a floor stand with a stuffed green parrot inside and a wooden globe atlas.

She looked again inside the sparsely fitted bedroom, gazing wistfully at the large iron-framed bed, still with white coverings over the top but no mattress. It was very clear now how her Uncle William had been living, probably for many years, in his reclusive mode. This whole area was a kind of self contained bedsit, relatively easy to keep warm, once that fire was lit, enabling him to probably ignore the rest of the place, so heaven knows what state that must be in. She reckoned that the massive main sitting room could have once been a ballroom for dancing and partying as small orchestras and jazz bands began playing in her head, forcing her to smile nostalgically.

"That is a genuine four poster steampunk bed in there," Julian joked. "I write about them, but it doesn't look like it's been tried out for some time does it."

She looked at the bed then back at him, and pondered for a second, when suddenly a loud crash and flapping from somewhere upstairs made them both jump.

"Jesus, what the fuck was that, Julian," she shouted, feeling an immediate cold fear filling her veins up as her heart started pounding again. "Sorry for swearing."

He shone the light back out towards the hall. "Perhaps one of the window boards has come loose or something and a bird has got in. Let's take a quick peep."

"Do you think we should?"

"Think logically and scientifically Victoria and what makes the most rational sense. Don't believe in ghosties do you?" proceeding to make loud whooing noises.

She felt hot and cold all over. "Don't Julian, please stop it, it might make the … sorry … I mean it feels sort of disrespectful somehow."

He sensed she was anything but appreciative of his humour and stopped. "I'm sorry, honestly I didn't mean to upset you, a silly schoolboy prank," and kissed her on the cheek. The banging and flapping started again only louder then died down.

She smiled. "Apology accepted this time. After you Endersby-Finnis," putting on a lady of the house voice.

He laughed. "You know Dr McKenzie, that rather suits you." as more clattering began.

They worked their way carefully up one wide marble stairway coming round to another long spacious corridor, which continued either side of the house for what seemed like miles. In front of them a smaller staircase led off to the third floor, but with a heavy door in front of it firmly locked.

"Servants quarters would have been up there," Julian proffered, both peering at the dark oak door with strange inscriptions over it."

"They look like painted on Egyptian hieroglyphics," Victoria added, sliding her fingers over the polished surface. "How odd."

"Perhaps the McKenzie clan have been global travellers over the years. That was quite common in the 19th century with the rich, and at some point in the evolution and history of this house, some people in your family were indeed very rich."

Victoria thought immediately about the amount of money set aside in the trust that Aunt Eveline had casually mentioned, still not believing that could be possible. She would keep that strictly to herself. But looking at the grandeur and wealth around them, perhaps it was. But how could she live here for a year to claim it? The place was nigh on impossible for modern day habitation, without lots of money behind it … On the other hand the services of an experienced restorer and self confessed do it yourself fanatic could make the hardship possibly a little more bearable, she sniggered quietly.

"You've got cheerier again all of a sudden. This place is going to need some work on it," he said wistfully.

"Thinking of volunteering, Endersby-Finnis?"

"Must say there is a likely mountain of interesting history here as rich writer background material, but it would have to be worth my while," he whispered, grinning mischievously. "Let's try these doors."

Quickly they discovered they were all locked, except the first two. Inside the first was a massive bedroom with double floor to ceiling windows, chock-a-block with antique furniture, exotic carpets, rugs, more books and all kinds of other paraphernalia, dumped and left for storage from around the house. The better stuff had sheets carefully drawn over them. As they opened the second door, facing the rear, a flood of light, hit their eyes, making them both squint, and the torch instantly caught the staring inquisitive green eyes of a pair of wood pigeons, sat, pink-footed, atop an old teak wardrobe. They immediately flapped and flew crazily around the room then out of a broken window, where the boarding had fallen inside, leaving evidence of attempted nesting. Her heart finally stopped pounding and she looked around. Another room full of furniture, less than the other one, but also she spied a load of old brightly coloured wooden trunks, piled high on each other or scattered around, together with ornaments, table lamps, and small matching coffee tables. She lifted the lid on the first few, stuffed with curtains, clothing, some old dresses and men's clothes. Near the small Adam fireplace, inside one initially locked, but the key fortunately still in it, was filled with old papers. She took the first paper out carefully. It was some scientific treatise, written by who she couldn't make out as the bottom was faded, but recognised some of the chemical formulae immediately, despite the quaint old fashioned ink handwriting. They were definitely coal tar derivatives, families of dyes, which could be seen clearly from the pattern of carbon, hydrogen and nitrogen atoms relating to aniline and benzene.

Drawings of distillation apparatus and practical diagrams were carefully sheathed in between.

"Oh my goodness, research papers, details of experiments, results, all dated between 1860 and 1866. There must have been really interesting science work going on then. I can't wait to go through all these, I must handle them carefully." she exclaimed, her eyes wild with pure joy, as she replaced them gently.

Julian sauntered over, having unsheeted a beautiful antique walnut desk, which looked to him like eighteenth century woodwork and marquetry, and shone the torch into a deep drawer to see a great mass of paper documents, old ledgers and diaries of all shapes and sizes.

"This is astounding in here Victoria and probably worth a small fortune. Who lived here last? Do you know?"

The house belonged to my Uncle William, elder brother of my Aunt Eveline from whom I learned of all this family inheritance and background bombshell for the first time yesterday. He died six months ago, a total recluse, aged 103. William and my father were apparently twins, but they were all estranged for over eighty years, until Eveline broke the spell and visited William three years ago before he died."

"And your father? He was a lot older than you wasn't he?"

"It's all a long story," she sighed. "I need to explain but later and there is a huge amount I don't know."

"Mmm ..." he replied thoughtfully, before going over to the fireplace and picking up a heavy poker. She looked up, immediately feeling a huge wave of trepidation.

"No, not to batter you to death, you'll be pleased to know," he jested again as she glared. "Temporary hammer, I'll just go and tack that board back in from the inside, keep out the winged squatters."

She continued looking through the papers, all on the topic of coal tar dyes, when she caught him staring hard out of the open window.

"My word, there are some brazen so and sohs out there. There's a guy on a black horse and a woman on a white horse, slowly trotting in your drive towards the woods. There must be a bridle path to the road or something. Odd though, they could be just out of my novels the way they're dressed, and that purple shawl wrapped around her head at this time of year, weird."

She jerked her head up out of the trunk sharply, her eyes wide and her stomach on fire.

"Oh Julian, you can see it, you can see it too, oh thank God for that … it isn't just me then … oh Julian, Julian …" and ran to him throwing her arms wildly and tightly around his body, her head buried in his chest, chuntering ten to the dozen, tears flowing down her cheeks.

"Jesus Christ Victoria, hey what's all this about? Hey, hey come on slow down, stop, stop, stop," and gently lifted her arms off, looking her straight in the eye.

She dabbed her eyes with a piece of red velvet curtain, covering it with black mascara and stood aside, suddenly embarrassed at her own uncharacteristically emotional reaction. She glanced out of the window, but there was absolutely nothing … and it dawned on her. The mystery woman in the purple shawl was no longer alone. She had a companion. Who, what and why? And in particular why was Julian so special?

"I'm sorry Julian, there's something else I need to explain, well something … I don't want you to think I'm raving mad, but all in Orsbrick Hall is not quite as it seems."

"I can see that ..." he replied and grinned. "And I love it, a real 19th century mystery ... or could it even be a supernatural mystery? This is manna from heaven for a steampunk writer."

"Actually," she replied sombrely, "I believe now something has happened here, something perhaps not very pleasant and I need to find out."

"Well, Dr McKenzie-Watson, Mr Endersby-Finnis-Holmes is here at your disposal, that is if you want him."

She laughed, feeling the tension drained away. "You're really daft aren't you? Yes I do ..."

It was his turn. He wanted to kiss her badly, looking at her coquettishly turned up mouth and those gorgeous staring dark eyes. He leaned forward ... when a loud crash stopped them both in a micro-second as a tall wardrobe at the far end suddenly fell over lopsidedly against the wall.

They both stared at it, dazed, then he peered at the base, all torn away. "Mmm... a bit of woodworm has got to that, have to watch there isn't any more."

"I could do with some air Julian," she sighed. "I think we've seen enough for today and that torch is fading ..."

As she turned the key in the second lock and they walked towards the beast, that odd feeling of total peace and tranquillity, always after some ... sighting ... suffused her entire body. Julian was fiddling about with the bag which he had been wearing over his shoulder.

She looked over the breathtaking view, seeing Parbold Hill clearly and unencumbered rising up in the distance, with the dark Pennine mountains behind, rolling green and golden fields in front interspersed with clumps of dotted trees, occasional farmhouses and the odd barn. It was quiet, tranquil

… and inviting, so inviting it was desperately eating her insides out …

"Hey … what are you rooting about for in that man-bag of yours?"

"Catch." He pulled out two cans of coke and threw her one which she fielded with aplomb, having had years of practice with Abby. "And, that's not all. Which do you prefer? A couple of bacon butties or a cheese sandwich and a portion of salad? Oh and an apple," placing them on the bonnet. "I thought you might get peckish sometime. Wasn't sure what the plans were as I thought we were going to be floating off into the Irish Sea on a ferry."

She was mightily impressed with his caring, culinary domesticity, especially as no man in the last ten years had ever done likewise, in fact not since Antoine in the commune. Picking up the carefully wrapped cheese sandwich in aluminium foil and a compact tupperware box of fresh salad she replied gaily. "I'll leave you to the cholesterol buster, thanks."

"Fine," he said, staring ahead towards the wooded area where the mythical horseman and woman were said to have been heading. "Tell you what, it's a lovely afternoon, shall we just do a quick walk over there and see what there is and eat our sandwiches?"

She was as intrigued as him. "Yeah, why not, no hurry. There's some sort of meadow there as well. I think too it's time to fill you in on what I haven't filled you in on."

They began to wander over when he grabbed her arm and pointed to the dusty ground. "Look there's hoof prints, I was right, must have been somebody locally in fancy dress."

154

Clearly identifiable, there were as she noted the distinctive markings of the shoes and the large shape of the hooves, petering out into the grass. "But there's no horse muck …?"

"True … mmm … perhaps they were a bit constipated." he replied, in a deep voice, studying the ground with intense determination.

She giggled stupidly. He was serious, and quaintly insane without a doubt, and becoming quite adorable.

They soon reached the edge of the wood and took in another magnificent view, as she realised how well sited the house had been some three or four hundred years ago, sitting on a small hill with a stunning three hundred and sixty degree perspective. She hadn't realised, hidden initially by the gable from the front, but there was a circular domed tower with tiny windows, high up on the roof between the two chimneys, offering a likely amazing vista of the countryside for miles. She was dying to climb up to it then thought of all the practicalities needing doing, not least getting some power on in the place.

"Julian, how are we going to get the electrics working? Although I even noticed some old gas lights still on the wall too."

"Good question. I noticed as we went out, there's a small porter type reception area near the inside of the front door. Probably the first port of manned call for receiving guests and then tending to the horses. I saw a meter on the wall, so it should be straightforward to get connected by the Electricity Board, although what those radiators run on for heating is anyone's guess. Oil I would think."

"Maybe even coal?"

"Possible? Or solid fuel? Depends how old the boiler is. Look there's a pond over there. Shall we sit down and eat the food by it?"

Victoria suddenly remembered. Aunt Eveline had casually mentioned a large pond, a focal point for past family life, where she painted the water lilies with Uncle William fishing. As she reached the edge, next to a cornfield, it was exactly as her aunt had described and truly remarkable. Water lilies of all kinds of gorgeous colours were indeed unfolded between large green leaves and she saw the shape of a couple of large fish swimming through the stalks, perch or maybe even a pike. Quiet, tranquil and so very romantic ...

As she was sat on the grass, munching through her apple, their jackets on the ground in the warm afternoon sun and daydreaming, he took her by surprise with his arm planting firmly around her waist. She turned, closed her eyes and their lips finally met in a passionate embrace, his kisses warm and sensuous. She had been dying to do that over the whole of the last twenty four hours if she was being truly honest ...

A very tiny rustle behind him, caught her attention and she opened one eye, looking over his shoulder whilst he continued gently, unabated and in another world ... and she was there. Alone a couple of feet away, wearing exactly the same outfit and purple shawl and grinning as she did in the fish and chip shop. The woman waved her arm playfully as if to say, don't stop on my account.

She closed her eyes again and continued to enjoy his kissing, but now sensing phase one of their long awaited embrace was coming to an end. ... phase two she would need to think about ... and certainly not now.

He withdrew and gazed into her eyes, her emotions mixed between lust and trepidation when the sound, loud and clear, resounded across the pond from somewhere in the woods on the other side.

"What's that Julian ... can you hear it?"

"Yes, it's a horse galloping away somewhere."

They listened as the clip clopping gradually faded into the distance and the tranquillity and total quiet except for some birds twittering returned.

She held his hands ... and said. "She was here, behind you, grinning happily, like she did in the chippie."

"Who?"

"The woman in the purple shawl, you saw earlier..."

"And her horse by the sound of it? Sorry, did you say chippie?"

"Time for the full story. Drink your coke. Then I want to take you to a garden centre not far away which has a lovely cafeteria. And I'm going to treat you to a meal out tonight because you have been absolutely wonderful today."

"Approved, Dr McKenzie-Watson. Serious sleuthing starts tomorrow. My word that methane suddenly smells a lot," he murmured, looking at the pond.

"Err ... methane is colourless and odourless, it's rotten vegetation you're muddled with, common misconception. But what you're smelling is neither. It's coal tar distilled aniline."

"Aniline? Mmm ..." and they got up quietly and walked hand in hand back to the beast, as Julian prattled on aimlessly about the things they could find in the garden centre to help restore the place ...

Chapter Eight

Inside the garden centre was the moment, Victoria thought, he became serious. Serious about the woman in the purple shawl because he believed everything without question when she had told him all she knew and had happened. That she wasn't going completely stark raving crazy was falling away, a huge relief, like water off the scales of the big oily fish she peered at wondrously every Saturday in Rotterdam market. And maybe he was getting a little serious about her too, which upbraided her insides with a thick bead of frisson she wanted to cling on to, perhaps for the first time in her life. And he did seriously amuse her when he said with the straightest of faces that the good news was she finally approved.

"Sorry Julian?" she replied loudly having a distinctly odd memory crackle of the wife at home she hadn't quite heard him tell her about. "Who has approved what?"

"Her of course, approved of ... well ... "

"You're blushing, out with it."

" ... Me kissing you ... you said she grinned!"

Victoria laughed so hard, she grabbed the bottle of water and downed a large swig, at last seeing the funny side of her new ethereal friend, not only giving the thumbs up to her diet of fish, chips and peas, but also the new man of the moment. Gosh, Abby has a ghostly competitor, but pity she can't speak as there was a lot to catch up on - like a hundred years of gossip?

He took off his glasses again and rubbed them gently on his scarf, which she also noticed was a pale purple-red, and grinned, obviously embarrassed despite his world weary fifty three years of vast experience. "I don't usually make women laugh so much?"

"My peculiar sense of humour Julian," she grinned back, seeing that twinkle again in his eyes now the specs were off. But actually, as her scientific brain began to kick in, one important logical conclusion overrode the flippancy, and she was not usually flippant either, far too serious a woman about town. If both of them were having ... well ... experiences ... then both of them must hold the key to identifying the reason in the first place and they both did need to work together and pool brain resources. His agile historic research mind was more than fortuitous, for whatever reason it was an integral part of the whole thing. Now she had to get him off the banter and onto that research ... but where to start? Although from the expression in his eyes and the way he gripped her hand again on the table, he didn't seem an unwilling participant.

"Julian, tell me how can we find out more facts, figures and data so we can get to the bottom of the hypothesis of what has triggered these appearances?"

He pondered, with his serious academic frown and quaint air of disassociation with reality, well he was a writer so that had to be forgiven today. "I suggest a three pronged pitchfork plan of action. Inside the house, there may be evidence in those papers you found, and possibly other things around. We haven't even looked yet. Secondly, local information, parish records, births, marriages and deaths, census data, old newspaper cuttings, that sort of thing. Lastly tapping the living. This whole enterprise was kick-started with meeting your Aunt Eveline. There may be other elderly people in the area who know things, have memories which with a jog could bring out a gem of information."

"Well I have to say my initial scepticism of pitchfork business planning, not on my known list of management speak has evaporated as quickly as the aniline. I like it, but ..." she sighed, "there is so much work to be done on the place if I want to live in it for the next year?"

"Not as much as you might have thought, from a more experienced eye. The place is fundamentally looking very sound, what I couldn't smell anywhere was the death rattle of wet and dry rot and just a couple of patches of damp. Despite the reclusiveness of your Uncle William, he had made some effort into ensuring Orsbrick Hall itself was well maintained, the internal decoration is pretty good. Not sure about that green office carpeting downstairs, where he lived, although there seemed to be a lot of nicely polished boards elsewhere. No, once we get the window protectors off Orsbrick it will start to look magical believe me. Do you really want to live there for the next twelve months?"

She hadn't meant to say that, kicking herself, but she liked the "we" and he seemed remarkably incentivised. "You know just how to cheer a girl up don't you?"

After another quiet and serious lull he continued in a deeper voice. "Actually Victoria ... there is something I want from you."

She looked up from her carrot cake, wide-eyed ... this guy certainly moves along fast ... her brain running extracurricular ideas in rapid succession, none of which she could even tell Abby let alone him. "Mmm ... well?"

"If I help you, and I think I must ... can I sort of use the rights from the experience to write up as my next steampunk novel? ... I'll dress it up a bit, you know ... maintaining anonymity and all that … but I can sense a rare opportunity to turn real history into great fiction …"

"Why not, absolutely Julian, love it … err … is that all?"

"Of course," he replied pulling at his scarf suddenly jammed in the table leg and around his neck. "What else would I want?"

She smiled. Excellent, his brawn and brains and no distractions … at least not yet. "Shall we head off to the pub and celebrate? It's nearly six o clock! But where to go around here …?" she ventured still feeling peckish.

"I know a place in Ormskirk actually, if you fancy? Not been for years but they used to do a mean gammon and fried egg. And on the canal too. The Red Lion."

"Let's go then," she replied jauntily, rather liking the canal setting concept …

Getting out in the car park they were amazed how full it was, having taken the last space, just, with the beast. Boat people and their horses certainly took far less room up in those days. Sauntering into the two hundred year old building, they could see a melee of happy-hour drinkers lining the bar, noticing that a folk group was on later as well. But she liked pubs like that too, reminding her of home …Rotterdam? … Or was that actually home? Lots of pitchforking to think about. He hung her jacket up on an elephant multi-tusk coat stand and they sat down. "My turn for drinks and I'll get a menu," she said and glanced over at the bar. "Oh my God … I don't believe it … it just can't be Julian, not here."

"Who, what … it isn't … you know … her again is it? She has a habit of popping up in eateries," he replied, looking there nervously.

"No, no ... the guy serving behind the bar ... he is the absolute spitting image of my solicitor Lynton Grey ... Oh gosh, I forgot to phone Abby like I said."

She grabbed her phone and dialled but it rang and rang and then went on the voicemail.

Hi, it's Abby. Sorry to disappoint you but I'm very preoccupied right now. Leave a message and I'll love to get back.

"I bet. Where are you chuck?" she answered. "I'll try later." She turned to Julian. "Now I'm going to ask that guy if he's got a twin brother."

"I think I'd better just come with you Victoria."

They threaded their way towards the busy bar, shoving through a noisy crowd of bearded hairy bikers with matching molls and finally reached the counter.

The barman looked up casually from washing a couple of beer glasses and eyed her up and down. "What can I get you?"

"Two of those Belgian lagers please," she replied, pointing to the real ale pumps. "And can I ask, do you by any chance ... have a twin brother?" seeing Julian looking distinctly uncomfortable next to her.

Unfortunately the rest of the bar, barman and half the pub became distracted as they all turned to the sight of a scantily clad female dressed in a tight apron, waltzing in with a tray of food, followed immediately by a loud and familiar voice. "Kebabs anyone?"

She then turned, completely incredulous, to see Abby, speeding towards them, her tray masterfully balanced in the air. She looked back to the barman who was laughing uproariously at her face and then said. "I'm sorry Victoria, I can't keep this up any longer, no twin brother, the real thing, welcome to my inn."

"And to the guest chef for tonight, especially as the regular cook is off sick and the place is heaving as you can see," Abby added. "And, I assume Vikki, this is Julian," she cooed flirtatiously, shoving her tray of hot food in front of his nose, his glasses instantly steaming up. "Hi Julian, you look like a man who likes to wrap his mouth around a tender chunk of meat. Have one ... on the house."

"Err hi ... yes please ... mmm ... delicious," he replied enthusiastically, Victoria completely dumbfounded and open mouthed, watching as he began to guzzle down the kebab whilst the other staff began serving everyone else again. Lynton very slowly and meticulously poured out their lagers, and a waitress came and started handing out the kebabs to everyone.

"Julian, this is Lynton Grey my solicitor or at least I thought he was and Abby, my friend, has already introduced herself," giving her a short glare, as Abby smirked back.

Mouth emptied, Julian wiped his greasy hands on one of Abby's serviettes she handed him then shook hands with them. "Great to meet you both. I used to come into the Red Lion many years ago, which is why we popped in tonight. I don't think you were the owner then?"

"No, only just bought the place actually, bit of an investment to add to the business portfolio. Victoria, it's my birthday today, fortieth, and Abby and I have been ... err ...celebrating ... and doing my etchings, so tonight we thought we'd finish off with a bit of a bash. Drinks are on the house for the next hour and free kebabs. And I am still your solicitor, I hope," he continued laughing. "Abby said you would be coming, great to see you both. I assume you have had a fruitful day around Orsbrick Hall, Victoria?"

"Very fruitful," she replied, with a noncommittal expression.

"Excellent. All final legalities are now prepared at my office, I've spoken to Eveline so anytime you want to go ahead, up to you, just let me know."

"Tomorrow?"

"Super."

Business concluded, he then turned to Julian. "Now, Julian I understand from Abby that you have in-depth expertise on Victoriana and nineteenth century art, and are a writer too which is absolutely fascinating. In the quarters behind the bar here there are some interesting features and collections I would value an opinion on. Want to come through?" He lifted the bar hatch.

"Love to ..." Julian replied enthusiastically, before looking at Victoria's face and adding. "Err, is it okay with you Victoria?"

"Of course, enjoy," she smiled, sensing a sooner than anticipated opportunity to have a little one-on-one chat with her best friend. Julian and Lynton set off to the back, chatting ten to the dozen.

"Those two are getting on like a house on fire already, sort of real men thing isn't it?" Abby chirped, knowing from past record that a volcanic grilling was about to explode.

But in fact Victoria, having now scraped herself off the ceiling and appreciating the fun, was feeling very relaxed, especially after the amazing day she had experienced and was simply pleased to see Abby, throwing her arms around her with a quick and unexpected hug. "Just good to see you again in the flesh," she chuntered. "That outfit's a bit sexy for a chef isn't it?"

"That's all Lynton had behind there, I need to work on him," she replied laughing and relieved.

"Listen, I've got just one question, how did you know I was coming here? Victoria asked genuinely quizzical.

"I won't put you off by saying I'll tell you later or anything else. Quite simply, I just knew exactly inside, later this afternoon, and I don't know why but I'm just heightened, you know ... much more sensitive ... and I've tracked down stuff I need to understand too this morning at the Central Library. Lynton has been a hoot all day. He is very amusing, and seems to be well, a bit besotted, God knows why? He's also a widower, has a nineteen year old daughter at University, amazingly. It feels good but I'm taking it slow and careful. He got damaged when his wife died and is throwing his money about to compensate, you know ... Anyway Julian is quite a dreamy dish. How did you get on at Orsbrick? I knew from your face you were going last night and you didn't need me, no problem."

"Yes, understand. Thanks ... much appreciated. Really interesting actually. The place is massive, needs much work doing but ... I like it ... and I am definitely going to sign up tomorrow to own it and go from there."

Abby hugged her. "That's super, chuck. And Julian, what did he think?"

"The same, he used to be a conservator for the National Trust for a time, like a hobby now with his writing, he was very taken with it and ...

"You saw her again didn't you and so did he."

Victoria looked up startled. "Yes, but how did you know?"

"It could be the only explanation for why I am suddenly heightened in psychic awareness, and I dealt another row of tarot cards today which confirmed it, for me anyway. Julian is linked Victoria, how, why, or when I don't know but he is part of the mystery as are you. I don't think bumping into him was so random, more ... how can I say it ... suggestively engineered."

"By whom?"

"That now is what I suggest the four of us need to find out. Look at the range of skills, knowledge and experience between us, an amazingly powerful intermix isn't it to solve ... well, the mystery which I believe for all of us now needs, in our own ways, to be done."

"You're sounding scary Abby."

"Sorry not meant to ... but we all have a stake somehow so let's all work together. I haven't said any more obviously to Lynton, but once you've signed that contract, then I can test him out. He has more paintings and other textile art objects from Eveline, all done in the period 1860 to 1900. I saw some of them, popped into his gallery in Southport before we got here."

"Now you mention it, we never saw any pictures on the wall actually, which thinking about it was a bit odd."

"That's because Lynton has them all ... and the few I saw tell even more of a story than the Rossetti on Eveline's wall. You and Julian will need to see them."

"Rossetti?"

"I will need to tell you that later and more about Eveline. Look they're coming back and I need to return to supervising the cooking in the kitchen. Whatever you both want to eat is on the house."

"Thanks, I really appreciate everything you've just said and I agree, time for the four musketeers to get to it! ... Excuse the pun but much food for thought isn't there?"

"Definitely, now let's forget the serious stuff for the rest of tonight, time for fun ...hey you guys," she shouted to the two men, walking back animated still in conversation. "Got to get back to the kebabs. Lynton, the folk singers have just come in. Can you get the amplifier, speakers and mics set up over there for them and ask James to move those tables out the way at the front."

"Sure thing Abby," he burbled back happily, turning to Victoria. "She's hugely organised, got all this lot booked and arranged this morning for me, and I need some of that in my life … both of you order what you want from the bar, it's already on my tab. Looks like this place is going to get pretty lively in a minute, and Abby says she'll do some karaoke later."

Victoria smiled, knowing that when he hears her Lady Gaga voice and dance routine, especially in a tight apron, any semblance of resistance left will crumble away.

"I'll just go and order your gammon, egg and chips, and I'll have fish, chips and peas, bread and butter, and some more Belgian lagers. Nice end to a hard day's work Julian?"

"Definitely," he beamed, squinting at the floor lights and rubbing his glasses again. A good sign … but Julian will have to drink her lager now because she would have to drive him home later.

Chapter Nine

The soft buzzing of her phone alarm combined with a sharp ingestion of bright sunlight through the tiny Georgian windows was enough to make her stir from the deepest slumber she imagined possible, totally disorientated and her aching brain wallowing in a deep and thumping fog. Despite the greatest reluctance, she pondered, struggling to remember anything of the night just gone, she would have to open her eyes, force herself out of this bed, have a pee and drink a gallon of water or even better a big pot of Earl Grey tea ... with no milk.

She moved her arm and suddenly felt it, bare skin, warm and soft next to her, and the owner of the hairy back emitting a very gentle snore. Oh my God, flashed immediately around her head ten times and then where am I and where are all my clothes, before it all came flooding back.

Sadly Julian didn't drink all her lagers, in fact she ended up drinking all of his, and once Abby got on the floor and started her personalised Poker Face routine, the whole pub went wild until all she could remember was being buried in the arms of Julian, in another world, pecking away at his delectable shaved cheeks, whilst the karaoke rounded up with the whole pub loudly joining in with the folk singers, and Julian slurring that he was hugely impressed with the woman in the purple shawl, doing Maggie Mae on stage with the mike ... She smiled ...

then she opened her eyes wide and stirred at the ceiling … hello brain, wake up, did he really say that? … Oh no …

The equally large naked body beside her suddenly stirred with a groan and wrapped his arm around her, with a slow sounding mutter … She looked at Julian, lying there peacefully and out of the world. Thank goodness his glasses were sitting undamaged on the bedside table, and she smiled happily, as the very final part of the night came flooding back into delightful perspective, and what a fantastic ending that was. Hey ho, a bit quicker than anticipated. But never mind the earth moving, more like a complete stellar cluster doing the dance of a supernova

She gently heaved herself out of the large double bed, impressed with the decor of Lynton's range of period guest rooms, low ceilings, genuine windows, white painted walls and brown woodwormed beams. She worked her way into the ensuite, wrapping a dressing gown off the door around herself and reflected on all the things Abby had said, now wanting as quickly as possible to get back to Orsbrick and start some research. She began to systematically run through all the things she logically needed to do, writing a mental and clear list. She was back in management mode and starting today with driving into Liverpool and Lynton's office, when she heard a kettle whistling. Back in the room, Julian, in a matching but pink dressing gown, as she had grabbed the wrong one, made her giggle, but she decided, watching him carefully pour out two cups of Earl Grey tea in Lynton's guest china cups and saucers, that he was shaping up to be her sort of man.

"Hi …" he grunted looking up, his voice hoarse … you look ravishing. I feel like shit."

"Mmm … you're almost acceptable, and before you say it, last night, and I mean all of last night, was wonderful. And

Abby and I have a plan. But next time lay off mimicking Robert Plant on stage, it doesn't really suit you."

"Yes, I agree … err what plan?"

"Over breakfast, I'll be two minutes in the shower, then you can have your turn," gazing at the unexpected sight of his and her clothes respectively piled up and neatly folded, in order of quick divestment, on each of the matching upholstered chairs with the Queen Ann legs.

He took longer of course … as she made her way carefully down the stairs, finally looking respectable with her best makeup applied, which at long last she found in her bag, to a wafting upward scent of bacon cooking.

"My goodness Abby, considering what you were up to last night, you look amazing, even with a frying pan in your hand. What's the secret?"

"Attitude, yoga and the gym," she replied deftly with her trademark grin. "There's some porridge cooking in that pan; grab it now before it burns, honey over there and berries in the fridge. Nice big pan this, I'll just put the mushrooms and eggs in and heat up some beans. I can see Julian is an all-day-breakfast kind of guy."

"Where's Lynton?"

"Left for work, I've had to get the entire troupe of cleaners sorted first thing and the bins emptied but the place is looking spick and span out there now. He had to get a move on, early client. He suggested eleven o clock for your appointment, I said that was okay."

"Sure," she replied looking at her watch and realising she had better speed up. "Is this personal PA bit going to become a permanent luxury then?"

"No, make the most of it. Can I assume that the luxury double room which Lynton specially selected for you two to be thrown into last night was up to your usual standard?" Abby chimed grinning naughtily.

"Mmm ... yes ... and don't ask any more ..."

"I don't need to. Good morning Julian, the full monte for breakfast then?"

"Yes please Abby," he replied enthusiastically, immediately rubbing his glasses, picking up the broadsheet Lynton had left and immersing himself straight into the Arts reviews, Abby smirking back at Victoria ...

Having signed off with a flourish the five contracts which Lynton had laid before her, *and* forced down a glass of champagne which he characteristically insisted they should toast, she left him to it, noting on exit, that he had started a new posh speaking receptionist, Dorothy from Woolton. Abby had already found her from a top agency in the city centre. A celebratory cappuccino and cupcake on her own in the small quiet coffee shop down the road was decisively called for.

She had dropped Julian off at the Pier Head. He needed to get back to his house to meet a journalist and change his clothes and she had managed to do the same back at the Adelphi Hotel before seeing Lynton. She had left the consideration of the one year living at Orsbrick Hall proposition open for the time being, and he was fine with that notion, no clock was ticking for a month or two. But inside she was hugely elated, but also daunted, now being the proud owner of a small stately home. She had enough savings and her salary presently to keep going for a while, but she urgently needed to get herself and the others into her usual highly structured, scientific organisational action mode and start writing up a project plan, pulling out a pad of paper from her bag. If she worked through this using her expertise, like she was good at back in the refinery, then when they all met up later on for a meal at the Adelphi, she would feel much more confident.

Her mind flashed back to the ghostly woman in the purple shawl. Who was she and what awful thing had happened and why? She now felt a strong obligation to try and solve the mystery, a conundrum buried somewhere hidden deep inside Orsbrick Hall, her hall, and maybe find closure and peace for the woman. If only she had a name ... and who was the companion? Clues? ... My kingdom for the right clues and a horse please too. Dinner later should be interesting to say the least ...

Chapter Ten

Standing outside in the car park with the key in her hand, whatever trepidation she felt the last time she was rooted in that spot, and frightened to look up, down or sideways, had miraculously gone. She patted the beast; he could do with a permanent owner. Perhaps it had been the final signing over of the deeds, or maybe it was the realisation that those childhood fears of Orsbrick Hall had been turned topsy-turvy. And the ghostly resident and she had a common cause; they were each in their own way trying to find closure from a bad time, in her case the whole of her childhood, rooted in a foundation of lies, subterfuge and deceit. She would never forgive her step-mother, if she ever turned up, now she knew the truth of who her real mother was … and then the thought really came home to her like a hammer in her head. She didn't actually know anything about anyone. Her parents had lived a make believe false, plastic world of unending lies. And apart from Aunt Eveline, she had no immediate family anywhere … maybe except for her companion in the purple shawl. Her mind could now focus on facts, reality, proof, and she would confront the knowledge, however bad it was, because she and her purple shawl companion were alibis in the same cause … they were fighting the same war, to reveal the ultimate truth.

She looked around for Abby, feeling some concern because Abby was uncharacteristically quiet on the way up from Liverpool. Something was on her mind, or in her psyche, which she was trying to work through and understand. Julian and Lynton, joking and laughing all the way were a good counterbalance to Abby's sobriety. She had told Julian, before he had kissed her chastely on the cheek leaving the Adelphi, as they both had rationally agreed to take their time, not rush things and get to know each other better, about Abby's … senses … Julian had calmly replied that Abby was simply psychic and that he knew because his sister was the same and she displayed the same acute observational disposition of describing things almost before they had happened.

It had been her, Victoria, who had the difficulty … but now she had learned from both of them a new outlook, that being scientifically rational and logical could sit happily with believing Abby was psychic … She had her new friend in purple to thank for the unexpected damascene conversion, although she still retained some level of scepticism in parts. But that was healthy as it promoted questions, even when there were no obvious answers.

But where had Abby gone to? They had left Julian and Lynton down the road after Lynton had shouted through the window … "there, there—stop, stop, I'll get it." They had been debating a cost effective way of quickly getting those boards off the windows, job number one, when Lynton saw a big bright yellow JCB digger, parked on the side of the lane with its bucket up in the air, like a male pheasant plumage, with a sign hanging from it … hire me please, I'm lonely. The fact that neither of them had ever driven one didn't deter them from haring off to find the farmer.

Abby returned around the corner, her face a little grim.

"Where did you go to, I'm just about to go in and we have a torch each now?"

"Sorry Vikki, you didn't mention it so I assume you'd forgotten, but there is a small graveyard at the end of that outbuilding over there, which is probably a family chapel."

"How did you know it was there?"

"I didn't, but worked it out from what Eveline had said ... and found myself needing to walk there immediately. The area is overgrown, very neglected, and only one grave was clearly legible, with a shiny black gravestone, your Uncle William, 1907 to 2010. There are fresh flowers on the grave, someone else is coming here."

"Mmm ..." she replied concentrating ... "Wonder if it's the housekeeper that Aunt Eveline mentioned, the daughter? Although heaven knows, she must be getting on." Then it clicked, when Julian was drawing up his list of to-dos and suggestions— someone who may know something. In fact she may know plenty. "We need to find that housekeeper Abby, I'll need to try and ring Aunt Eveline later."

"Okay then, turn the key, let's see inside this mighty inheritance," Abby replied, now smiling and looking her usual self again.

But before they had a chance a great roaring and bumping sounded up the drive, puffs of exhaust smoke billowing around as Julian, with Lynton hanging precariously on the side cavaliered in driving the bouncing JCB veering uneasily from side to side. Some ladders had been strapped to the other side. They shuddered to a halt, next to the beast, both BMW and JCB eyeing each other nervously, or so she thought, as she was decidedly nervous herself once Julian jumped out of the cab waving a crowbar.

"Lynton can talk the hind leg off a donkey. Not only have we got the JCB for a week and for a song, but the farmer threw in a massive tool-chest on the back and a triple set of ladders!" he shouted triumphantly, like a warrior back with his spoils of war.

"That's what lawyers are for guys ..." Lynton added. "Ripping off the unsuspecting ... oh sorry Victoria, I didn't mean you" ... seeing Abby's face.

Victoria laughed back. "No offence taken Lynton, now I can reduce the bill by twenty-five percent," making Abby roar alongside with even more laughter. She turned the two keys simultaneously, having got a copy made which cost her fifteen pounds. "Let's get the place lit up," she cried, looking back at the small diesel generator which the beast had been towing from the gypsies outside of the Ormskirk Boogley Hire Shop ...

The end of the day was approaching and Abby and Victoria were sitting outside, in the warm sun, drinking tea around the old iron patio table and four matching chairs, they found in a storeroom. They looked up to see the amazingly ingenious Julian, electric drill in hand, precariously balanced at the top of a three stage ladder, which itself was standing in the bucket of the JCB, also raised to its highest level, so he could get to the last two window boards on the third storey of the main building. Lynton was sat in the cab, looking distinctly nervous.

"He told me not to worry," Lynton shouted across. "He learned extreme climbing techniques in the TA, but there is no way you'd find me up there."

"You're a wuss, get to it and join him," Abby chided him playfully as he scowled.

"Okay everyone keep out of the way, I'm going to have to throw this down," Julian shouted as Abby and Victoria ran back and the final plywood board tumbled with a crash onto the gravel. Revealed now in their full splendour, the tall sash windows and the surrounding paintwork looked in excellent condition. On the ground floor the splendour of the massive bay windows could be fully appreciated. It had taken them all day, although the rear was much easier because of the huge first floor balcony running along the length of the main building and its extensions. Finally, after careful lowering of the ladders Julian swung down in the bucket, Lynton grinning as he manipulated the levering. At last they could switch off the noisy engine, the only sound left being the quiet chunter of the diesel generator by the front door, which Julian had skilfully hooked onto the main meter feed wires, so the place was indeed now lit up temporarily.

Abby had gone inside for more tea and mugs and came out with a steaming fresh tray full.

"How did you get on with the Electricity Board, Victoria?" Julian asked, supping his tea, whilst large triangles of jam sponge cake were handed around.

"They'll be a week, because they have to organise a special trench machine and a cable, but it's all booked and they said they could put it in underground."

"Yes thought as much," he replied pointing towards the pole on the other side." Somebody has disconnected the original cable feed from that pole transformer down to the side of the house, probably to keep the sticky hands of the metal robbers off the copper … Good job we borrowed that old three-phase fairground generator. We've got 10KVA of power, plenty to work the lights and a kettle."

"And," Lynton added, "I found a pile of logs around the back in a woodstore, presumably for the aga, so we could cook as well."

"Kebabs later?" Abby cried, and they all spluttered, groaning into their tea.

Julian continued. "The rooms we couldn't first get into Victoria upstairs, they look fascinating inside. Some are completely empty, but many have period bedroom furniture in them which haven't been changed for many decades, there is a whole wealth of antique stuff around."

"And, as you all know," Lynton continued, "I took charge of a van load of paintings from Eveline West, who had them taken out when brother William died, all quietly hanging in my gallery for the time being. You need to see them too Victoria."

"Yes, I'm looking forward to that," she replied, looking at Abby. "And thanks for loaning your entire pub cleaning equipment Lynton. Abby and I have managed to clean and dust all the original living area, bedroom, kitchen and further rooms along, unused but with beautiful furniture there."

"Yes, I saw inside those rooms through the windows on the bucket," Lynton added, "and my guess is a lot of that stuff is 1920s from the decor and furnishings. It all has a remarkable feel of the Great Gatsby and F. Scott Fitzgerald and all that jazz, so to speak. There's a record player and a rack of old vinyl in one of them."

"Yes, we saw that, all 1920 and 30s 78's then it stopped, like somebody was having a ball then suddenly got bored with it all." Victoria commented.

"Or became severely traumatised by something bad and then went into a reclusive shell."

They all looked across at Abby, as Victoria frowned, then remembered of course, Eveline's comment. "Oh God, William and Alicia, I'd forgotten for a moment."

"Who are they?" Lynton asked, intrigued whilst Julian wiped his glasses nervously. Victoria then described the story of the horrific suicide drowning in the canal of Uncle William's girlfriend Alicia in the late 1920s after allegedly seeing something in the house and how the roaring twenties for him ended with him living the rest of his life like a hermit.

"But, the question is what did Alicia see that would make her dive in the canal?" Lynton asked, quizzically. "This should be fun, like following a mystery trail as more of the house is uncovered. How come everyone is looking so glum?"

Victoria shuffled in her seat. Lynton of course knew nothing about the woman in the shawl, which was obvious, Abby was, if nothing else, a fortress bastion of discretion. Julian was looking distinctly ill at ease, which Abby caught immediately and knew what the reason was, because she may have inadvertently created a psychic wave, which Julian was feeling a subconscious chill from, even though he wasn't naturally blessed with that acuity. It must, Abby thought, have been the graveyard. Because when she found Uncle William's recent and well tended grave, next to it, after she rubbed at the stonework, she could make out Alicia van Gruyff, died suddenly April 20th 1929.

At that moment of discovery Abby had felt a frightening chill running down her spine and a very cold breath of wind pass across her face followed by the faint sound of organ music coming from the small chapel. She knew, she was experienced, and she had expected something because that was why she had been drawn in the first instance to the resting place, before she had hardly got out of the beast. She was breathing in and out deeply, staring down at the inscription on the gravestone when she saw something even she jumped sharply at. Inside the stone, like a faint hologram, was a woman's face, contorted, screaming, terrified beyond belief, a face, captured within some living hell, that was crying out for help, salvation, for something or someone to save her ... Abby then felt a rumble under her feet and stepped back smartly, as the ground she had been standing on shook, cracks opening up across the earth and the soil started sinking, as she watched, mesmerised. The small black vase of flowers on William's grave fell over and the top broke off. The sinking earth, forming a visible depression, stopped. And coming from William's grave, she smelt it again, that horrible bad fish stench of aniline seeping into her nostrils … before everything then cleared instantly. The birds started singing again and all was still and peaceful, her inner senses having been turned around from turmoil to peace.

Abby knew the significance of what she had felt and seen. Whatever had happened and however it was connected to the woman in the purple shawl, Orsbrick Hall contained a terrifying and dark secret that had lingered long beyond when it first occurred sometime during the 19th century, and probably resurfaced again when Alicia died.

"I think we're all just tired Lynton, it's been a long first day," Abby retorted, doing her best to uplift her voice and be cheerful.

Julian caught on. "Yes, I'm definitely knackered, but we've achieved a huge amount. Not quite got the stamina I had twenty years ago in the territorial army."

"Really Julian?" Abby replied with an innocent grin across her mouth, staring next at Victoria who blushed bright red, and at which point they all laughed heartily, tension evaporated.

But Abby remained in a difficult dilemma. There was no way she was going to mention the face in the stone and instinctively knew that there would be no repeat, the message had been conveyed. But she had also worked out, whilst hoovering Uncle William's former bedroom that seventy odd years had elapsed between Alicia's death and the present time, and that seventy years before that took her to around 1860. She thought about Eveline's painting and comments about when

Victoria's great-great-aunt, surrounded by water lilies, would have been painted. Rossetti was artistically very active between 1860 and 1880. The maths was beginning to stack up at least giving them a window to focus their researches on. Then another chill passed through her. What if those seventy years was a proxy period for the next incident, that evil restless spirits, whoever or whatever they were, needed their next jolt of revitalisation from the living? It was too late for Eveline, but not for Victoria ... oh God, she pondered, that chill sweeping over her stomach. But what role has the woman in the purple shawl got? ... They had to get a move on and find out ...

Victoria immediately jumped up smiling. "Okay, now seeing as everyone is exhausted and thank you all so much for helping out today, I can't tell you how much I've appreciated it ... actually yes I can. Bar meals are on me tonight and the venue of choice will be the George in Burscough, one of my precocious teen-scene drinking dens, when my father and Sergeant Hargreaves weren't in there. I'm curious how the place has changed. So let's get cleared up. Lynton? Abby tells me that you've booked out some days leave to carry on?"

"I sure have Victoria. Tomorrow Julian and I, now that we can see everywhere at last, are going to do a full building repair and maintenance schedule, and make some estimates what it would cost to get this place shipshape. At least he is; I'm going to follow him around and write the notes!"

"And Victoria and I are going to start assembling and filing those papers she found and any other documents we discover, so we two can begin the research," Abby added now feeling chirpier again, but looking for the first opportunity to get Victoria alone, to update her including her stepmother.

"Yes, sounds good," Julian replied. "I'm just going to put all the tools back into the house. There's a small barn at the rear, ideal to leave the JCB in, probably an old stable once, but with padlocked doors, just like those rooms upstairs. Pity really, wish I could get in ..."

"Da-da," Victoria piped up waving a large bunch of keys from her pocket. "Found all these in one of those desk drawers and they include two big padlock keys!" throwing them to Julian, who grinned like Father Christmas had just come by, as he and Lynton sauntered off.

"Vikki, can you help me bring that pub cleaning equipment out, we'll have to get that back to the Red Lion," Abby ventured, pulling her into the main doorway.

"You're in a hurry, what's up?"

"A couple of things, whilst we're alone. I'll be quick. You're mother, sorry you're American stepmother Beatrice that is, won't be a complication any longer in your life."

"Eh? Why not?"

"Because she's been dead for the last three years ..."

Victoria looked at her friend blankly, then Abby summarised what Aunt Eveline had confessed, as well as the background to the Rossetti painting of her great-great-aunt. Abby decided to keep her experience in the graveyard to herself, at least until she had done some more research, a likely veering now into esoteric aspects of seventeenth century witchcraft, curses and spells, in the Central Library and on the internet.

Victoria was sanguine and calm about her stepmother, her feelings unaltered, like a sort of frozen deal emotion, realising it had always been like that. It wasn't just the serious neglect as the obvious alcoholism got worse but that constant feeling their relationship had never been right or normal since a child, like she wasn't really wanted. "You get out of life what you put into it Abby, I'm glad that chapter at least can be finally closed. I just wish I could have talked to my father and developed a normal daughter relationship … pity my father was not Uncle William."

"Some things are just not to be for a reason Victoria, but don't ask me what they are!"

Abby had decided, like with Alicia, to withhold the details of the autopsy and the purple bloated liver, because she was now certain that the death of Victoria's stepmother was also not just alcoholism … she too had seen something here … and Aunt Eveline knew. "Hey, now who are those two strange men outside waving at us with rippling torsos, sexy stubble and lantern chins? Okay, forget the lantern chins."

Julian and Lynton joined them in the grand sitting room, going from wall to wall, both chattering animatedly about art, frescos, decoration and original marble carvings. Abby then took Julian into the kitchen to see the progress she had made on the aga, all wood-primed and ready for lighting and cooking, having unblocked the vent pipe and cleaned the soot up A large range of original copper and iron pots and pans, were neatly hanging again on hooks on the wall.

Lynton quietly sidled up to her. "Victoria, whilst Abby and Julian are outside, I've been thinking. This lot is going to take some money to get back into at least a liveable-in condition. I'm going to look at that trust fund again and see if there is any small-print provision for release of some funds solely for repairs to the house, not uncommon a hundred years ago in situations like this. Also, you probably didn't get the significance when I mentioned it, but because of the age of this building, between 1700 and 1840, it is automatically classified as listed, and is a Grade 2 category, so we could apply for grants in due course from English Heritage to match funds. Julian is amazing with his skills and knowledge on building conservation; he's like your personal consultant so I'm confident we will be able to nail an accurate cost. That way, if I can release funds legally, you could get this place sorted and live in it comfortably ... for the ... err ... twelve month period ... err if you want to."

Victoria went silent, that difficult decision was coming faster than she hoped, she had to get practical ... and Lynton made real sense, but ... it still depended on whether they could find out what had happened, and she still had some sort of stupid hankering in her head to go back home to Holland too, or was this going back home ... she was confused ... and what about Julian ...?

"It just depends, I understand Lynton, but ... I have to think ... I'm sort of torn as well, perhaps I should go back to Rotterdam, I don't know with so much ..." looking up casually in the fading light at the ornate mirror hanging behind his head ... when her eyes widened. Oh God no. She was standing behind her, her reflection clear and unambiguous, those sharp dark eyes, burning down, and she wasn't smiling. A tear had begun to trickle down her cheek. She breathed in hard and continued to stare back at the reflection of the woman in the purple shawl.

"Are you okay, Victoria? You've gone quite pale and you're shaking. Shall I get you a glass of water?"

"No Lynton," she replied slowly maintaining her gaze at the reflection. "Overexertion and overexcitement, bad combination for me. You know, I think I've decided," she replied steadfastly. "I'm going to stay here ... let's get the grants ..."

"Excellent, Victoria, just what I hoped you'd say and I've got some colleagues who specialise in this area of heritage so we should be able to ..." He stopped because Victoria obviously wasn't listening, instead she was watching the face in the mirror immediately stop crying and a tiny smile make its way across, then the face faded away and vanished. "Here, sip this bottle of water anyway."

She looked back at Lynton and guzzled some water and her colour reappeared. Julian and Abby were coming back in chattering about food. "Thanks, I always get like this when I'm tired and hungry," Victoria replied. "Julian, are we all sorted?"

"Yep … JCB is safely tucked away in the barn, generator is in the hall, you just need to lock up."

"Time for the George then everyone, let's go."

The George, a small former drinking haunt of the local boat people, was a complete contrast to the urbanised and rowdy in-crowd Red Lion. Whilst some reluctant efforts at decor and furnishings modernisation had taken place and the sawdust had long gone, the basic poky bar for regulars still retained that time stood still effect, although numbers were low and the atmosphere was deathly quiet. A more comfortable and larger restaurant lounge, which Victoria recognised from her teenage binges, was open at the rear where they went into and sat down. Abby strode to the bar to pick up the menus, and at the same time a small family party walked in, with an elderly white-haired lady wearing a large bonnet, slowly and carefully led to a suitable chair, where she struggled to sit down, as they fussed around to make sure she was comfortable.

Victoria looked across idly. The person in charge was likely to be the woman's grandson, given the close facial similarities, although she looked as old as Eveline, in her nineties. The man's wife and a couple of teenage children then sat down around the table. Victoria didn't recognise them. In fact she didn't recognise anyone in the pub at all, not the landlord and his wife behind the bar, although she did notice a picture of

Sergeant Hargreaves over the fireplace. He must have passed on some time back, but he was a keen off-duty regular.

"Drinks everyone, my shout," Julian said and stood up. "Four lagers?"

They nodded and he set off walking to the bar, as Abby commenced organising everyone to choose their food. Victoria became distracted by the people around the family table, as she watched the old lady suddenly peer hard at Julian, becoming seemingly agitated, not taking her eyes off him whilst he stood waiting for the drinks. The grandson looked across at Victoria and then at Julian, as he began to walk back with a tray, the old lady's eyes, following his every movement, her head slowly swivelling from right then to left and back, muttering incoherently to herself, with an expression of distinct fear and alarm. As Julian put the tray down, completely unaware as always, a loud crash sounded as the woman shot up out of her seat, her stick flying over the table and smashing the wine glasses, shouting she had to go immediately. The wife and daughter took each side and slowly began to take the lady, who had turned deathly white, out of the exit quickly.

Julian turned around as the man walked over, looking very aggressive. He stopped in front of Julian, staring him in the face. "Who the fuck are you pal? You've scared my grandmother half to death. What the fuck are you doing in here?"

Julian raised himself to his full six foot five, already switched into automatic defence and repel mode, which his former army training dictated. Victoria felt palpitations arising. He looked exactly the same as when he rescued her from the muggers in Liverpool; hellfire the last thing she wanted was to witness a blood bath in the George. Lynton and Abby were staring, silent and wide-eyed.

Julian immediately addressed the man, in a quiet, non-confrontational tone, obviously wanting as much as Victoria to defuse the situation whatever it was. "I'm terribly sorry, I think there's been a case of mistaken identity I'm afraid. I don't know you, your grandmother, or in fact anyone else here and I've never been to this public house before in my life. We're simply visiting."

The man scowled, red in the face, but looked up at Julian's controlling, fixed steely gaze, and immediately decided to back off, as the landlord pulled up the bar trap to come over.

The man started to walk reluctantly away, before turning back from a safe distance and howling, "I know you, you don't fool me, and you're not fucking welcome in this town. Stay away for your own good," and vanished.

Julian sat down, and picked up his lager, unabashed. "Cheers everyone. Here's to Victoria and her new venture, and one less head to rip off tonight."

"Yeh," Lynton replied jauntily, raising his glass. "I get that reaction often too, especially when angry husband's wives mistake me for George Clooney." But the only response he managed was a sharp glare from Abby.

Victoria, still concerned, rubbed Julian's arm. "What was that all about?"

"Heaven knows. I must remind that half-wit and his family of someone," Julian replied perkily, seeing Victoria's order of three steaks and chips and one fish pie and peas being brought to the table. Abby however remained silent, because she realised another key part of the jigsaw had been unwittingly confirmed. Julian also had a secret. Was he deliberately hiding the fact, or did he have a strong family connection to this rural Lancashire locality, despite his London accent and background from Wapping? Abby glanced at Victoria ... who glanced back with a knowing frown ... also having immediately deduced the same conclusion. But nothing was going to spoil a relaxing evening any further as they tucked hungrily into their food ...

There was no doubt, Victoria noted with a pleasing inner smile, that Abby's notoriously persuasive and organisational ways were working well on the lonely Lynton, as she dropped Julian and him off at the Red Lion. Lynton was, in fact, living there rather than his luxury apartment in Southport, which Abby had quickly prised out, because he was still struggling with the loss of his wife and too many memories there to cope presently. Undoubtedly Abby was doing a remarkable job of bringing a bounce back into Lynton's step ... and Victoria was beginning to realise that they were unexpectedly very compatible, despite their stunningly disparate backgrounds, and sensed a fast and serious ramping up of their relationship. She also felt increasingly happy about Julian, but would remain measured and steady. Too many bad and painful memories from the past, when relationships always ended up in tears the moment she become too enthusiastic and committed. She wasn't in a good place to cope with that as well. And she sensed intuitively, Julian was happy to do the same. He hadn't talked much about his past, but she knew, when he did, from his expression and body language, that a lot of pain also lurked in there. Indeed both of them had obviously, for years, shared the same thing in common ... flitting aimlessly from one easy noncommittal relationship to the next, both frightened of being hurt again. But he had that determination and commitment in his eyes to help her through the challenges ahead of Orsbrick Hall.

At the Red Lion, Lynton announced that he wanted to provide some practical support and to offer his pub as a free base to lodge for as long as it took. There were lots of unused bedrooms. Prompted quietly by Abby, who already had worked out what her best friend would choose, he offered Victoria the luxury room she had already slept in and Julian, a quiet small eyrie in the attic, with a desk, where he could also write when the urge took him. Victoria didn't ask where Abby would be sleeping, having realised the now obvious, but she welcomed the gesture warmly as did Julian. It gave her breathing and working space to think ... and ... decide if she really could or would live at Orsbrick?

Driving back to what would be their last night at the Adelphi Hotel and to pick up their things, Abby seized the moment as Victoria turned onto the busy dual carriageway into the northern Liverpool suburbs.

"You need to question Julian."

"I know, but watching his reaction to that incident, and my instinct, I believe he genuinely has no idea of any possible family connection in the area, although it may be crossing his mind now?"

"Or he may just be a plain liar, Vikki."

"For what reason? No, I suggest we continue the plan. You and I start delving into my own family history and those papers and other information, perhaps photographs, paintings, anything which might throw up something. Then I will ask him. I trust Julian."

"Mmm ..." Abby replied, annoyed because her instinct and her natural tendency, from all the bad which had also happened to her, was to mistrust ... but perhaps ...

"Good news too," Victoria continued in an upbeat mode. "Tomorrow the telecoms company Zinger is coming to reconnect a landline and install broadband. I asked some advice from Marlies which was invaluable when I phoned them this afternoon. She's offered to come for the weekend and set up an infrastructure for us to work with. I'm glad we brought our laptops."

"Marlies?"

"Marlies van der Wege. She was Head of IT Services at the refinery; we were quite close at work. They made her redundant last week; Ahrendolie really is going down the tubes fast. I hope they continue with my promised salary for the next six months. Also, you remember those nineteenth century scientific papers I found with Julian? Although I got a gist of what they were relating to, it isn't really my field. I don't want to get bogged down with extra research."

"What field are they?"

"Coal tar dyes and old industrial processes."

"So what are you going to do then?"

"I've already done it," Victoria replied after a moment's silence. "I ... err ... phoned Eva. Of course she's on school holidays but was so keen to help ... so she's offered to come as well at the weekend ... for two weeks."

Abby looked, at first startled and then erupted with a growing fury. "Is that really such a good idea, bringing Eva of all people to Orsbrick Hall? Anyway, what about her wife?"

"Err ... no wife ... they split some time back, Eva is in between things, you know ..."

"Jesus Christ, Victoria, I can't believe it ... and what about Julian? Do you really want to hurt him at this stage? You know how you and Eva were, and she was in a relationship then for fuck's sake."

"Julian and I are good friends. Okay, I admit we've had some benefits, I just don't want to rush things ... and Eva and I are good friends too and that's it," Victoria replied primly, but now biting her lip and wishing it was the morning before again.

Abby sulked in her seat, hugely annoyed, but it wasn't just complications of Victoria's love life now. Her mind had rattled back to one hundred and fifty years before, and a chill ran into her body. She stayed quiet and neither spoke. Victoria fiddled with the radio, irritated with the banalities on every station, as the beast plodded on steadily and smoothly. At least, Victoria thought, she had done one good thing today and taken on the beast as a continuing personal monthly rental ... she wasn't giving him up that quickly.

"I want you to consider one other factor Vikki," Abby began suddenly after the prolonged lull in conversation. "Your other friend may not be very happy either, and that could have consequences."

"What other friend? Oh gosh Abby. No, stupidly that never crossed my mind; I need to get a grip. I'm sorry for being terse before, it was uncalled for."

"On the other hand, if Eva really does crack on and speeds up the scientific detective work, then it could be ghostly fish, chips and smiles all round?" Abby replied light-heartedly, diverting her concerns and causing both of them to laugh and relax back to normal.

"I may also be of some use in this complicated tangle of emotions," Abby continued, "because Eveline indicated the likely links with art, and textiles ... which go with dyes like fish to water. So I'll make an effort and get on with Eva, gritted teeth and all that."

"Thanks. Eva is very much into history, culture and writing so she should get on well with Julian too, which will be a great team."

"As long as she doesn't decide to switch to the other side. Don't worry, I'll be keeping an eye on her and batting for you. Given the way you swoon quietly over Julian's muscled restoration and conservation genius, alongside his willing apprentice, Lynton, I assume you have their roles pigeonholed into the grand action plan rollout too? I always knew you were happiest conducting the orchestra rather than playing the tuba."

"Yes, all of that. And thank you so much, I don't know what I would have done without your help. You love him don't you?"

"Shit, is it that obvious?"

"Only to me, but Lynton has definitely found a zing in his step, from when we first met him in that strange building of his."

"I'm getting that sorted ... but yes ... why not? It doesn't have to take years and he does look a bit like George Clooney doesn't he, that mature greying look, like Julian?"

Victoria smiled back, contented again, for the time being, but it all made her ponder hard ...

Chapter Eleven

The rest of the week went remarkably quickly and smoothly, almost as if her childhood guardian angel was back ... mmm ... a guardian angel with a disposition to purple and who likes fish and chips? She pondered. Was it Friday already? Rarely did Victoria smile at the efficiency of utilities, in fact if she was honest she had *never ever* smiled about utilities, but the electricity was on, because the Board had acquired their trench machine three days earlier, and the landline was connected with broadband. Although she was waiting for Marlies to arrive in the evening to sort out the wifi, and Julian discovered there was even a water meter and a huge stop cock in the porter's cabin, which was read for the water company and turned on.

Julian was deliriously happy and constantly whistling, up to his armpits in paint, plaster, varnish and filler, going from room to room touching up this here and that there. Abby had rigorously polished every single wooden floor with Lynton's pub machine, and they had both inspected every room and amassed a huge pile of papers, documents and old folders, from drawers, chests and desks, all carefully laid out in Uncle William's old study, becoming now the research war-room. Unfortunately they only had Lynton for the first two days, as he had to get back to client work in the office. But, chivvied on by Abby, who praised Lynton every moment she found, he managed to work like a demon with the JCB, after a quick lesson from Julian, moving debris and rubbish into a pile away from the house, and finally he cleared the immediate vicinity to absolute perfection, right down the drive to the gates, so the whole entrance from the road looked respectable once more.

She and Abby finished off the rest of the cleaning, including the living carpeted area, and finally Julian had completed his initial assessment of further work that could qualify for a listed building heritage grant. She loved her project management role working the orchestral baton, gently of course. But that was what she was always good at, although she successfully managed one personally supervised restoration task, and painted the rusty gates shiny jet Hammerite black, until they shone and glinted in the sunlight, like they once must have done a hundred years back, when the horse drawn coaches, full of rich arty and science people pulled up outside ...

Evenings were relaxing recuperation time, but they all lost their appetites for the George, despite the good food, and instead went to the Liverpool Arms, on the canal bank. It wasn't that far from where she once lived but she would leave Cinderblack Lane for another time. She had zero curiosity, except to eventually find some down time and visit Annie's hippie parents in the next village, who had been so incredibly good to her before she ran away from home.

Lynton had asked her to tow the generator back to the gypsies at the fairground near the Red Lion, and, once Julian and Abby were immersed in their next tasks, he jumped into the beast beside her. They slowly edged out between her splendid new gates and onwards towards Ormskirk.

"Sorry I can't spare any more days, Victoria, but I will help over the weekend. I understand you have a couple of friends coming?" he began, glad to have some time on his own with her. He had some interesting news, for her ears only.

"Yes Marlies should be arriving, a Dutch colleague from the refinery, who is going to get all the broadband functioning and also Eva, an old friend, who will help me and Abby with the scientific analysis. She has a science brain like a planet … I'm sure you and Julian will get on well …"

"Great. Abby is fabulous isn't she … next week she is going to meet Judy who is coming home for a couple of days."

"Judy?"

"My daughter, first year at Oxford doing PPE. I hope they get on."

"Abby gets on with everyone, don't worry Lynton," Victoria replied cheerfully, her brain and ears now alert and thinking… Lynton was definitely moving their relationship along a pace too; hopefully neither of them will burn out painfully and prematurely, but they are both grown up adults, it was up to them … thinking wistfully for a second about Julian … and then Eva.

"Now, an interesting development. Rebecca my new legal assistant who Abby also found in the temp agency, I gave her some demanding work for day one, the small print of your trust fund, to see if there are any flexibilities. To be honest it's a turgid fifty page document, and I had put the thing to one side for later. Rebecca has found a hidden clause which allows the trustees discretion up to a maximum tiny percentage of the fund, for use solely on necessary initial building repairs and restoration and related expenses, as long as the trustees agree.

"Who are the trustees actually?"

"Eveline West and Betty Grable."

"My goodness, at the care home?"

"Yes I am legal administrator, so I've already popped in to see them, which is why I was late this morning, and they agree, so I've set up a special escrow account for you to draw on, literally up to £25,000. Cheque book is here, credit card shortly. But all receipts need to be kept and handed to me regularly."

Victoria was so taken aback she could hardly breathe and pulled into a nearby lay-by, throwing her arms around the blushing Lynton and kissing him wildly on the cheek, murmuring a long string of thank yous. It wasn't a huge amount of repair money, but with her own funds as well, she would match her bonus to it, an endorsement of belief and confidence by Aunt Eveline in her commitment to bring Orsbrick Hall back into shape. And that meant a lot.

Finally when he caught his breath, he continued. "Eveline is really excited at what you are doing and the progress we've all made. She said to not waste time going over yet to see her, she's very busy. Her friend with the cello was waiting at the door, bow in hand, as I left. But she didn't seem so pleased when I mentioned the graveyard."

Victoria stopped and stared hard. She had forgotten about that, so much to do inside. "What about the graveyard?"

"Well, as I was doing the grounds with the JCB, I made sure I kept only to the edges, consecrated ground and all that. It's in a pretty poor state though, only small, and the railing around it needs replacing, although the chapel looks very sound like the rest of the house. But I noticed, there was a large hole next to one recent grave, I assume Uncle William. I didn't get that close, a bit tricky in the machine. I did mention it to Eveline and she got rather agitated, but then quickly calmed down, after some deep thought and was back to her normal, smiling self. As I said to her, the ground has probably sunk a bit with the rain or age, so nothing to worry about. Oh … and as I left, she had a special message for Abby. She insisted that you have to tell her to look and listen … I don't know what that was about, do you?"

Victoria contemplated ... the graveyard could wait for the moment ... but of course ... the Eveline and Abby tête à tête art road show ... Eveline must know there is more music and art artefacts to be found, as she explained it back to Lynton who agreed.

But as they drove back from the fairground, she continued wondering uneasily ... but this was soon overridden being massively pleased about buying more stuff legitimately to get the house right ... in fact she even wished she had seen her new ghostly friend, but not a hint of aniline all week. Hopefully she was a friend ... then thought again of Marlies arriving and Eva tomorrow. She looked at her watch and panicked, she had to get to Lime Street Station fast and pick up Marlies.

The evening was relaxed, giving opportunity for her new Dutch arrival to meet Abby and Julian and take an initial perusal of the layout of Orsbrick Hall from both a security and wireless network perspective. Marlies, a tall, confident twenty nine year old, with shoulder length brown hair and an arresting smile, quickly proved to Julian, who had that sceptical, glasses rubbing aura again, her knowledge of IT, computers and security systems was exceptionally deep. But then, Victoria mused, he should have worked that out from her position, although he was yet to understand exactly how senior she too had been in her former job. Marlies quickly dispelled any nostalgia for Ahrendolie, by confirming that she had told the pompous CEO, Joss van der Dyke, to stick his job up his rear end and been fired on the spot ... she knew her marketability and was taking a break before walking into the next equivalent position. Demand was high for her computing skills and Julian quickly became an instant devotee; Abby, as usual, had worked all that out in one minute flat.

Removing a fast, top range internet router from her bag, with Ahrendolie stamped on the bottom, Marlies clarified to Victoria that being only a mile from the local telephone exchange meant they should be able to access a fast broadband service, especially with the extra goodies she had brought, including filters, amplifiers and a range of signal distributors to overcome any barriers of transmission through old, thick and tall walls. Job was effectively done, and they had only been there half an hour, at which point, looking at the flagging body of her master conservator, Victoria called it a day, locked up and everyone was driven at speed back to the Red Lion.

Abby had already booked Marlies and Eva in, and courtesy of Lynton, they had a relaxing dinner and long discussions of art and music, when an exhausted Victoria was thankful for Julian and Lynton to take centre stage. Cases unpacked, rooms filled, a round of hot chocolate and a peck on the cheek from Julian and she was very thankful to put on her long nightdress, crawl into bed in that gorgeous double room again, with the space to stretch her long legs and think undisturbed with her latest kindle novel, without worrying about a mildly snoring body next to her; although she looked wistfully up at the ceiling, knowing that Julian was directly above her. As she lay back on the soft white pillows, working through, step by step, the enormity of where she had now arrived, from what a few weeks back had been a total catastrophe and near death experience, she could hear it. A little tap-tap, then a respite and more tapping on a keyboard … all coming from the eyrie above. He was writing again into the depths of the night, obviously inspired by Orsbrick Hall, or maybe even her … as she smiled, closed her eyes and dozed quickly into a deep sleep, the kindle still in her hand …

"No problem at all Julian, we don't need wired up passive infrared sensors, a real nightmare in here. All the trigger devices are discretely compact and wirelessly connected to the alarm master system. Already checked the specifications and you can pick this system up from a specialist retailer in Ormskirk, today," Marlies retorted, laying her iPad on the antique desk, as they all peered up at the tall ceiling, having been given an in-depth lecture from Julian over bacon and egg earlier about the security necessities and the massive problems of installation in a listed building.

"Technology has advanced enormously," Marlies continued. "The 21st century now meets the 19th ... what a beautiful synthesis of compatibility, don't you think as a steampunk writer? Sorry, before you ask, checked you up too; three books published and doing well looking at the sales figures Julian?"

He smiled ... chastened but not beaten, and shut up.

Victoria glanced at Abby ... both thinking the same ... How will the woman in the purple shawl come to terms with the arrival of modern technology? Everything in Orsbrick Hall had been in a virtual time-warp for more than half a century. Do ghosts do twitter?

Marlies finally provided the icing on the cake, in the shape of an equipment list for Julian and Lynton to go and buy a small CCTV system, including a number of security lights for the outside, cameras and a recorder-transmitter, to feed back to Victoria's iPhone, so that any potential intruders would be captured and relayed in real time. Linking directly to the police remained a future option. Gosh, Victoria thought, life was getting simpler by the minute.

"Don't waste your time with external alarms. Who is going to hear the wailing from here? Anyone in the town would just think the resident ghosts were out and about," Marlies joked, to laughter from Julian and Lynton.

Abby stared back again at Victoria ... laughing was the last thing on their minds. Victoria's phone pinged as she looked at the message.

"Abby, Eva will set off soon, she'll drive straight here for lunch."

"In that case," Abby replied, "I'm going to cycle into town and get us all some cold drinks and sandwiches."

"Cycle?"

"Yep, look over there in the kitchen. Found that green beauty in the coal shed. It must be a 1920s model and been carefully and regularly polished and maintained by somebody. Only the tyres are relatively modern—even a wicker basket, cool. I'm beginning to feel the part."

"What part?"

"Head cook of course. Revive our fast food diets with some historic delicacies. Calves-foot jelly anyone?"

From the simultaneous groans, they were not yet ready to take such a gastronomic leap into the unknown, although once that huge aga was lit she could cook them all kebabs until they came out of their ears.

Victoria clapped. "Okay everyone, listen up. This morning, Julian and Lynton are to get all the security and fit it up later, Abby into town to get lunch, Marlies and I will set up the wireless network and Eva is coming at lunchtime to help me and Abby start on the science papers."

"All on board captain and shipshape," Julian shouted across saluting heartily, with everybody laughing as they moved out ... when suddenly the hat stand in the corner crashed over with a loud bang.

Victoria whispered to Abby. "Forget the calves, better stick to a fish pie."

Chapter Twelve

Watching Eva and Marlies working together scrutinising pages and pages of almost illegible scientific text and obscure diagrams of ancient apparatus, gave Victoria a major boost to an impatient need to achieve her plan as quickly as possible. She hadn't discussed her next objective with anyone, instead trying hard to quell her inner apprehension about doing it. She wanted to stay the night, and very soon, now believing that how she felt the following morning after would determine her ability to continue … but knowing in her heart that as each day went on, she wanted more and more to stay. Orsbrick Hall was her home. She was surrounded by her real family heritage finally and after all those years could carve out a new life, something desperately wanted for so long.

Abby came in and also cast a glance at Eva and Marlies, and then smiled inside immediately as she observed something patently obvious. She also knew that Victoria, gazing with nostalgic thoughts over at Eva, was still actively resisting what was plain to see.

Sidling up to Victoria, Abby whispered. "What are those two discovering? Anything, I wonder, we can use alongside the private papers upstairs which I think you should look at?"

"Not sure yet," Victoria replied, watching Eva carefully picking out specific handwritten areas to be scanned, and then transcribed by Marlies with a word processor, likely missing words or phrases being filled in by both of them. Marlies was also tapping furiously through her database of search engines to draw comparative inferences, which she then passed on to Eva for comment. Their system was certainly working efficiently with the first two folders already gone through.

Victoria began to head upstairs, before turning to Eva. "Just to say ... I like your new hairstyle, it really suits you."

Eva looked up, smiled, mouthed a brisk thank you, and then continued unabated onto the next scientific folder.

Abby pulled up a small sheaf of letters out of a heap of private bound document folders, from the trunk they had both earlier discovered. "Much of this stuff is household inventory," she began. "You know bills, orders and day to day requirements signed off by the then head of household, a Mr James McKenzie. The dates start around 1860 and run through until 1866, but then they disappointingly tail off. All absolutely fascinating historic material, especially the huge amount of food ordered and consumed weekly, pork, chickens, beef, vegetables. There is a mountain of research here for Julian, I'm sure, which relates to the upkeep of the place then. A lot was spent and work done. Your family were proud to ensure the stately pad was a desirable magnet for high society I reckon."

Victoria glanced quickly at one folder, 1866, noting the meticulous accounting pages, done monthly with a yearly total, spotting that a subfolder related to the mystery outside factory, with all kinds of entries for significant ironmongery, sheet metal, piping and related fabrication equipment, as well as orders for coal to a J Whitting, Wakefield. There was a spike of expenditure in the summer of 1866, then a rapid tailing off. Entries for the factory began in the first 1860 folder, relating to distillation equipment, but unfortunately there was a lot missing for the next five years.

"Abby, this may be significant, the factory is mentioned here. They called it a distillation plant, which makes sense, given what Aunt Eveline hinted at. They were definitely distilling coal for tar and derivatives, at a sufficient scale to either be or try and be commercial. Orsbrick Hall was of course well placed to import cheap coal from Yorkshire mines off the barges on the canal, and export any products made, either to Liverpool or to textiles mills either way along the canal including Manchester which had a linked waterway. If this all worked, no wonder they made a lot of money. I know the first coal tar dyes were discovered in the early 1850s, fairly rudimentary colours I assume, I don't know a lot more, need to check against what Eva is finding."

"So who was James McKenzie?"

Victoria contemplated. Without more accurate information, maybe from census data if it went back that far or parish records, it was difficult … mmm … early 1860s …?

But Abby had an immediate mind flash back to the special Rossetti family painting of Aunt Eveline's beautiful grandmother Lydia McKenzie, the absolute identical image to Victoria. She was the niece of Victoria's great-great grandfather, who had owned the engraved cigarette case. Her mind was reeling with the family tree complexities so she grabbed a pad and pencil and scribbled the names, with arrows, in order, whilst Victoria continued fiddling amongst the folders.

"Abby, guess what, there's another folder here at the back, not much in it but it described the chemist shop which belonged to my grandfather and grandmother, with old sepia photos, similar to the couple which Aunt Eveline gave me. They were called Harold and Jesse, isn't that wonderful?"

"Thanks, just the job, I've solved the mystery."

"Pardon?"

"Come and look at my family tree, lots missing of course but it's a main link. There's no doubt in my mind that James McKenzie was your great-great grandfather, he was likely the money maker in the family.

Victoria stared at the tree diagram. "Who is Lydia McKenzie?"

Abby blushed, she had forgotten to mention the Rossetti painting … came clean and explained, especially about the facial likeness. But Victoria was distracted elsewhere in her head, mentally busy rationalising and boiling the data down to manageable conclusions and suddenly blurted out.

"Abby, I'm certain that whatever happened here, was connected with James Mackenzie and his niece Lydia, I can sense it, the logic is sound and if that's the case then we have a small focus of time to concentrate on, don't we."

Abby nodded, and smiled, but inside her head, her brain had gone into a weird rush of indescribable dizzy turmoil, like clouds scudding across her vision. Something was happening and she could feel it but couldn't explain … she needed to get a tea and calm down.

"Victoria are you there?"

They were both suddenly disturbed from their respective thoughts by the booming voice of Julian, obviously excited about something. "Can you come down? I want to show you something."

She looked quizzically at Abby. "Yeah okay …" and got up to follow him down the stairs and outside. He walked her to the end of the house, next to an attached brick outbuilding with double doors. "This is the boiler-house, both the original and then later modified for Uncle William's restricted use of the property to save money."

They walked inside, into a large and well lit area. "Gosh it's bright in here, Julian," she uttered, squinting over at a large white floor standing boiler.

He patted it lovingly, having given it an inspection and a cleanup. "This is a forty kilowatt oil fired boiler, probably around thirty years old looking at the make. There's actually an oil tank outside cleverly hidden amongst shrubs and almost full. I'm amazed it hasn't been siphoned off."

He took her hand gently and led her to it. "Press this red button please."

A gentle whirring and whoosh was heard and the boiler immediately fired into life. A beaming Julian leant over and kissed her on the cheek. "I could see you were getting chilly and uncomfortable so I got it working. The pipes only connect to radiators in Uncle William's living and bedroom area plus those two rooms upstairs. The rest of the house is all piped too but shut off by valves, over at the end there, and the radiators drained, which is why all the other rooms were locked up. Never been used probably for many, many decades. That lot used to be run from that monster over there," pointing to a huge antiquated coal fired boiler in the corner. "I'll leave that for another day, but now you can feel warm and cosy again."

She turned to him, and softly said. "You're wonderful … I am all warm and cosy now actually …" and gently wrapped her arms around his lithe and slightly smelly body, and pulled his head towards hers. Their lips met, gently at first until their kissing gathered into a passionate whirl of moaning and deep embrace.

"What's all this about?" he whispered, trying to catch his breath, her arms all over him, pulling and stroking. "I thought we were going to …"

"Sod that, I've been missing you so badly Julian, especially since that warm-up in the Red Lion ..."

He smirked ... and began to pull up her jumper, throwing it carefully onto the workbench. He began to slowly undo the buttons on her shirt as she followed suit, and both quickly landed on top of the jumper. Finally she undid the clasp on her bra and threw it through the open window in a wild gesture, as it wrapped around a branch, wafting delicately in the breeze. He pushed his hands under her breasts and slowly began kissing her large brown nipples as she closed her eyes.

Both now naked, she grasped his hard erection as they continued kissing passionately and he began to back her towards the boiler.

"I've never been made love to over a boiler?" she whispered earnestly, staring into his eyes, wild with anticipation.

"I doubt anyone else has in here either before, perhaps it's time to make history," he replied panting. "Mmm ... just nicely warm on the ass."

He leaned her against the front, pushing his fingers inside her, wet and aroused. She made a loud sigh before she widened her legs, pulling his hard manhood fully inside her, his hands firmly gripped around her bare white bottom. His need and frustration was palpable, grunting loudly as they began to make love frenetically, and she screamed out with abandonment, one orgasm following the next ...

Outside, Abby was walking over with a mug of tea in each hand, when she heard the commotion, then spotted through the slightly open door, a bare male backside, gyrating backwards and forwards at a rate of speed which could only burn whole images of unfettered lascivious pleasure across her gaze.

"Oh, my God," she uttered, not sure where to look, when she felt the left hand mug being taken from her fingers. "I think we'd better go back Lynton," she said firmly, still staring, but feeling an embarrassing blushing surge coming on. "Lynton?"

She turned around ... and her eyes widened so large they could have burst open. Staring in front of her, she dropped the other mug straight onto the grass. The woman in the purple shawl ... Abby was seeing her for the first time, exactly as Victoria had described ... brown wool skirt and some sort of corduroy buttoned matching linen top and nice silk scarf. Abby's attuned fashion design and textiles expert eyes and knowledge clocking immediately the expensive cut of clothes, small leather tightly bound boots and slim figure. The woman, aged no more than twenty, was very beautiful but the facial features, the hair, blonder but a similar thick texture ... and those eyes and serious expression ... she was staring at Victoria one hundred and sixty years ago.

Unable to utter a word, frozen on the spot, Abby stared with total disbelief as the woman drank the tea, which vanished into nowhere ... and then handed her the mug back. The woman turned her head gracefully towards the continuing commotion, getting louder and louder and grinned. Abby also looked back, where a crucial change of moaning grunts indicated it was time to go, turned back ... and the woman had completely vanished. Time for her to do the same, as she ran back panting into the front entrance to see Lynton, back from his gallery, and standing on a stepladder, putting one of his gallery paintings up on the sitting room wall and a glint in his eye.

"I found this amongst a small additional set of wrapped up pictures that Eveline gave me last time I saw her. I thought Victoria would appreciate it, given her scientific background, obviously one of her forebears. No name on it. Eveline didn't have a clue who it was, but mid nineteenth century I would hazard."

Abby looked up and breathed in deeply. A serious looking woman, mousy hair in a tight bun, was standing in a dingy, chaotic looking room, next to a bench, holding a glass flask with purple liquid in it alongside various pieces of apparatus in the process of being heated. A small heap of coal was visible on the bench. She was wearing a long white coat, not that dissimilar to a modern day laboratory worker, but the rest of the environment was anything but a modern science laboratory, the gloom being lightened by a pair of gas lights in the background. The likeness to Victoria was very apparent, but far more immediate was that the face was suddenly very familiar. She had just stood next to her outside.

"Hey everyone, how's it all going?" Victoria breezed in with Julian quietly following behind. Eva and Marlies were tripping down the stairs.

"You two look a bit red, like the cat that's just found a gallon of cream, where've you been? You'll never believe what we've found," Eva shouted down the sweeping staircase, jauntily.

"Err ... we've just been fixing the boiler, can't you feel the warmth already?" Julian replied, trying to look as normal as possible but shiftily hopping from one foot to the other.

Abby began to cough away an immediate splutter.

"You don't like cats Abby," Victoria said in a monotone to her friend, pondering momentarily ... when she looked up at Lynton's painting and gasped out loud with surprise. "My goodness, now I can't remember anyone painting me in the refinery," she joked as they all laughed. "I wonder who that is."

"Well, obviously there's science somewhere in the genes, Victoria. I thought you'd like it as I'm sure Eveline does too, she gave it me," Lynton replied with everyone nodding and umming. "But we haven't a clue who she is."

"Tea break everyone?" Abby called out cheerily, heading for the kitchen.

Just as Victoria was going to follow the rest, Julian gently grabbed her arm. "Just remembered, there's something else I wanted to show you, outside that boiler-house."

"Oh yes. Got any energy left then?" she smirked happily. Now she knew for sure, she was falling in love with him.

"Don't be daft ... okay later ... maybe ... no something else very interesting, come on, we can get tea in a minute."

They wandered back down there, the sun was out again after earlier drizzle and those skylarks could be heard, carousing over the cornfield near the pond. It felt idyllic as she clasped her hand around his.

At the rear of the boiler house, Julian pointed down to the ground, freshly disturbed. "Lynton got a bit close to the wall here with his mechanical shovel the other day, clearing all that overgrowth, but look what he's uncovered."

He bent down and scraped some more soil away as she peered and the glinting in the sunlight immediately gave it away. Glass, the top of a window and frame, very dirty and buried under the topsoil.

"There's a cellar down there," he continued. "But no sign of any stairway anywhere. The window area runs right along this side, but nowhere else. The ground at one stage has been banked up to hide it, so my conclusion is it runs underneath the boiler-room at least, maybe further back under the next room, which looks like it was a scullery or something going by the tiling on the walls. Follow me McKenzie-Watson."

"Sure thing, Endersby-Finnis-Holmes. My goodness that is a real mouthful. Has your family always had double-barrelled names?"

"To be honest Victoria, beyond my grandfather who was born in Wapping, I have no idea ..." he murmured. "Too busy researching everything else to be bothered with me, I'm sure we were boring and non-descript. Victorian London working class in Dickens time, who were fortunate to have survived beyond childhood."

Taking her hand he led her through the former tiled scullery, with a couple of old black pots still hanging on hooks. "Now what do you see on that wall?" he asked her, pointing down one side.

"Paint, a bit of soot, okay, nothing out of the ordinary."

"Come closer, now tap here then here.

She tapped down the wall, and the dull sounding thud of solid brick was evident behind the plaster, but then it changed to a hollow echo. "Gosh, Julian a false wall, but very cleverly done, I would never have know."

"Yes, a craftsman lime plasterer I suspect, but to the eyes of a conservator, it can be spotted," he chuntered, pleased with himself.

"Okay know-it-all, now what?"

"I think the entrance to the stairs is here and has been closed up. Why who knows. But with your permission, as owner of this stately abode, I'd like to belt it one with my trusty sledgehammer over there and find out, and I promise faithfully to restore it as good as new if I'm wrong."

"You'd better ... my word Julian. Go for it."

He picked up the heavy sledgehammer and swung it hard against the wall as she stood well back. The wall shook with a loud bang and cracks shot up and down the plastered area.

He stood back, panting and fished into his rucksack for a drinks can, taking a large swig. "Irn-Bru!" he shouted over and began to peel off his shirt. "I'm going to have to give this some welly."

He swung the sledge hammer again with a great thuck and the covering in the middle cracked from top to bottom. She gazed at his muscular sweating six foot five half-naked physique, all tanned, rippling muscles and biceps and sighed, feeling suddenly as hot and clammy again inside as she did earlier. By now the others, hearing the noise, had all trooped down, led by Abby, mugs in hand, and walked in.

"No Abby," Victoria grinned, fingers to her lips, seeing Abby staring, mouth dropped open at a muscled half-clad Julian ready to give the wall a third mighty belting.

"What's going on?" Eva shouted as they all stood around at a safe distance. The third whack produced a belly in the wall and a large horizontal zigzagging hole, chunks of plaster dropping off. A thick piece of wood could be seen behind.

"Just watch," Victoria shouted back as they all continued enjoying the show with Julian preparing to give another monster swing. Gathering momentum with a whirl of his feet, he landed a massive fourth hit. The wood cracked apart, taking the rest of the plaster with it and a flimsy brick covering behind collapsed, a great cloud of muck and debris rising, showering Julian with red dust but missing everyone else.

Everybody stared into a huge black hole in the wall. Lynton pulled up all the sash windows and the dust cleared, as a distinct cold draught began running over everybody's face.

As Victoria approached, Julian pulled across his arm to stop her. "Me first, must be careful."

An original brick and tiled wall could now be seen at the back of the hole and the top of a stair-rail leading down into total blackness, when Eva shouted. "Look Julian there on the side, it looks like an ancient bakelite switch like my grandmother had in her old house."

Julian pulled the switch down and a flood of electric light went on below, the light pouring upwards from the void. He peered down. "Jesus fucking Christ. Sorry Victoria and everyone, I don't normally swear, I just cannot believe ... let me go down first to be sure the stair isn't rotted," ... seeing Victoria surging forward, eyes wide.

They heard him clump to the bottom, with Victoria now at the top and staring down. Her whole body trembled; it was an amazing and unexpected sight. "Oh my goodness," she shouted. "You're not going to believe this, Eva you especially, but there's a complete science laboratory down here," now edging her way down the wooden stairs into the well lit area.

Soon everyone was in the cellar, but really it was a very large basement, at least forty feet long and twenty feet wide, running a good length under the house. Earth and sand had been piled up outside, against the small windows near the ceiling and it was clear to everyone that the cellar, and the laboratory, had been clearly hidden at some stage in its history, by someone. But why and when?

Marlies was staring up at the array of electric light bulbs, hanging in holders in rows, from a master cabling system fixed to the ceiling, which was oddly high for a cellar, probably twelve to fourteen feet. Perhaps it had been purpose dug out originally. "I did my masters in electrical engineering on the evolution of electrical motors and lighting. At the time I was looking for clues from old methods a hundred years back, reinterpreted with modern technology to write a thesis."

"You mean like the wind-up radio?" Eva immediately interrupted animatedly, Abby looking on and taking in the body language ... now even more happily.

"Yes, exactly," Marlies replied, smiling back. "These light bulbs are very old. This is the first time they've been on for many decades I suspect, and they're frosted. From the design and the shape and pattern of the filaments, early tungsten. I would say they were one of the first of their types available commercially, inert gas filled, and given their relatively short lives, I would say mid to late 1920s or so. Frosted bulbs were invented in the US in 1925."

"Okay," Eva continued. "But look, cough drop ... sorry, Victoria ... at the state of the apparatus and benches, the glass jars on the shelves; goodness there are many still with liquids and powders sealed up. This is like observing an exhibition in the Science Museum, with 19th century objects and artefacts. The lighting was put in later. At the time they were probably using gas mantles, given the abundance of coal gas. We are looking at where the experiments took place that Marlies and I have finally documented, with amazing results. My word, over there are ..."

"Flagons of concentrated sulphuric and nitric acid, which combined with distilled coal tar products like nitrobenzol and aniline, produce ..." Victoria added ...

"Dyes!" Abby finally chipped in, getting bored with the Marlies and Eva talk show. "Look at that shelf with those bottles over there, all kinds of coloured liquids, various hues of mauve, orange, yellows and greens. I know a lot about the history of dyes and if this laboratory was running in the 1860s they were very advanced for the time, maybe revolutionary ..."

"They were." Eva cut in sharply before turning pointedly back to Victoria. "Marlies and I have now transcribed what I believe are the most illuminating scientific papers, between 1863 and 1866 and left them with notes upstairs. I am quite amazed as you will be Victoria. And the female laboratory assistant in the painting? I think we've identified her name, again another eye-opener."

"So what is her name?" Abby cut in again, determined she would not be shut out of this discussion by Eva with her increasingly apparent attitude problem.

"Mauveine."

Victoria stared blank and Julian and Lynton also looked at each other baffled. What a peculiar name.

"Not so strange though is it Eva," Abby replied stiffening up, her face reddening. Lynton noticed and squeezed her hand gently.

"No Abby, given the research she was doing, no it isn't."

"Sorry both of you," Victoria intervened now sensing some sort of stand-off between the two of them, in her cellar, or should she say, personal laboratory. "Excuse the French, but what the fuck are you both talking about?"

Julian gently squeezed her hand too from behind, as Marlies stiffened.

"Dyes," Abby continued, her gaze remaining fixed on Eva. "I know this is not your strong point Victoria, but the first synthetic chemical dye was discovered in 1856, accidentally by a student, William Henry Perkins. He was looking to try and synthesise quinine for malaria treatment, but ended up messing about with coal tar derivatives and made stuff to produce a purple dye, called aniline purple that by the end of the decade had been given the French name mauve which the scientists labelled eventually mauveine. The colour took off in 1862 when Queen Victoria appeared at the Great Exhibition in a silk gown, dyed with mauveine. Mauveine kicked off a European race later in the textiles industry for bigger and better dyes and colours."

"Absolutely correct. Abby has an extensive historical knowledge of dyes for a non-scientist Victoria," Eva responded.

"I have a PhD in dyes and textiles actually, Eva," Abby replied coolly.

Julian diplomatically intervened, stepping forward to break the tension as they all stared at his tall frame, shirt loosely slung back on and glasses, which Victoria had been holding, well wiped. "You mean that the laboratory worker in the painting was called Mauveine, the same as the dyes that she was experimenting with, in this very laboratory we are standing in?"

"Yes," Eva responded. "But whether it was a nickname or why, we don't know. Perhaps that is elsewhere in other papers or private diaries, we don't know exactly who she is." A text ping punctuated the contemplative silence and Eva looked down at her phone. "Sorry, have to go outside and make a call."

Julian shook his head, disturbed in some way.

They continued to look around, intrigued by the way the laboratory had been left, which apart from the gathered dust, was as if it someone had been in the middle of an experiment and then the whole room had been frozen in time. Shelves lined the walls with old chemicals in bottles and apparatus. Evaporated liquids leaving solution stains lay inside test tubes and flasks in holders and on stands. A large Wolff bottle stood majestically with some sort of acidic yellow gel in the bottom, next to a copper retort, a Bunsen burner underneath still connected to a gas tap with the tap still on and the heat collar on high. Victoria sniffed hard, not a sign of gas, coal or natural, nor any lab notes or papers. A pile of other similar equipment lay everywhere.

Marlies, Julian and Lynton were admiring the ancient large glass fronted fume cupboard, laughing and sharing old school chemistry experiences, as Abby sidled alongside Victoria, who was still pondering heavily.

"Incredible find isn't it, but something has happened here. This room was deliberately shut up and hidden away very quickly, but why and when? From what Marlies has been saying it must have been later than the 1860s. I've been thinking. Remember what Eveline said about your Uncle William's girlfriend Alicia who ran from the house screaming and drowned herself in the canal, and from that moment he became totally reclusive? Look, Uncle William was a Cambridge scientist who came back and reopened the house in the mid 1920s. This laboratory would have been here. Perhaps he starting dabbling again in the former family science work, you know, dyes and stuff, the factory was still here then too, coal plentiful, a good business opportunity. And at that time there was a growing economic boom in the UK, post World War One, the bubble didn't burst until the early nineteen thirties when the depression took hold. For a high society household, pillar of the community, it was the roaring twenties, music, parties, fun as Eveline hinted at. Then Alicia dies … she's buried next to him in the graveyard incidentally …"

"Really? I don't want to look there yet; don't ask me why, I need to feel more comfortable in here, although it's coming. Carry on Watson, you have an amazing brain inside that head of yours, it makes a lot of logical sense to me too."

"I know, when I can be arsed to do something sensible, but don't worry about the graveyard, I understand … it can wait … Anyway, do you see where I'm heading?"

"Yes, Alicia experienced something, perhaps in this very room and fled and then William wanted to shut it out of his life

217

forever. He probably did the boarding up. Oh God Abby ... I'm frightened to be honest, but also my curiosity and need to get to the bottom of the whole conundrum is so strong, and necessary, I have to keep going with it ..."

"We both do, so I'll be sticking close by you. Hey where's Marlies going now?"

Marlies had dashed up the stairs and out and Eva hadn't returned either. Victoria called everyone and they decided to finish in the laboratory and wind up for the day at the Liverpool Arms, all pleased to be heading out again from the dank cellar into the fresh air. They began to walk into the entrance to fetch their things when Abby pointed towards the far end of the car park, and tapped Victoria's arm.

"Wonder why Eva is sat in her car, with Marlies?" seeing both in furious worried discussion. Victoria nodded her head nonchalantly and they continued inside, animatedly admiring Lynton's lady in the lab coat painting once more, now with a name, Mauveine, as Eva walked back in, Marlies silent some way behind, both very concerned about something.

"Eva, what's the matter, are you not feeling well?" Victoria immediately asked putting her arms around her former partner and planting a kiss on her cheek, not caring who sensed why or what. Julian and Lynton had already headed for the kitchen fridge to pull a beer and find some crisps. Abby went back outside.

"I'm sorry Victoria," Eva replied. "Just had some bad news, I'll have to go. I can't believe it. My head teacher has just been taken into custody for serious fraud and some idiots have broken into the school and done real damage, principally wrecking my office completely and spray painted graffiti all over the walls, would you believe bright purple. That was the chair of governors; I'm now in charge being first deputy, so that's the rest of the summer gone. Marlies has volunteered to come back with me and sort out the security and computers, which have been selectively smashed up ... I can take her back to the airport when she needs to return to Holland. I'm really sorry, good luck with this project. It's been wonderful to see you, you look ... happy and at ease. I'll be in touch. Must fly. My stomach feels terrible too with that strong smell of naphtha lurking in the laboratory. It needs some air in there."

As Eva was speaking, Marlies had sidled up to Abby in the front. "I'm going back home with her, there's been a serious crisis at her school."

"I know?"

"How, Abby?"

"Just sensed it somehow, don't ask. Anyway hope it all works out and gets sorted, sorry for earlier but she just got under my skin."

"You know she was prissy, don't you. Eva knows that it's all over for good. It's obvious to the world and his wife that Vikki's falling in love ... I've known her a long time in Holland, and I'm pleased."

Abby smiled back. "Me too, good luck ... both of you ..."

"Can I just say quickly," Marlies added. "I got the security CCTV Julian put up working so you can check it tomorrow. The scientific stuff is fascinating, everything I transcribed into readable English is in the pink folder. I also found some personal letters and put them in an envelope inside, didn't mention it to Eva. I think you should read them first."

Abby's eyes narrowed. "Thanks Marlies appreciated, you're a treasure. Eva is waving, you'd better go, don't forget to pick up your things at the Red Lion."

"No, cheers, Abby, and remember there's a wealth of information on social media for your research. I've checked you out, you're on everything unlike Victoria, so use it," and with a wave Eva and Marlies jumped into the car and were gone.

Victoria looked at Abby. "Did you smell naphtha down there?"

"No, I didn't smell a thing, bit damp that's all."

"Where's Eva and Marlies gone?" Julian shouted, walking over, another beer in his hand, whilst Lynton was quietly inspecting the wooden carvings on Uncle William's old walnut desk.

"Crisis at home, tell you later," Victoria replied, quite matter of fact.

"And, I know everyone is sick of chips and kebabs," Abby said joining in on seeing all the glum faces. "So … my treat tonight. Curry and rice, it looked really good last night," she added, to a resounding chorus of cheers and renewed smiles.

Walking out of the door, a flood of light immediately lit up the complete front car park expanse, the shiny beast and the dew covered gravel glinting back in various hues and colours. A tiny discrete camera on top of the high porch, visible only by the red led dot, swivelled into place, with Lynton staring up and waving stupidly.

Jumping into the driving seat, Victoria's iPhone pinged distinctively. "Mr Grey, you're on 'candid camera.' Hurry up, we're famished." She turned to Julian. "That makes me feel a hell of a lot better," planting a kiss on his cheek.

"Me too, thank goodness it all works, Marlies is a genius."

"And so are you," she whispered … happily, Abby in the back noting with relief, that Eva was not just gone for the night but finally gone for good.

Chapter Thirteen

Fourteen days later:

It was going to be her day of reconciliation, the moment to truly feel the fear. Victoria was convinced now the sooner she faced her inner demons the better. Today she would stay the night, her first in Orsbrick Hall. And without any hesitation, Julian had volunteered to be there with her, for protection of course, but what she really wanted was his endearing comfort and the physical feel of him near her. She noted that his enthusiasm had risen ten-fold when the furniture van arrived in the morning. The cast-iron bed was once more reunited with a companionable luxury mattress she had ordered online, and adorned with a new set of white drapes, thick cotton sheets and soft luscious pillows, carefully selected and amazingly arranged by Abby. He had turned up the thermostat a few degrees and lit a huge log fire in the massive fireplace. She felt cosy, contented and happy, reflecting that this was how her ancestor James McKenzie, living in Orsbrick Hall, must have felt during that heady social heyday and whirling parties in her ballroom, of the 1860s. Abby and Lynton had discretely returned to the Red Lion. It was another folk night again and she was needed ... Lynton in a panic.

Julian was in his shorts, upstairs with hundredweight bags of plaster and a large bucket, carefully repairing and artexing a damaged ceiling, having already plastered and repaired the damage caused around the entrance to her mystery science laboratory in the cellar. She could sense he was very happy restoring the house. Using his hands creatively was a necessary physical release and he had left the detail of the rest of the research work purely to her, simply taking in the summary at the end of each day. But she could see, the moment he rubbed his eyes and ran his hands through his thick grey hair that he was cleverly absorbing all she said, methodically and meticulously into that quiet scatty brain, because every night for an hour before he joined her in bed, she would hear him tapping away in his eyrie in the Red Lion attic, alone, quiet and transported into the world of his nineteenth century characters, completing another two thousand words. She didn't ask him what or who was inspiring that endless flow of words on a virtual page, and he didn't offer, but she knew it was Orsbrick and being with her.

She was waiting for the aga to heat up to make traditional scouse and vegetables, and a bramley apple crumble with real scientifically mixed and measured custard, as Mr Bird himself made in 1837. Curled on Uncle William's original long sofa, with a linen throw comfortingly wrapped around her legs, it was a perfect moment to reread, still in disbelief, the original science papers and draft letters of great-great grandfather James McKenzie, which Eva and Marlies had transcripted …

March 17th 1866 - to Dr Friedrich Kadolfsky, Frederick William University of Berlin.

My dear friend. It is so long since we enjoyed the pleasures of the intellect together, and I must add, with some nostalgia, the pleasures of the flesh too, as I assume you still remember that raucous night when we met those ladies from Norwich, in '52 at the Cambridge

Station and all of us running down the road chased by the Station Master and his assistant, brushes in hand!

But enough frivolity, I want to update you on my progress and elicit your opinion of the said works and results as I believe I am on the brink of an important way forward. I have as you recommended, garnered a valuable working friendship with the talented dyer Mr Thomas Wardle and his new friend, artist Mr William Morris. Morris is married, I must say to the most beautiful woman I have ever seen, Jane. Alas their marriage, unlike my own with my departed Susanna, does not seem as full of joy as I would expect, but creative men can be fickle; we scientists have robustness in our blood, I believe.

My discussions with Wardle inspired me to rekindle old research into natural dyes again, forcing me from the work I started on expanding the colour range of the purple mauve dye, now as you know made popular by the display of our blessed Queen Victoria at the Great Exhibition of '62. My assistant has been most assiduous and helpful in this respect, with outstanding research and I concur new discovery. Her intellect and dedication is first rate for a woman and she has taken everything in, and more, from all my personal teachings and knowledge over the past three years. 'Tis the damned pity that those bigots and idiots at Cambridge still refuse the entry of women. I pray and support that with my political work, this ignoble dissonance will one day be righted. Anyway I digress. My assistant's travail has thus freed me in my journeys so as to confer with other chemist entrepreneurs and bring new ideas back to her laboratory for consumption.

I must also add a little story before I summarise my conjectures for your valued opinion, which I have not told you before, but always gives me pleasure to think. When I discovered a newly born baby girl, left on the side of the canal water to die, twenty furlongs from here, Susanna and I could do no more in my clearest conscience than to take her in and look after the child, wrapped as she was in a purple shawl. As my studies then, as you recall, were occupied with the research for mauve and indigo dyes, later in '56 of course announced formally by Perkins, so I named her Mauveine from the French, sounding much like my close cousins, Madeleine and Eveleine. She has since transformed into my adopted daughter, and is my beautiful and intelligent assistant I refer to above. I think my good friend, with your humour, you will find this tale congenial and I will introduce you on your next visit to England.

Alas, my rambles have as usual, deflected from the objective of discourse on my new dye discoveries and time has run out, but I send you this as a taste for precise outlines next week.

With sincerity - James McKenzie

Victoria felt an immense sense of excitement but also discomfort from that chance discovery. The painting and the laboratory were all attributable to this beautiful Mauveine, James McKenzie's adopted daughter. At last she knew who the mystery woman in the purple shawl must be, now with a name, odd but pertinent though it was. She was another chemist, a scientist the same as herself and remarkably similar in features, but obviously coincidental as Mauveine was found abandoned and adopted. But what was driving the restless spirit that she, Julian and Abby were seeing? What had happened to not allow her to rest? She wanted to discuss this immediately with Julian and Abby but would need to wait until the morning. She picked up the next paper.

March 24th 1866 - to Dr Friedrich Kadolfsky, Frederick William University of Berlin

My dearest friend. As promised the latest findings, but it has been a very difficult week, with tension and bad words between the staff, myself and Mauveine. They are jealous and petulant of her position, believing she is merely a boatperson and not deserving of my attention and indulgence of her talents, all coming to a head as she can read and write fluently and beautifully, unlike those illiterates on the barges, except of course for my head butler. I think she could have been an artist too, if she had dwelt in the household of my new friend and painter Rossetti, a close confidante of Wardle and Morris and his wife Jane. Rossetti wanted to paint Mauveine in the pond, with lilies and in some state of undress, which I could not of course permit, but I allowed him a quick session in the obvious place, her laboratory, the result being quite pleasing. There is a reason for this apparent diversion, please bear with me, my friend.

Now, my new preoccupation, with alizarin, which as you know has been used throughout history as a prominent natural red dye, taken from the root of the madder plant. The dye is being studied by Wardle and Morris to find better textile application with mordant and colour variations, one affecting the other. The plant of course, grown in enormous quantities, is the only source of this valuable dye and paint pigment.

Mauveine and I, in our collaboration over the last twelve months, have discovered a process, hinted at as a possibility and rumour in some chemist quarters, but all going down a dead end. This process, which we have replicated in the laboratory, has established a relationship between alizarin and the coal-tar hydrocarbon anthracene, which Mauveine has assiduously demonstrated to me. Key to this relationship was Mauveine's ongoing dialogue with a Dr Anderson who in '62 established the formula for anthracene of $C_{14}H_{10}$ and this set her thinking, as it is a solid with relationship to benzene, and may have useful applications if better researched.

Anthracene has very little known about it and although produced from coal tar has no applications and is not prepared by tar distillers. So I agreed with Mauveine that if she pursued more research I would use our coal distillation plant, which I permit for all our commercial dye production trials, to produce sufficient quantities of anthracene as well, being very fortunate on having access to any quantity of coal and coal tar I need from the local gas works, which I also own and manage. Normally pitch is distilled to acquire small quantities of anthracene, a tedious, expensive and time consuming process, but I have discovered that by cooling off the last runnings of our tar stills, we can filter out crystalline products which form the raw basis, with further heating and purification, of anthracene itself, in commercial quantities which would amaze you.

But now to the nub of my discourse. Mauveine has found through judicious permeation of dissolved anthracene with bromine and some further induced oxidation, that a bright red liquid is produced. With careful distillation and testing of the substance, she has produced the solid red colouring matter itself which is identical in composition to alizarin and its chemical relative purpurin, the two colorants within the madder root itself, discovered by Robiquet in '26.

Now, you will see the outstanding importance of this discovery, because Mauveine has produced the very first natural dye by artificial means. I am aware of other researches in Germany on similar lines and will forward some names later, but I wonder if you might then have the time and disposition to elicit how far they have progressed, because my desperate plight is to quickly produce a full paper for the dying and textile establishment and establish our precedence for England in this discovery.

Indeed even more significantly, Mauveine has found that replacing bromine with sulphuric acid, not only produces a more conducive reaction but the quantities obtained have, with refinement, the real potential to be produced on a commercial scale. This would be an economic goldmine for us here at Orsbrick, especially combined with my commercial tar production of the raw material anthracene. If this became established then certainly the whole madder plant industry would disintegrate, but the world of dyeing would expand massively in scope and scale.

To this end Mauveine has also been conducting side experiments with the synthetic alizarin compound and by fusing with certain alkalis used as a fixing mordant, and leaching with anthaflavic acid, has noted that the colorant is not pure but has proved to be three in number, one of which has the composition of the other madder root dye, purpurin. The third she is still testing using potassium chlorate as a stabiliser. She has an astounding gift of being able to mentally discern patterns and linkages across these compounds and is confident of increasing the scope of colours by including cyanine and other nitrobenzol derivatives in the mix, although I have to gently curb her enthusiasm, as I worry about the toxicity of these substances with their overuse in the laboratory.

As you will well understand, the introduction of a hydroxyl into a body by the fusion of its sulphonic acid with alkali, then a monosulphonic acid should be the proper outcome to produce an alizarin formula, but Mauveine is convinced that the oxidation could be improved considerably and is testing new applications with …

At this point the paper was torn and illegible. She could find no further references, in fact had this letter even been sent? Or was it just a copy which never got further than his desk, noting the crossings out and spelling errors corrected. The one later letter of April 20th 1866 gave a clue. It was another fragment, the beginning and ending had been made illegible with either damp or water over the paper, but she could make out a correspondence between the two friends over another

Mauveine discovery of a range of orange, yellow and green dyes which Thomas Wardle and the painter Rossetti were going wild over for their possibilities in clothing and art.

She thought harder about Mauveine and did some quick superficial historical science searches on the internet Not only was she beautiful but Mauveine was a genius before her time having preceded the eventual published papers and discoveries of these dyes years later and in some instances thirty years later. In fact some of the other papers, written in 1865, indicated that Mauveine was already on the track of commercial production, identification and uses of dyes and pigments, which are being followed in the present day. Her discoveries were incredible, mind-blowing for the time, almost unbelievable that a self-educated woman could evolve into such an amazing scientist, in such a short period of time. But the papers stop at the April 1866 date, no more could be found. What had happened? And was this the time when something happened to Mauveine, to cut her life short and her incredible potential off at a stroke?

She was feeling dizzy, frightened and heady, with all kinds of possibilities and scenarios working haphazardly through her mind. What she needed to do next was work through the private papers upstairs and see if anything was forthcoming. She needed to calm down, breathe deep and take a break desperately. The aga should now be heated up nicely, Julian having done a tremendous job in cleaning it out further with Lynton and the pair of them getting it to work again.

She set off into the kitchen and opened the fridge for two bottles of Belgian lager. It was time the workaholic Julian knocked off, cleaned up and relaxed, perhaps an early beer would be the best catalyst, then a nice traditional meal and …off to bed … mmm …

But in the background, her attention was caught by an odd sound. It was music of some sort. She listened harder and realised it was old dance band jazz music, the sort played in the 1930s or later but where on earth was it coming from? But of course, she realised, it must be one of those old 78's, goodness, Julian must have also got that old record player actually working, heaven knows how.

But the sound was coming a little way away, towards the end of the house. Putting her head out of the front door, she saw the light through the cellar windows, now cleared before the JCB went back. Julian was obviously down in the science laboratory with some surprise to show her. She shivered a little in the chill air outside but then wearing a flimsy cotton summer dress was perhaps not the best of choices, and slowly walked down, dusk rapidly approaching, tripping the security lights.

Opening the door of the boiler house the sound suddenly got much louder. The new door to the cellar laboratory was wide open, the light flooding up the stairway. Julian was down there, but all that racket, she thought, must be making him deaf the volume he had turned it up to. She began slowly walking down, trying to adjust her eyes to the glare.

"Hi Julian, I've got some beers here. What have you found to show me, apart from the record player which is amazingly clear? It makes you feel just like being in a 1920s club coming down here. Julian, where are you?"

She got to the bottom and put the beers on the bench, looking around and then she saw him, partly shadowed right at the far end. The whole space seemed twice as big, when she suddenly realised he had got the nailed up partitioning freed up and opened. There was a huge extended area beyond, and the lighting was weird, a dull bluish spectrum, like a nightclub gone wrong, realising that the bulbs were, for some reason, very old mercury vapour lamps, which she had seen operating once in the Science Museum. In the gloom she could make out all kinds of large metal distilling appliances, buckets, barrels and interconnected pipe-work. There were industrial benches along one wall but this was no science laboratory. Obviously they had added a small proof of concept commercial plant, to test out results on a larger scale following Mauveine's work in her laboratory. A clever idea. Old rusty chains, clamps, ropes and wooden pulleys were hanging everywhere, on the walls and ceilings, and a huge round black vat sat at the very back underneath a chimney vent. Then she made out a reddish glow, like some sort of coke fire underneath the vat burning. There was a smell in the air too, a cross between aniline, naphtha and smoke. What on earth was he doing?

"Julian, where are you? This is pretty amazing down here just like a museum. We could make a fortune giving tours I reckon. Sorry Julian, I can't see you in that gloom. How did you get that coke lit?" She could feel her voice wavering, it was chilly despite the coke fire, but she was feeling a little apprehensive.

A rustle from behind startled her, but when she turned Julian was standing there, smiling. She stared at his attire and laughed. "I have to say, you steampunk writers certainly have an imagination. I never heard you getting cleaned up. I assume you found those clothes up in the servant's room; it's a bit of a surprise, but a fabulous idea for our first night here together. You look just like an old family doctor. When we go back in, I know where there's a trunk with some 1920s dresses inside, so I'll try one on and match you, then we're really getting into the swing of the place." She peered over at the bench. "Can you turn that music down a bit please?" she pleaded, watching the old record revolving at a fast 78 speed.

She smiled as he bent forward and slowly turned the volume down, trying to work out whether the smart black jacket and matching waistcoat, crisp striped cotton shirt, red tie, polished black brogues and those interesting looking baggy fine corduroy trousers were 1860s or 1920s as she wasn't that fully au fait with the fashions of either time, wishing Abby was here too with Lynton to share the fun. They could have all dressed up and had a party.

He still hadn't said anything, but slid under the light, out of the shadow, pulled his pocket watch up and stared at the time, and it was then that it immediately struck her. His glasses had changed, and they were not his sleek bifocals but something with much heavier frames and very thick bottle lenses.

"Julian, where are your glasses? How on earth can you see through those lenses?" she said in a jaunty but increasingly apprehensive tone. Something just didn't feel quite right.

He looked up slowly, ignored her and gazed to the back at the coke fire. "Well, are you going to or not?" he uttered, his gaze boring into her through the bottle lenses, but not the usual Julian sexy undressing stare, but with a hard malevolence she didn't recognise.

"Sorry, do what Julian? Okay, let's cut the play acting now and the funny voice. I'm impressed, but shall we grab those beers and go back up because I need to put the scouse pan onto the stove."

Suddenly he leapt forward and grabbed her shoulders hard his face close to hers. Why was he frightening her so much? She tried to move but his strong grip was too overpowering, as he held her firm.

"You fucking whore, Mauveine," he screamed in a deep and heavily Lancashire accented posh voice, the voice of a much older man. "You've been doing it day in and day out with that bloody loser in the stable; I've seen you, slag, in the straw, undressed and naked, with that uncouth lout. You knew how I felt about you, and how much I wanted you. Well, he's not having you, and neither is anyone else." He grabbed a rope, pulled her arms together and began binding her wrists tightly.

She was petrified, she couldn't understand, nothing made sense; why was he calling her Mauveine? Oh God … Julian …

When he removed his glasses, she knew. His eyes were watery, yellow and narrow, like a wolf, and his teeth were tobacco stained and discoloured, with deep lines in his baggy pockmarked eyelids. The rest looked like her Julian, the hair, the build and the features were identical, but this person was not Julian. He was someone else, from another time, another dimension, even another world …

The full horror hit her as he shoved her forcefully over onto the dirty floor, hitting her head against a wooden cupboard … staring like an old lecher at her exposed thighs. She screamed loud and piercing, the noise echoing round and round the vast, bare walled enclave, but all he could do was laugh; a low, hoarse and throaty laugh, coughing deeply as he expunged the sounds, like he had some bad chest complaint. She screamed again and again, helpless and disorientated, feeling her body weakening and her head pouring blood. Her legs were being dragged forward, she had no strength to resist the pulling and jerking as another rope was being bound around her ankles until she couldn't move. Her voice was hoarse, she had no screams left …

He looked at her, pained, his mouth dripping saliva, panting with the exertion of an old man but in a young body, and his foul breath stinking of stale tobacco. The room was becoming hotter and hotter. Even in her flimsy cotton dress she was sweating buckets, the coke fire really catching up. He threw off his jacket impatiently onto a bench and carefully rolled up his

232

white silk shirt sleeves, securing them with elastic metal arm bands, waistcoat still tightly done up. He then walked slowly, almost painfully, with a pronounced limp towards the vat, wiping his brow continuously with a pale pink handkerchief.

The sides of the huge black enamelled container were high, up to his shoulders, as he stood on a stool and dipped a large metal ladle into the liquid contents, drawing it up into the air. Tipping the contents back, she watched and shuddered. Bright purple liquid, already warm and steaming, plopped down with a splash inside. He was heating up a huge vat of dye, purple dye, mauve dye … Mauveine …

She managed to let out another scream, which hollered for half a minute using all her breath until she stopped exhausted, croaking, "Julian, for fuck's sake, snap out of it … it's me, Victoria, Victoria McKenzie … Julian, listen to me …"

But her remonstrations were fruitless. She couldn't move as her body was now tied to the iron leg of a furnace. He ignored her totally, before returning and standing over her, still panting, but she could smell a putrid, filthy stench from his body, like state sweat but ten times worse. Fumes from the vat could be seen rising into the chimney, shimmering in the odd noisy lights, some form of ancient, carbon filament mercury vapour bulbs, hissing and buzzing on thick, black cables. And those fumes had a familiar smell. Aniline, again. He was boiling up some dye mixture with an aniline base.

"You know something Mauveine, you have a strong pair of lungs on you, the same as the day you were born and they brought you in here. You can scream all you like, so go on; there is not a soul in the house. They've all gone out to the races, so no one will hear you. I like your screams and seeing your frightened face; not so snobbish and particular now are we. You can beg too, but I warn you first, it's too late."

Her mind began looping back to things that had been seen, said or conjectured, running superfast, like a digital data stream outpouring into the ether, her brain bytes and bits shooting around her head ... settling on what Julian had observed that first day ... he had seen Mauveine too, but not on her own. She had a companion, a young man, who was he? Why had she not thought of it since, and in particular why hadn't he spoken of it again? And the horses too? Julian had said there were horses, one white and one black and that they were riding away out of the estate ... what did that mean? Oh God, she wished her Julian was here, and Abby and Lynton ... where are they? ... Please help me ... Her brain tracked back to the Red Lion, and then the George and that horrible incident ... whoever those people were, they also knew he was not Julian. Who was this person that inhabited Julian's body? Or is this the real Julian? All along surreptitiously working his way into her confidence, planning this whole thing carefully, a massive clever subterfuge, even making her fall in love with him ... shit, shit ... She wanted to cry, she sobbed and a tear rolled down her cheek.

He frowned and bent down, wiping the back of her head with a rag gently, pushing her hair up first to try and make a bun, and then tying it methodically into a ponytail with a piece of cord. The blood from her head wound was now stopping, it was the blow that had jarred her and was making her head ache badly.

She tried another tack and began to ask him questions. "Who are you? Where are you from? Why are you doing this? This is the year 2010? Who the fuck are you, you bastard?"

But it made no difference. It was like he was stone deaf, totally ignoring her as he checked the vat of dye again and started fiddling with the stiff, rusty chains and wooden pulleys hanging on a moveable gantry from the ceiling nearby fixed to a kind of iron track, used, she pondered, to once haul up buckets of chemicals or materials to tip into the vat. It was that conclusion which immediately sent a deep chill throughout her whole body, from head to toe, as the end game became clear, and she cried, and screamed and sobbed and shouted, all to no avail.

Her brain finally began pulling the facts and conclusions together at breakneck speed. She had to understand, she had to know. This was how Mauveine had died, murdered, boiled alive in a vat of boiling purple dye by this sadist in 1866, who now needed a repeat performance, because she was now Mauveine again. She had become a weird, satanic sacrifice, necessary to perpetuate something resoundingly evil, which had gone on ever since that terrible event in 1866 ... but of course ... the music, the nineteen twenties dance band, Alicia, the unexplained suicide. Alicia had come out of somewhere in the house screaming hysterically and then dived headlong into the canal and drowned ... She was here, Uncle William's girlfriend. Perhaps she had found out something and for whatever reason, hearing the music of course, came down to the science laboratory, expecting to find Uncle William. But instead she found a version of Uncle William, this evil monster. And whatever he did or said, hadn't worked because she escaped ... then killed herself from the unbelievable terror of what she saw ... oh God ... the flashback ... the canal bank when she was fifteen, the pointing hand and the purple floating pig ... but it wasn't a pig ... it was Alicia, found dead the next day ... oh God, please help me ...

He came back again, leering, calm and assured. "I calculate we have about fifteen minutes, Mauveine. Mmm ... that lovely white cotton dress of yours? Time to demonstrate your so called genius Mauveine, that this dye really sticks well with the mordant you invented."

She watched him, wide-eyed and silent, as he walked again to the vat and pulled out another two-handed huge ladle of the hot dye, tested it with his finger, returned and instantly poured it completely over her head. It was like stinking hot bathwater, warm but not scalding; it made her jump as she coughed and spluttered, whilst he wiped the purple liquid away from her mouth. She looked down and she was completely dyed purple, her hair, skin, legs, feet and her dress, soggy and wet, clinging to her tightly, as he slathered again at the sight of her shaking her head and body.

"Oh God, no ... Julian ... no, no, no ..."

"Well Mauveine, as I said they brought you in covered in purple, and fittingly of course you will be going out the same way. Have you ever seen a frog, Mauveine, placed in a pan of water which is then heated to boiling point? For some reason they just sit there as the temperature rises, never moving, resigned to their fate. Never understood why that was so, but I expect Mauveine, inside that pretty genius brain, you know the full answer. Must be the same for humans ... time to find out don't you think, being the consummate experimental scientist?"

She began to struggle and scream, but her voice was hoarse as he put on a thick pair of gloves and carefully untied her weak, wet body, raised her arms and wrapped another thick rope tightly around them. Pulling and shoving as the contraption was heavy, he pulled the gantry along with a rope until she looked up and a hook on a chain was hanging over her head ... with a quick movement of the pulley, he placed the hook over the rope and began to carefully pull it taut, raising her arms as she felt her body being yanked painfully and slowly upward, in small jerks, to her full height, as she wriggled uselessly, like a swinging sack of sugar being loaded into the hold of a ship.

He stopped the moment she was fully vertical, her toes just touching the ground as she tried to shake herself off, skating across the slippery, oily floor to no avail. Her voice was almost gone. He held her firm, his face opposite and close, so she could again smell that awful breath of rotten teeth and gums, the purple dye dripping onto the floor from her dress and body.

"One more ladle, Mauveine," as he repeated it, and she screamed with the shock of the hotter liquid.

"Now," he said. "Last rites; I will naturally pray for your soul but you must understand Mauveine, there is no choice in the matter, it has to be done as decreed. All that lascivious lechery, with that bastard Isi, cannot be condoned, but I'm sorry to have to tell you, he won't be doing any more either. Already too late for poor old Isi, hanging there all lonely, but you'll be joining him soon won't you. Must do the horses though," he grunted, pulling out a knife.

"Isi?" she wailed at him. "Who is Isi?" before spitting intro his face.

He grimaced, slowly wiping his chin with the pink silk handkerchief, before spinning around and slapping her viciously across the cheek, her head jerking back hard with the impact. The room span and a sharp pain shot through her neck, as she spluttered and coughed, crying and moaning.

"One final thing Mauveine, we don't want to boil you up before revealing the truth about you and your nauseous sister Lydia."

She stopped coughing and looked at him silently. Sister?

"Good, glad to see your mental faculties remain as sharp as ever. Like father, like daughter, of course. McKenzie reverted to his lecherous and lascivious drinking ways too after Cambridge, down at the George with those filthy boat whores from the barges. Both before and after the death of his lovely wife Susannah. No respect, no piety and no self discipline. Yes, your contrived discovery was a well planned and executed secret, but I found out, always my job Mauveine to know the parish. You were found by your real father, James McKenzie. He will feel true, deep pain tomorrow for the rest of his life, but that will be his penance, to atone for those unforgiveable wrongs, especially to Susanna."

She stared wide-eyed. Mauveine and Lydia were sisters? Lydia was therefore her great grandmother, not her great great-aunt, which explains the near identical family resemblances, in the paintings, and why she has become Mauveine again, to be murdered, in the same way as 1866 ...

He looked at his watch. "Time's up, we're ready. Dye is nicely warmed up now, took longer than I thought but I must get a move on, McKenzie will be back soon. Up you go Mauveine."

Wheezing and coughing, he began pulling on the chains again and her body was jerked off the ground. She wriggled in the air, but it was useless as he slowly raised her higher and higher, her arms feeling like they were being wrenched out of their sockets ... she screamed, one final and long drawn out wail.

"Mauveine, where are you? Help me ... please help me ..."

Another rowdy night was ensuing down at the Red Lion, music wafting through the opened steamy windows, the usual crowd of local revellers enjoying themselves. Abby had pulled out all the stops and got the staff fully organised with food and drinks, and watched Lynton, happily behind the bar once more pulling pints and joining in the fun. She felt so good with him and she was sure for definite, she wanted it to go on, they were so incredibly compatible and complimentary. He was a man, who for the first time in her life, knew how to really wine, dine and romance her in the best restaurants in Liverpool, and excite her intellect with his amazingly wide knowledge of paintings and the visual arts. A man genuinely interested in her passion for textiles and fashion, which she had also found rekindled. Lynton had even suggested helping her to restart her business again, which had excited her so much she could hardly breathe.

But something else was bothering her that night. The pain had started early in the afternoon, strong feelings inside her brain, and she didn't feel good in herself. She decided to finally slink off back to her room and peruse the rest of the files Marlies had quietly passed to her, now that everything in the bar and lounge were organised and in full control.

It was all down to Lynton a few days ago that they had jointly solved one conundrum unexpectedly; but they wanted to surprise Victoria and Julian, following their first snuggle night together at Orsbrick Hall. She picked the folder up with the photo Lynton had run off on the colour printer and read it again. Unknown to everyone in the George, whilst all the kerfuffle was going on between Julian and that bizarre family and old woman, Lynton had snapped them all on his phone. A full image, looking towards the camera, of the teenage grandson helping his grandmother out of the pub was clearly visible. A quick call to Marlies for advice did the trick, after downloading her image recognition software with extensive scanning through Facebook. There was a good match, identifying a nineteen year old Andy Rimmer, living in Burscough, his grinning image clear on her laptop screen. The name meant nothing to her or Lynton, but the rest of the family, including obnoxious father, Peter, sister and even great-grandmother Agnes were unmistakably identifiable amongst his photo album and various recent entries, no privacy security having been set by the dork. However the name might ring a bell with Victoria or Julian.

She idly began to sift through the small bunch of letters, which Marlies had advised to be perused by her eyes only, and carefully undid the bow of the ribbon and unfolded the yellowing papers, marvelling at the clarity still of the dark spidery black-inked writing ...

To James McKenzie August 16th 1876

Dear Mr McKenzie - it is with a sad heart that I have learned of your recent debilitating illness, which on top of your other ill health endured for the last ten years, is a tough burden to shoulder, being now confined to a wheelchair, although I understand from relatives that your commitment to the local community and town has remained undimmed. I was also pleased to read in the press of your extensive work in the arts which I hope has given you much needed solace from your dreadful loss.

I was sorry to leave your employ, after the tragedy, but the opportunity in Leeds to oversee the engineering for the new Sedridge spinning mill was, as you agreed, too good an opportunity to turn down, especially as my wife and four children were ailing with consumption. I remain forever in your complete debt and gratitude for teaching me to read and write, and paying for me to partake of the mechanicals course at Ormskirk technical school, as without such lift I would have remained, for the rest of my days, illiterate on the boats.

I apologise for the great length of time writing to you, I have been so busy, but I thought you may be cheered to know that I am now general manager of the whole mill, in charge of three hundred people and the most advanced equipment possible, and have been offered a partnership by the owner. He has asked for a former reference, for legal reasons, and I would, if you are not too unwell, be grateful if you could supply said reference, for when I ran your distillation plant. I was sorry we closed it down so quickly, but I understand how, after Mauveine's death, you no longer had the stomach for further science and manufacture.

I want to finish with a matter which has bothered me for many years. I always knew, from the moment she was found, that you were Mauveine's real father. I do not need to tell how I came about such reveal, but I want you to know that I never held any inner malice or bad thought, and was pleased and proud of the way you and Susanna brought her up, instructed her in the sciences and nourished her pioneering spirit and inventiveness. She was in all respects, unlike her younger arty sister Lydia, but instead the mirror image of your scientific ambitions and aptitude. And when you formally adopted Mauveine, I felt proud and happy for all of you. I could never have done that, and given her the opportunity, as you will remember, especially as my first wife, Mauveine's mother, died soon after.

Finally, I want to state how badly I still feel, not only of the unwarranted death of Mauveine, but the ongoing sadness that the wrong man, Isaac Fazackerley, a talented and kind man, who could have made her a fine husband, was blamed. I remain as you do too, that we suspect the real culprit, but nobody would have listened and real evidence could not be found. I pray daily that justice will eventually be served.

I remain forever your servant and friend and hope your palsy remains manageable and reacts favourably to the new cure.

Jake Gibbons

Abby stared in disbelief at the revelations. Mauveine had certainly sadly died suddenly, perhaps an accident in the laboratory and this man Isaac Fazackerley took the blame, possibly wrongly for someone else who caused it. But even more astounding was that Mauveine and Lydia were sisters and both true daughters of Victoria's great-great-grandfather, James McKenzie. This was without doubt the Lydia in Eveline's picture and shows why the family likeness to Victoria of Mauveine and Lydia and probably Eveline in her youth, are so strong. But none of this explained why Mauveine's restless ghost haunted Orsbrick Hall. There had to be more, something darker and deeper, the timelines were definitely running back to her death occurring in 1866.

Abby's psychic imbalance was also continuing to increase during the day. She had no explanation, and her unease was driving her to continue the reading, despite Lynton's likely disappointment that she had escaped the party melee and come upstairs. She decided to play around with the local heritage group websites Marlies had emailed her, the first being the archive section of the former Orsbrick and Burscough Herald, a popular local weekly paper, which had died out in the 1960s. Local media enthusiasts had scanned and filed online articles and news of historic interest going back to the 1830s when the paper was launched, providing a treasure trove of local historic information. She went immediately to the winter of 1866 and began perusing articles. She found it slow going, working steadily through week by week, as the typefaces used and the structure of press English in that period were proving a real challenge. But the entry for the end of June 1866 caught her eye immediately. It was the front page headline and printed in massive large type ...

The Orsbrick and Burscough Herald June 29th 1866

Ghastly Murder at Orsbrick Hall
Dreadful Mutilation of a Woman

In the early hours of the morning of June 26th, the naked body of a young woman was found by family Head Butler, Harold Rimmer, floating in a vat of purple dye. Investigations by the Preston County Police Force and medical evidence of the state of the body from the local doctor, confirm that she had been perniciously assaulted and boiled alive in the dye during the previous evening. The woman, known as Mauveine, was the seventeen year old laboratory worker and adopted daughter of the honorary Mr James McKenzie, owner of Orsbrick Hall and the associated tar and dye works in the grounds.

Later in the morning, workers from the plant found the body of gardener and stables manager, Isaac Fazackerley, aged twenty-five, hanging from a rafter. One horse had been badly mutilated, since died, believed to be owned by the deceased woman and the other, a black gelding owned by Mr Fazackerley has disappeared and not been found.

A County Police Chief Inspector is now working with local police officers on the case and whether there is a link between the two deaths.

Sadly, Mr McKenzie, on hearing the news, suffered an immediate seizure and is now recovering slowly in hospital, but has lost the use of his voice.

The family is in a state of grief and shock, no further comment will be made and they have asked for their privacy to be respected.

Abby could barely contain herself. Now she understood the appalling severity of what had happened to Mauveine. The front page entry the following week was equally compelling.

The Orsbrick and Burscough Herald August 6th 1866

Deaths at Orsbrick Hall
Woman murdered by lover

In a rapid resolution to the case of the deaths at Orsbrick Hall reported last week, and from corroborated evidence found later at the scene, the Police Superintendent has concluded that Miss Mauveine McKenzie was incontrovertibly and horribly murdered by Mr Isaac Fazackerley in a jealous lover's rage. He then fatally mutilated her beloved horse and finally hanged himself with remorse. No further suspects are being pursued and the case has been formally closed and the coroner notified.

Mr James McKenzie, remains in hospital and is improving slowly.

Sitting back in her chair, Abby could only feel her head pounding louder and her whole body shaking and sweating with the shock. It was immediately clear, that after all these years of the facts being hidden and buried, why Mauveine could not rest in peace. Abby realised and understood fully. Poor Mauveine, both she and her lover had died tragically, a terrible crime of passion. She had to tell Victoria immediately and would drive over there. This information could be the necessary trigger for a peaceful end to Mauveine's restless spirit, if Victoria knew the truth. Everything was making sense at long last. She began to enthusiastically put on her ankle boots, Lynton would have to wait, when a flash of something odd and unsettling crossed her mind - the name Harold Rimmer, the butler who found Mauveine and the throw away final comment of James McKenzie's plant manager. Rimmer was the family that were convinced Julian was someone undesirable. There had been suspicion, not formally aired, of a misdeed and that Mauveine's lover, Isaac Fazackerley, was not the perpetrator of her death. Could this be the real key to finding peace for Mauveine, perhaps Jake Gibbons was correct ... oh God. She had to think more, wishing her pounding head would cease being on fire. Back to her laptop, she began a scour of the other heritage site and access to births, marriages and deaths which Lynton had enabled for her online ... useful his brother was an archivist in the related government office, so she had access to secret public census data beyond 1900 right up to 1951. They were still digitising beyond that. Fazackerley and Rimmer ... as she looked at collections of family trees assembled by volunteer enthusiasts. She found the death certificate details of Isaac, as stated by the local paper, but no details of Mauveine. Where was she buried? Lots of Rimmers too.

She ran through more family links, this was complex and head splitting, like doing her PhD all over again, and noted that Isaac had many younger siblings, boat people, ... something ... was it instinct or ... a push ... made her go back to the online paper and look around the period Jake Gibbons had sent that letter to James McKenzie. As she ran through the front headlines, she got to December 1876 and her eyes froze.

The Orsbrick and Burscough Herald December 21st 1876
Fatal stabbing at the George Hotel
Former Orsbrick Hall butler dies

A series of fights took place on the evening of the 18th December, between drunken boatmen, members of the Fazackerley and Rimmer families at which Harold Rimmer, aged sixty-six, a well known former butler for many years at Orsbrick Hall, was fatally stabbed. It was alleged that the fight started over a comment concerning a long held grievance and that Mr Rimmer attacked a Mr Nathanial Fazackerley, aged twenty-seven, in a frenzy with a knife and that in the ensuing tussle, as Mr Fazackerley attempted to defend himself, Mr Rimmer sustained fatal injuries to himself. Mr Fazackerley was unharmed. It appears that the whole pub then erupted in a mass brawl necessitating the calling out of all police officers from the Burscough Police Station to quell the disorder with many still locked up in jail, including Mr Nathanial Fazackerley. Considerable damage has been done to the public house and the landlord, Mr Henry Manchester, expressed concern that he may not be able to open for Christmas. However, unanimous eyewitness statements, including the landlord, confirm that Mr Fazackerley was merely acting in self defence and that Mr Rimmer fell accidentally onto his own knife, but convictions for disorderly drunken conduct and affray are expected at the next Magistrates Court. The Fazackerley family maintain, due to poverty, they will be unable to pay any reparations and express regret for the damage caused to the George, blaming the Rimmer family for starting it …

Abby's brain was buzzing along fast and drawing the kind of logical, scientific and rational conclusion, which falls like leaves off a tree for Victoria … Perhaps the feuding between the Rimmer and Fazackerley clans had continued, through the following generations, especially in a close knit rural community with strong family bonding, akin to Catholics and Protestants hating each other in Northern Ireland, as she had experienced too as a child in Manchester. Perhaps the modern day Rimmer family had thought Julian was a Fazackerley because he looked like one, or maybe because … he was one.

She rummaged about next online with census data, firing up the special user name and two access codes, Lynton had "borrowed" from his brother. She recalled the other week that Julian had mentioned his family came from Wapping, tapping into various search engines Endersby-Finnis, almost a unique brand rather than a name and easily finding his date of birth confirmed, exactly as Victoria had said, aged fifty-three. Gosh he looked fifteen years younger she sighed to herself. Lucky Vikki, although Lynton was definitely pretty cool and a hot male contender for an equals prize. And she definitely loved Lynton. Julian also had two older brothers and a kid sister. Then she spotted on Julian's birth certificate: mother - Finnis, father - Endersby. They had double barrelled up when his parents married a year after his birth, naughty, well for the time. She searched further, wishing this genealogy was easier, scribbling names and another skeleton of a family tree, then the entry came home to roost. Julian's grandfather. Died Endersby in Wapping, former name Fazackerley, born Burscough March 5th 1911. Hell … Julian was a Fazackerley! But … surely not possible … as she went into the census, births, marriages, deaths and finally the local heritage site again and traced his great grandfather, a boatman and his great-great-grandfather … one Nathanial Fazackerley, brother of Isaac Fazackerley, Mauveine's lover found hanged but both possibly murdered by someone else, perhaps a Rimmer …? Oh God … no!

An unexpected connecting link had shot across her mind; Alicia, girlfriend of Victoria's Uncle William found drowned and the strange happening with Alicia's grave that she had kept to herself. She tapped furiously into the keyboard again for the online paper and went immediately to 1929 and began the same front page headline trawl as before, week by week from January 1st … she hit the end of April.

The Orsbrick and Burscough Herald April 26th 1929
Woman drowns in canal at Orsbrick Hall
Unexplained suicide

On the morning of April 20th, a Miss Alicia van Gruyff, a London debutante, aged nineteen, was found drowned in the canal at the rear of the Orsbrick Hall, behind the coal tar plant. Mr Richard Rimmer, head butler, who found Miss Gruyff, commented that he and his staff had been searching during the night after he had heard a scream around midnight and she was not in her room. Miss Gruyff, a close friend of Mr William McKenzie, owner of Orsbrick Hall, was on a hunting holiday there with friends. Mr Rimmer also confirmed that she had been seen earlier drinking heavily and had confided to his female staff that she was feeling depressed and letters to that effect had since been found in her room. The police could find no evidence of criminal misdeed and the coroners court has ruled accidental death by drowning and likely suicide.

Abby jumped out of her chair, her breathing rapid and her head in turmoil ... she had to find Lynton quickly and explain everything, she couldn't keep all this to herself ... Rimmers ... all butlers ... both find Mauveine and Alicia dead ... Julian is a direct descendent of Isaac Fazackerley ... suspicions, allegations and more deaths ... what if the last Rimmer butler was still alive? Or his son or grandson and they were the ones who had been keeping an eye on the house because somebody had ...? They had keys ... oh God ... Julian and Victoria could be in serious danger, especially tonight ... and all the time Mauveine was trying to point the way to a wrongdoing which had gone back in time ...and maybe even before that. Abby instinctively had wider and far deeper suspicions.

And she too had prepared, assiduously, as a precaution ... there had been too many psychic warnings and signs, all that time spent in the central library unearthing family curses, witchcraft, death, burnings at the stake. Orsbrick Hall went back at least another 150 years before 1866, what if this had been a cyclical curse … that was even worse … Victoria and Julian were in more than danger of being attacked, they were in peril of potential eternal damnation, of the unleashing of evil so awful the consequences were indescribable … and that was the real reason for Mauveine's appearance … she had been a victim of such an evil doing, and so had Alicia, and Isaac … Mauveine was a warning, and this night would be the only opportunity to prevent Victoria and Julian following Mauveine, Isaac, Alicia and probably others before into some zombie eternity of the netherworld, where souls never rest and find peace but remain forever suspended and tortured, between the living and the dead. Eveline sensed and understood the danger but didn't have quite enough psychic perception or knowledge from the internet and social media, to square all the circles and interpret.

Her head was pulsating inside and she could feel a new sensation, giving her a needed strength of purpose and drive. It was Eveline. She knew, she had joined forces to help, it was down to her. Oh God, this effort could kill Eveline … if only …

She heard the door knob rattle and a knock and Lynton suddenly marched in, beer bottle in hand, his face lit up with an over-strenuous bout of karaoke and jesting with his crowd of lawyer friends celebrating someone's birthday party in the bar.

"We're having a ball down there, and I love you and … would you like to come down and join in the fun? …My word, what on earth is the matter? You look terrible."

She looked up, feeling weak and her head pulsating … and he just said he loved her for the first time … which was so amazing … but what could she do?

"Lynton … I love you too … we must get over to Orsbrick Hall, now. Victoria and Julian are in serious danger, trust me, I've discovered everything on my laptop."

"Hey Abby, I'm sure they're fine. They'd phone us if there was a problem, sometimes you worry about ..."

A loud tap, tap, tap, commenced on the outside window. They both looked up startled, then at each other. They were two floors high. The tapping continued again. Abby walked over and threw back the heavy velvet curtains, then looked down and her eyes widened, and she drew breath. It could not be possible. She yanked the latch and forced the tight window open, as Lynton joined her and they looked down below.

"Who the fuck are they, Abby? Sat on horses in fancy dress and waving this time of night? Christ, there are some odd people around here."

"We must go Lynton ... can you ride a horse?"

"Yes of course, the benefits of an expensive public school upbringing and obscenely affluent parents. Sorry, being stupidly facetious again, but who are they?"

"You can see them?"

"Yes of course, as plain as a pikestaff, whatever that means. Who are they?"

"It's Mauveine and Isaac, they've come to take us, come on, no time ... hurry."

"Pardon ...?" he muttered as she grabbed his hand and they clattered down the stairs, tripping and stumbling, Abby running for all she was worth.

They got to the backdoor and he undid the bolts then turned to her, his face going pale. "Abby, you said Mauveine and Isaac ..." he whispered hoarsely, trying to catch his breath. "Mauveine, and I assume her friend Isaac, have been dead for a hundred odd years!"

"No time to explain, trust me Lynton, now I know why they need you too," she hollered back, stuffing an envelope into her coat pocket, shoving open the door and finally running outside hand in hand. They stopped in front of the large white and black horses, quietly standing there patiently. The woman, in her purple shawl, clearly Mauveine, had demounted and was standing smiling, holding the horse, steam coming from its mouth. Her companion, a tall handsome man in brown breeches and thick jumper looked down, also with a friendly grin, from atop his black gelding. They said nothing. He then jumped down and held out his hand, steadily, to Lynton, turning and pointing to the double saddles. Lynton looked aghast, up into his face and then realised the same as Abby already knew ... he was looking at Julian, a younger version certainly, a kid brother, but the likeness was remarkable, and then staring at the woman in purple, recognised the same woman in the laboratory painting, named Mauveine, with another striking resemblance to ... Victoria.

"Bloody hell," he whispered. "What is this about? It scares the hell out of me ... Christ why aren't you petrified? ... This is weird Abby."

"Just get on the fucking horse with him Lynton and I'll do the same behind Mauveine. Trust me, it's fine, they're taking us to Orsbrick Hall."

"I think I'd prefer to go in the Merc if truth be known Abby ..."

"Get on it ..." she hissed, and jumped up into the stirrups behind Mauveine, holding her tight, or at least holding onto something an inch around her body.

He took Isaac's hand, now also on the black horse, except something was forcing him along, but it was not quite Isaac's hand, and did the same. Isaac and Lynton set off at a pace over the field at the back, with Mauveine and Abby in close pursuit behind but they were not following modern roads. In fact there were no roads, no cars, no people, only endless tracks, trees and fields, endlessly jumping over fences and hedgerows, through woodland, the clear full moon and cloudless sky, lighting their way well, as they hurtled past old farms with smoke billowing out, the whole world flashing by in greens and browns, ponds and gates ... the pace never relenting as if the horses had enormous boundless energy.

Soon, Abby began to recognise some of the landscape, they were getting nearer and she saw Parbold Hill, rising in the foreground, the moonlight carving out its looming shape clearly and unmistakably. The final fence took them past the woods and into the car park, the horses coming to a rapid stop outside the front door of Orsbrick Hall, their hooves slithering in the gravel ... but no sound. Abby jumped off, followed by Lynton, his face drawn and cold, their coats buttoned up tightly around them. They both looked up at Mauveine and Isaac, who turned the horses to face the end of the house and pointed ... a light was on which they immediately recognised was the boiler house. Abby knew straight away ... the wailing and driving forces inside her brain going into overdrive ... Victoria and probably Julian were in the laboratory. They looked back ... the horses were disappearing back over the fields ... it was now down to her and Eveline. She had to get this right and hope ... because now there was no turning back, for her or Lynton either.

She pulled out her envelope, tearing open the cover and handed Lynton a sheet of paper, whilst she scanned over her notes and sang a few high bars.

"What's this for Abby? What are we getting into? I love you and I trust you, but none of this makes any sense inside my dull lawyer brain. Although I recognise the words—they're a denouncement of some sort, written in arcane language. Who is Rimmer?"

"Lynton, I can only say this once. What you will see in there may terrify you and me, but we must hold firm, for Victoria and Julian's sake. You stay behind me. When I say so, you read out this script, which must be spoken clearly by a licensed legal practitioner of the Crown, which is you, and then I follow. If it works it will be the only way to prevent Victoria and Julian from an eternal hell and more. But you must promise not to laugh … promise?" she said, sternly.

"Yes, promise. But one thing. How do you know all this stuff? How do you connect? I can't fathom it out …"

"I was born with a psychic gift, Lynton, and Eveline has it too; we have had this since our childhoods. We recognised each other's capabilities when we first met, which is why she confided in me immediately. She is here now with us both, inside me, to give us extra strength. Eveline and I see and feel beyond what normal people … think of it like being able to see four dimensions. I can do it but you can't. Love me, and love my powers … easy."

"I do love you, I can see we have to get in there quickly, but I want to ask you something … here …"

He fished inside his pocket and pulled out a small box and handed it to her.

She peered at it, perplexed.

"Till death us do part, Abby, just insurance before we go in. Will you marry me?"

"Yes, you idiot, yes, yes …" she cried happily, his face changing from distinct worry, to an ecstatic grin, opening the box, to see a large ruby engagement ring, which she slipped immediately over her finger. She reached up and kissed him, whilst he ran his fingers through her pink, spiky short hair. "Let's go."

Opening the familiar boiler room door, they worked their way to the laboratory cellar stairs and began climbing down. A blast of heat hit them along with a stench of something awful and tar-like. They were hearing a lot of clanking of chains and general noise. They looked down the room, towards the unexpected opened out area bathed in the eerie mercury vapour lighting and saw a purple sack-like object, being winched up on a chain and then slowly pushed towards a large vat, a fire underneath roaring away.

"Oh God, quickly Lynton ... it's Victoria ... quickly before we lose her."

They raced down, clattering over pieces of metal and junk, the noise immediately attracting the attention of the person shoving the sack. He turned, stooping and panting with exertion, his horrible yellow eyes narrowing, and his dirty teeth exposed in a grimace seeing the unexpected intruders. She knew now for definite. It was him, and he'd taken over Julian's body. He stopped and Abby looked up to see Victoria, wet, dripping and bright purple from head to foot, dangling in a slow rotation from the hook, her head lowered and eyes closed, half dead but breathing still.

"Now Lynton ... read ..."

He lowered his script and began:

"Rimmer. On this day, and this moment, the 14th February 1666, by the legal power that rests in me from the Church and the Crown, I do declare that you are hereby excommunicated from this holy establishment of Orsbrick Hall, and that the evil and wrongdoings you have perpetuated to the McKenzie and Fazackerley families will now be judged by a higher power and sentence will be immediately passed and executed in accordance with the heinous gravity of your misdeeds, so help you."

He stepped back puzzled at the words, but Rimmer stood stark still, hugely distracted, his face growing perturbed and his body shaking. And then he growled, not a human growl but an animal like moan, deep and throaty, his body bloating out like a balloon, clothes splitting at the seams, and his face rounding, the yellow teeth chattering with a weird clicking sound. Victoria stirred and looked down at Abby, a smile forcing itself from her lips, before physical and mental exhaustion caused her head to loll forward again and her eyes close.

Abby began slowly and clearly, first a reading of incantations and spells, carefully assembled from the internet and the library, which had been used when accused witches and church heretics in the seventeenth century had been burned at the stake, the words interspersed with Rimmer's name.

She and Lynton watched in horror as Rimmer's motionless body began to dissolve, and drip thick smelly liquids onto the ground, all kinds of colours, purple, red, green, yellow, orange, like dyes, dissolving out of his putrefying skin.

Lynton horrified beyond normal reason, turned wide eyed in disbelief to Abby, who had begun ... to sing. She hadn't practised this style of choral singing since she was head chorister at her school, an elite public girls' school in Hampshire. The only activity she hadn't strangely rebelled at, but she was very good, a natural, following in the footsteps of her mother, a fifties club singer. Abby's voice was clear, penetrating and loud, the eerie tones echoing from wall to wall around the workshop, only the bubbling dye inside the vat disturbing the outstanding beauty of her voice. She sang modulated scales, with an unnerving and mesmerising precision and power; a form of Gregorian chant but written and uttered in such an arcane sounding Latin, that Lynton, despite his classics at Oxford, struggled to understand, realising this was a variant which could have been spoken in Roman times, or within an early plainchant, which monks and friars would be undertaking daily in their closed fifth century monastic orders.

The effect on Rimmer was equally hypnotic. It was as if he were an ancient Greek sailor being seduced by irresistible sirens and beckoning muses. Rimmer struggled to try and reach out his arms towards Abby and grasp her, but failed and groaned, a long, pitiful roar, as she continued her chants, composed now of ancient tarot rites and rituals, long lost in the deepest annals of history, the words and tones flooding into her brain, no longer from her researches but coming from elsewhere … through the additional strength, knowledge and power of Eveline.

The room began to shake, and a strange bright light lit up the rear behind the bubbling vat, as a spectrum change from the mercury violet gradually moved into higher frequencies and gathered all the lighting around together until only a vivid orange ball enveloped the vat and moved forward, inch by inch, towards Rimmer. He turned slowly and painfully, and the remains of his distorted bloated body shook violently. Lynton felt something grab his arm, and he spun his head fearfully to see Victoria, standing there dry, exhausted, in her white cotton dress, grasping him for support, whilst he held her tightly in his arms. The purple dye covering her had totally disappeared.

Abby finally screamed at Rimmer in old Latin. "Depart Rimmer, go forever, with your evil ways," wrapping her arms around Lynton and Victoria.

Rimmer stared first at her and finally at Victoria and released a long, curdling scream, the orange ball enveloping him. The whole room began to spin as a massive cataclysm of red and yellow flames shot from the ceiling, engulfing them all in a massive, blinding white explosion …

Chapter Fourteen

Gazing blankly out of the window, she shook her head hard, having gone into one of those silly daydreams where your brain totally shuts off and your eyes stare widely and idiotically into nothingness. Abby carefully watched Lynton, struggling in the dusk towards the front entrance with a large cardboard box from his white Mercedes coupe in the car park. The telltale tops of wire wound corked bottles poked out of the top. She looked down at her hand and gently rubbed the large ruby ring on her finger.

She turned and saw Julian, in his shorts, with white plaster powder in his hair and face, asleep and gently snoring on the wide wicker chair by the fireplace, the burning logs settling to a mass of red glowing warmth. Glancing through the half open doorway to the kitchen, she spotted Victoria, whistling happily, struggling to replace a large cast-iron black pan back onto the aga, the inviting smells of bubbling scouse wafting through into the sitting room.

Abby felt like she was both seeing and performing simultaneously in a theatre play, wondering and watching with awe and trepidation. Because her mind was crystal clear. She knew, she remembered, and she had experienced ... but her head felt like a ton weight had been lifted off, and a distinct lightness and satisfaction was permeating her whole body. She coughed slightly, her throat was very sore, then she realised, because she was being guided in her thoughts. Eveline was still there, but the intensity had changed ... and as Lynton walked in laughing with his box of bubbly she finally realised.

A chunk of time and space had been wiped out and reengineered in the unknown warps and wefts of those other universes which she was able to occasionally peer into. Victoria, Lynton and Julian were still in 2010, continuing seamlessly in time from where they had left off, totally unaware of what had happened, because that period no longer existed. The chants, the denunciations and the incantations had worked. Fortuitous it was, her finding and assiduously studying that old book in the upstairs library of Uncle William on church heresy abuses, and then finding the small illustrative piece, with matching engravings, where in 1666 a Josiah Fazackerley and Lucinda McKenzie of the parish of Burscough had been denounced as science heretics and witches for jointly perpetrating to the local community, the Copernican and humanist teachings of Galileo ... the denunciator being Friar Adam Rimmer, Abbot of the Orsbrick Priory. They had both been quietly burned to death together, by Rimmer and his monks, in the cellar of the newly built Orsbrick Hall.

Victoria came bounding back in, wearing the most gorgeous white cotton dress, showing off her ample figure to perfection. "My goodness Lynton, what have you got in that box of yours? What are we celebrating?"

Lynton looked at Abby and blushed, before blurting out. "Well, I sort of ..."

"He's asked me to marry him, outside in your car park, although he took a gamble that I'd say yes, having the celebratory booze already packed in the boot! But of course I said yes!" Abby replied happily, thinking fast on her feet. She threw her arms around Lynton and kissed him sloppily.

Victoria threw her hands up in the air and shouted back how wonderful it was ... but not before Abby caught a glinting diamond flash from Victoria's left finger and let out a howl.

"Oh gosh, Vikki, sleeping beauty over there has been rather busy hasn't he and not just plastering?"

Victoria waved her ring around in complete ecstasy. "Not quite as romantic as I might have envisaged, although he did get on one knee in his shorts and covered in plaster dust. Hey Julian, wakey-wakey," she burbled. "We're having a double wedding and Orsbrick Hall won't have seen anything like it for years!"

Julian stirred from his slumber, grunting and grabbed his glasses rubbing them gently on a floor cloth. "Double wattle? ... What wall material is that supposed ...?" then seeing Abby and Lynton entwined in each other's arms and his brain spun back into life. "Double wedding? Hey, you two, that is so fabulous," breaking into an instant grin spotting the bottles of champagne. "Come on Lynton, I'll just put these in the fridge. Scouse and bubbly later, what a combination."

They all laughed as Lynton, tottered off with the box and Julian into the kitchen, already in animated conversation, as Abby, in trepidation, caught him saying ... "And I must show you in a minute, I managed finally to get that partition in the science lab opened." She listened harder. "...but the whole area behind was completely empty, absolutely nothing, perfectly painted white walls, brushed clean and unlit. Must have become redundant for some reason ..."

Victoria checked the simmering stew, threw in some more chopped onions and carrots, and returned with some plates and cutlery. She sat quietly down beside Abby in the comfortable armchairs, facing the view of the woods and the pond through the lovely patio window, which Julian had repaired.

"We can open this now, just like Uncle William probably did when he first came here. After Julian proposed earlier, I felt a huge uplifting from my mind, everything felt good and happy. We're going to live here Abby, forever, both of us, this is my home and I will never move from it again. Something has changed and I believe, having been pointed to all those revelations in the papers and letters of James McKenzie and Mauveine and now that Julian and I are engaged it gives a final closure with ... err ... the spirits of Mauveine and Isi ... Julian and I saw."

"Isi?" Abby queried, desperately trying to work out what else had happened.

"Oh goodness, I haven't had time to tell you of course. Earlier today, Julian and I found these other letters, in that locked trunk in the wardrobe, you know the one you and I couldn't open, but he managed to prise the lid off."

"Well, Mauveine and an Isaac Fazackerley married and when her father, James McKenzie, died from palsy, they took over Orsbrick Hall. She continued her science work, researching on dyes and colorants and Isi ran the coal tar factory. They had one child in 1880, my grandfather, Harold, the local philanthropist and chemist shop owner. Aunt Eveline was a little confused with her family history. Lydia existed but she was Mauveine's sister ... and it was Mauveine who was sitting in that later picture of hers not Lydia."

"Really ... you mean it was Mauveine who was painted by Rossetti down by the pond with all the water lilies in the background, as well as in the earlier painting in the laboratory?"

"Yes! Sadly, Mauveine and Isi both died within days of each other in 1900 from cancer. Like for many scientists and engineers in those days, the health and safety of hazardous substances was not understood, look what happened with Madame Curie. But most amazing is that Isaac's brother, Nathanial, became head butler to James McKenzie, and that family tradition continued until Daniel Fazackerley, who had been head butler to Uncle William, left for London and changed his name to Endersby ... Julian's grandfather! There was a tragedy. Alicia had actually given birth, to William's daughter but she was sadly stillborn. That evening, in acute depression, she jumped in the canal and Uncle William was so upset and depressed, it triggered his reclusiveness which he never got over."

"That is all absolutely amazing," Abby replied slowly.

"So Julian and I are like cousins fifth time removed or something ... which is legal," Victoria added, fingering her engagement ring, her eyes glinting with pleasure at being able to tell Abby the full story at last. "I have to say ..." she continued. "I do remain a bit of a sceptic about you and your psychic stuff, but will now admit a genuine belief that there may be parallel universes out there we don't fully scientifically understand ... yet."

They laughed and giggled together and Abby poured out two teas.

"I think Julian's got plenty to inspire his writing with now," Abby whispered.

"Oh, one final thing," Victoria continued. "Then, I must show you what Julian has done upstairs, painting and plastering. He is truly wonderful, and then we can eat. But I will have to work on keeping him writing, because if let he'll spend all his time with his armpits up to cement and bricks, day in day out. I managed to bring myself, before you came, to look at the graveyard for the first time and found Uncle William's grave as you described. On one side of him are Alicia and Baby McKenzie and on the other are Mauveine and Isi. My grandparents are also there, a little further along. My father of course was, I believe, cremated.

Abby sat back in her chair, contented and sighed briefly, finally pleased that the family ghosts had been put to rights... and turned towards the table ... and her heart almost stopped dead ... as she saw it, unexpected ... and unbelievable.

Mauveine and Isi were standing there as she watched her smartphone rise up from the table, with both of them holding it, their faces curious and mystified in deep concentration, scrutinising the screen and playing with the buttons. Outside behind the patio door, the two horses were standing impatiently, tied to a fence post, steam pouring from their mouths ... oh ... no ... Abby turned to Victoria who was gazing, dreamlike out of the window, towards the horses.

"My brand new, expensive state of the art iPhone, Vikki ... oh fuck ...gone forever ..."

"What's the matter Abby? Your phone's there on the table."

She looked back ... and there it was.

"Sorry, of course, getting paranoid, thought I'd lost it."

She got up and grabbed the phone quickly and stuffed it into her handbag, noticing that Victoria was still staring out of the window. Outside, Mauveine and Isi were standing, hand in hand, smiling warmly at Abby, before they each waved, jumped onto their horses and started galloping off towards the woods. Abby continuing to stare at the riders, her mouth dropped in utter disbelief.

"You know," Victoria began. "First thing I am definitely going to do in the grounds is to clear that scrub by the pond and do up all around the woods again so it looks exactly as it used to when Mauveine was painted there by Rossetti. What do you think?"

Abby looked again at Victoria and back outside, seeing the riders and horses suddenly dissolve away, the woods clearly visible and skylarks once more singing over the cornfield. They were not seeing the same things ... thank goodness ... and her mind immediately cleared, Eveline had gone, nothingness, only a feeling of immediate joy and contentment. Closure had been reached as well for her.

"Super idea. My throat's really sore, I must be picking up something, probably all the dust from the cleaning. Have you any lozenges anywhere?"

"Yes, in my bag in the kitchen, I'll just go and have a look, and check the food," Victoria replied wandering back towards the aga.

Abby continued staring at the woods, visualising how amazing it really must have been when Mauveine was painted, and deciding she was going to open her own textiles art studio and about time ... when her phone pinged. She peered at the screen, and couldn't believe the twitter message, it wasn't from Marlies as she expected.

@missdyehead - love the phone, no wires, really cool science, must get one. Thanks for everything, we're eternally grateful. Hey, check out my new Pinterest site! Have fun - M and I

"Vikki? What's Pinterest?" she shouted towards the kitchen.

"I think it's some sort of new social media site," Victoria replied, "where you post up your own events and stories as photos and images, like a cross between Facebook and Flickr, but hey what do I know? I don't have time for any of that.

Marlies probably has it all fathomed out. My laptop's open on the coffee table, have a look."

Abby lifted the lid and typed in some search details and quickly found the new Pinterest beta site. And on screen, clearly pinned and displayed in order, were images of all the personal letters, Orsbrick and Burscough Herald newspaper cuttings, science papers and certificates of births, marriages and death which she had searched for and read earlier in the Red Lion, except the stories were completely changed, reflecting exactly as Victoria had just related earlier. Plus there were old sepia photos which she and Victoria had been perusing, including new ones of Mauveine and Isi in the laboratory, and factory and other gala and dinner pictures they hadn't seen of Orsbrick Hall in its glittering social heyday, including Mauveine and Isi happily holding a baby, Victoria's grandfather, together, and also Uncle William and Alicia dancing.

"Found what you're looking for?" Victoria called down, carrying in a large porcelain tureen of scouse and a bowl of pickled beetroot. "I'll just get the other vegetables, can you shout for those two upstairs?"

"Yes ... useful ... okay, but first I'll bring the champagne in. Definitely time to celebrate that double wedding!"

Or would it be a triple wedding ...?

Continued in Prism of Purpurine

Have you read the Rhapsody Series?

RHAPSODY OF FATE Book Three:

A fun holiday in Rome beckons for scientist and Cassini CEO Lauren Hind to forget the recent nuclear debacle in Sicily. Looking forward to a new relationship with Philippe, her Chairman, her business and personal life should at last become rosy and settled. One revelation changes everything, discovering her lost adopted daughter, Charlotte and new family. But will this upheaval be a force for good or an uncontrollable disruption in her life?

She needs to find out, confront the demons and reconcile her feelings and admit who she really loves. But unexpectedly, in China, the marital happiness she had sought and won is violently disrupted leading to unwanted challenges and distractions. She is forced to question Amélie, her best friend, who she had always understood and trusted.

Something oddly sinister unfolds leading to a set of destabilising coincidences and finally a kidnapping which even her worst nightmares couldn't have predicted. Never before have her technical skills and bravery been tested so much. Could there be a man even more evil than Luis, capable of lacerating her emotions and loyalties at a stroke? And why does she have to travel to the Arctic to find out? Many may die, the dice is thrown and she must finally make the ultimate decision, one way or the other.

But which way does she turn? And who really loves her enough to pull her away from the deadly consequences?

RHAPSODY OF FATE is the third book of the Rhapsody series, continuing the science adventures and romantic escapades of Professor Lauren Hind

EXCERPT … they were soon heading out of town and into the surrounding countryside. The wide city beltway had dropped from a major highway down to a series of small rural lanes. Lauren gazed with interest at the great expanse of landscape, a mixture of parched and green rough grass, undulating hills and some meadows, but also randomly interspersed were a number of flat desert-like areas, on which stood interesting large contraptions with long beams, bobbing slowly with a counterweight and some kind of motor. Lauren immediately began working through the physics of turning the fast rotary motion of the motor, through a crank to upwards and downwards slow reciprocated pumping. But what was being pumped? Presumably, she thought, oil, but there were a lot of them and she was under the impression that inland oil reserves in Texas were long depleted.

"I can see you are intrigued Lauren. They're called pump jacks or nodding donkeys. Most of what is coming up is water with a bit of oil, but it remains extractable as does the gas often associated which can power the motor."

"Fascinating," replied Lauren, quietly.

"Okay, I'd better warn you in advance. Lyell's father Doug, who you are going to meet, although everyone, including us, calls him DG, is not only a Senator but the family have been big in the oil business for four generations and made a lot of money. I was just getting going with my engineering company when I met Lyell, but all the family connections and expertise were so useful, which is why I supply specialist parts to the industry. DG was a big help, and when we got married he insisted on buying us the ranch as a wedding present, as all my money had gone into the business. I lived in a small apartment in downtown Dallas. The ranch is a fabulous place.

"Really big Grandma," added Lexi. "And we keep our own cattle as the ranch used to belong to a cowboy. And we have our own nodding donkeys as well."

"Yes, DG insisted we exploit the mineral assets which had never been done, and he got it sorted out. In the US, mineral rights belong to the landowner not the government, like many other countries. Now it provides a useful addition to our overall income."

"But Lyell never wanted to be part of the oil business then like his father?"

"No, he never took to it. He loves the outdoors, and is very physical. He was a bit of a rebel in his youth, which is why he ended up in the army when he left school, but did very well and yes; he was in Special Forces when we met. He is very talented too with computers and software when he can be bothered, and has written some software for me, which has got me a load of new business, but I just wish he stuck at it. But when you see his wood carvings you will see why he doesn't need to."

Lauren nodded, taking in the information, her mind ticking its inexorable way through detailed analysis then synthesis of the data. Charlotte didn't seem to have anything in common with Lyell, but then again, who was she to judge or comment, three time married and soon Philippe the fourth to be added, especially on her own daughter? Everyone has to find their own way in life, even Lexi and Kat. She thought of Svet and wished she was here to enjoy this outing and vowed to bring Svet the next time she and Philippe visited Charlotte, although everything was getting so busy and the original planned arrangements with Svet had gone astray. When indeed would she have the time? Many mothers with a daughter of Charlotte's age would be more carefree in their later middle-age — shit, she was just forty-three and Charlotte was twenty-seven, they were like sisters. Then she reflected on the twins, nine years old. Something wasn't mathematically quite stacking up.

Without warning, Charlotte suddenly swung the steering wheel to the right and she put on the four-wheel drive as they headed down a dusty and very bumpy track through glades of trees, more meadows and quite sandy soil. Lauren noticed a large blue lake in the distance, when they rounded another corner and came to a wide, but ungated entrance, flanked by two light grey stone pillars. An iron cattle grid was placed over the entrance which they slowly rattled over.

Edging around a final bend, the full extent of the lake fringed with beautiful willows and occupied by a small rowing boat and lots of ducks of all shapes and colours, came into view along with the Half Moon Corral. Lauren simply drew breath at the view and the size of the ranch, if you could call it a ranch at all. She had a picture in her mind of a typical Southern State cowboy ranch, with lots of brush blowing outside, rather derelict, and all wooden, with verandas and rocking chairs. Obviously, she realised, she had watched too many Westerns. A massive white walled, sprawling building, like a snake with a two storey extension on its head, wound itself into a rectangular shape, all gorgeous windows and fronted by a huge stone laid veranda going on forever, with the tiled roof covering held up by endless archways, like a railway viaduct. Fronting all this were a series of beautifully laid out gardens, blooming with masses of colourful flowers and various small shrubs. The driveway cut in through a well tendered lawn interspersed with majestic oaks.

As they stopped, Lauren could see, though the archways and entrances, the inside of a square courtyard, centre-pieced with a large swimming pool and all kinds of levels, stairways and tubs of flowers, leading to different inner building areas, including a spiral staircase up to the second storey building. She sat mesmerised before being distracted by Philippe, waving from a table on the veranda, perfectly placed out of the sun but catching the full view of the lake and trees from the house. Lyell was sat next to him, grinning, bottles of beer and plates of nibbles being consumed avidly by the pair of them. A third man in a large black Stetson almost hiding his face, sat next to them who she didn't recognise.

The main door opened and a tall, well built African-American man, possibly late forties or early fifties, in green overalls and a floppy straw sun hat walked briskly to the car as they all got out.

"Charlotte, great to see you back. I'm just cleaning up the pool, reckon you might be needing it tonight; it's been as hot as Hades here."

Charlotte beckoned the man over to meet Lauren. "Lauren this is Orlando, our gardener and handyman, who keeps this place as spick and span and as amazing as you can see."

Orlando shook hands with Lauren. "Glad to meet you Ms Lauren, something tells me this is the first time you've been to Texas. I hope you like big steaks; my wife Marcie is cooking the most delicious T-bone's you will have ever tasted in your life, all to a secret family recipe we had in my family since them old slave days. Charlotte here, she keeps wanting to buy it off me, but I won't sell that recipe for any amount of dollars!"

Lauren laughed and felt instant warmth for Orlando as she looked into his eyes and could see a man with a lot of hidden depths, especially his do-it-yourself and gardening skills, which she might be able to learn a bit about.

"That's true Lauren. One day Orlando and Marcie want to open another simple family restaurant downtown. It will be a big hit with her steaks and special pumpkin pie. Orlando, Lauren is a special guest — she is my mother."

Lauren felt startled inside at that admission, said so informally and off the cuff. It was oddly peculiar being called a mother. She looked at Orlando, who looked her up and down back, but never blinked an eyelid or appeared in the slightest bit surprised.

"Well now, isn't that just something Ms Charlotte, and can I see the resemblance. I thought at first you and Ms Lauren might be sisters or cousins. Hope you enjoy your stay here Lauren. We've put you and Philippe in the guest building, best view of the lake too." He pointed to the beautiful two storey end building with the spiral stone staircase winding up and wisteria splattered all over the while walls. "Your things are already up there." He began to head back inside. "Charlotte, I'll just get off and help Serena get everything ready for dinner."

Lauren looked casually around. The twins had already gone inside too, probably off to their rooms. Charlotte touched her arm and pointed to a Gazebo at the other end of the ranch. "Philippe looks fine in the company of Lyell and his father. I want to tell you something, let's walk over there."

"That's DG in the Stetson?"

"Of course. He thinks he's like JR Ewing sometimes and makes us all laugh, although Lyell doesn't see the humour so much. DG is always wheeling and dealing at any opportunity to make even more money…!"

RHAPSODY OF POWER Book Two:

Nuclear scientist Lauren Hind returns to Brussels to find her company, Cassini Power, riven by upheaval and turmoil and her Director role threatened. Confident in her adaptability and desperately needing a change of direction, she decides to face down her antagonistic Chairman, whilst seeking solace in a splurge of fashionable indulgence in advance of her expected big payoff. Appearances however can be deceptive and out of the blue an unexpected turn of events shakes up her perception and sets her off on a new path towards career possibilities and a world stage she could only previously have dreamed about. But threats and a puzzling technical dilemma shake her out of any cosy feelings of finally being in control of her life because she has to decide where her loyalties lie, and confront once again who she really is and her true feelings. Aspects of her recent past have not quite gone away as she had hoped and expected. A looming catastrophe, with enormous consequences for Europe and the rest of the world reveals the true extent of her capability to deal with serious dangers. To add to her confused feelings and foreboding, her Chairman is at the centre of the murky wheeling and dealing and she is summoned to engage in an adventure which could lead to her death and destruction. She badly needs help and there is only one person to turn to again - who could annihilate her in a moment. Can she let this happen or are the consequences and payback already drawn in the sand? And there is still her Chairman ...

RHAPSODY OF POWER is the second book of the Rhapsody series continuing the science adventures and romantic escapades of Professor Lauren Hind

EXCERPT ... Lauren saw immediately that Amélie was massively irritated and annoyed by what had been said in the first five minutes. "Honestly Amélie, I have not got a clue what all this attention is about. Listen, you can bank on me, once we get into the meeting, to step swiftly into the background, I'll back you up at every turn and when the time is correct follow your lead into what Cassini can do on fast plutonium reactors. And then let's sew up whatever deal we can muster; first and foremost to benefit you, remember just like we did in the old days? Anyway you look stunningly immaculate as ever, whilst I look like I've been dragged through a hedge backwards after that damned gust of wind outside. Have you got a decent hair brush?"

The tension in Amélie's face dissipated as she dug into her handbag. "I'm sorry Lauren for snapping. This deal is actually potentially more important to me than maybe I let on. Things have become a bit tricky back at the ranch, you know what I mean?"

Lauren patted her arm affectionately. "Of course, fully understood, you can tell me later. Hey, what are friends for. Now, let's get in there and give them the old one-two sales patter. I just hope my Chairman isn't there, I really do."

They strode out and over to reception where a smiling Valerie whisked them off to the lift and up to the fourth floor. As they stepped out into the executive corridor, an amazing view of the sea and the coast hit their senses, an immediate impact from the unusual design of the building, built like a glass atrium with a steep vertical wall immediately beneath going directly into the sea.

In a few seconds they entered the Board room to be greeted by a sea of male faces stood around the large buffet table, beautifully set out with an array of hot and cold food, salads, vegetables and sandwiches. Amélie immediately took a glass of white wine off the waiter near the entrance, with Lauren in close pursuit of the red, when a deep, clearly very English accented voice, familiar but unfamiliar, spoke out softly from behind.

"Ah … so you must be Professor Lauren Hind. I have waited quite a long time to meet you." Lauren turned around and her face dropped as she found herself shaking hands—with the UK Prime Minister!

RHAPSODY OF RESTRAINT Book One:

Professor Lauren Hind is a scientist who appears to have it all. Global recognition for her nuclear energy work, a doting designer husband who she loves and a mega salary in a large corporate so she can indulge in her joint passions of haute couture and mathematics. After leading a prestigious research conference, she unexpectedly meets up with the mysterious and beguiling Luis who lures her into a culture she had not experienced. Fuelled by drink and intrigue, a train of events takes off and Lauren finds herself desperately buffeted by a seemingly irresolvable kaleidoscope of emotional and confused outcomes, which threaten to violently overturn her well-structured lifestyle and relationship bearings. Trying hard to salvage her way out of the mess she has created and save her marriage, new and interrelated twists and turns throw her into further turmoil, entanglements and more betrayal as she is forced to question everything she has stood for and make fundamental choices. But someone else turns up who has the capability, passion and desire to take from Lauren whatever she wants. Lauren needs to find the will and strength to confront this additional adversity and resolve her own complicated needs ... but can she overcome the temptations ...?

RHAPSODY OF RESTRAINT is the first book of the Rhapsody series which tells the story of the intriguing scientific and emotional destiny of Lauren Hind. "Where romance and adventure meets nuclear fusion!"

EXCERPT ... she sauntered to the table already occupied by around a dozen other Sicilian men, some similar in age to Luis but many others younger. As they surrounded her, she sat down deciding not to take off her jacket immediately but flaunt her new outfit a little longer. They were dressed smartly, like they were all part of a group and were engaged in what appeared to be quite intense discussion on some hot topic or other in Italian.

"May I please ask your name?" He grinned warmly towards her. "We think you are the most interesting and desirable person to have crossed past our table tonight ... well so far anyway! It is nice to meet again in much more pleasant circumstances."

"I'm sorry?" Then she looked again and that minute before of déjà vu was confirmed with a jolt, the colour draining from her cheeks as her mouth dropped. He laughed vigorously at her seeming discomfort.

"Let's say my near decapitated legs in the airport are now fully recovered. Don't worry. I could see you were somewhat preoccupied then. Now tell us about yourself. I hope you're happy that we speak in English. I sense somehow that your Italian is less well developed."

"Gosh ... Yes thank you, please continue in English that's fine. I don't know what to say except to apologise profusely. It was rude and unacceptable of me to react that way when I had just arrived and ..."

He interrupted her gently. "My response back to you was not exactly civil either, so let's call it quits. No harm done and anyway I admire assertiveness in a woman and you certainly appear to have that in spades, as they say!"

Lauren, although embarrassed and somewhat taken aback with his immediate forwardness, nevertheless returned the smile and replied warmly, her composure returning quickly as she surveyed all the inquisitive faces.

"Hello everyone, I'm Lauren. I've been staying in the hotel over the last couple of days with the conference which has now ended. We've been doing some international exchange work in sustainable nuclear energy, networking, new developments all that sort of thing," she said clearly and deliberately.

She could hear herself sounding unnecessarily formal and not really knowing why she was speaking so wooden, when everyone around was being quite casual and laid back. She felt displaced with her thoughts, and especially with Luis who was deceptively and deliberately disarming her normal flow of reaction when meeting new people ...

Luis became immediately sensitive to the situation and took up a suitable response to relax her and make her more at ease. "Lauren, now that is an interesting name. Ahh ... you said the conference, on mmm ... energy ... in fact nuclear energy."

The group laughed quietly, understanding clearly the English and the irony of the conference being in Sicily.

After a pause, Luis continued. "Well yes, I'm afraid your delegate colleagues all seem to have totally vanished. We don't really know why they rushed off in a hurry, so it appears only you seem to be attending the invitation to the party, apparently. Perhaps they are a little boring for missing the fun do you think? And you have much more discerning taste choosing to come here with us. Tell me. What exactly do *you* do in your work?"